Some Hope

Some Hope

Jonathan Rix

ANDRE DEUTSCH

First published in Great Britain in 1993 by
Andre Deutsch Limited
105–106 Great Russell Street
London WC1B 3LJ

Cataloguing-in-publication data for this title
is available from the British Library

ISBN 0 233 98834 3

Printed in Great Britain by
WBC, Bridgend

I've got a lot of things I want to say, but not a lot of people want to listen, I mean, words just come out of me, they always does, and they shock people. That's them you see, that's why they're so stupid, they don't listen, they don't look – they answer. I mean they don't realise they're so predictable they're dead. They want things that make them feel safe. And I don't do that. I make them think they've failed.

So I'm leaving, I'm getting out of it, I'm going to meet the people out there, and it'll be good, like a laugh, because they won't know me, they won't judge me, they won't have ideas about what I'm like.

And watch their dead faces sag, watch them thinking I'm a fool, thinking I'll screw up, watch them wipe their hands and nod their heads and sigh, 'Ah. I see White's been excluded from Britain. Probably for the best, he was always a stupid boy.'

So this is to all of them, because they never listen, because they think opinions are rules, because they don't understand that all there really is is Mates. So this is to my teachers, to my social workers, to my family, to my employers, this is to the people in charge, this is to you, because none of you never gave a shit without wanting something in return. So here it is, dedicated to you, right in your fucking eye.

Thank you.

1

Introductions

Simon. You'd better meet Simon. He's my mate from years back. Known him since I was five and he was four. Known him since his Mum knocked on my Mum's door and this is her, 'My lad's going to the same school as yours', and then they starts gabbing crap, and we were stuck in the same piss small room and told to get on – so we did. Chalk and cheese. Chalk and cheese, that's how people see us, I mean they can't believe we're still mates.

Si's a frigging saint. All my life I've been told to be him. He's the creep who shut up. He's the creep who listened. He's the creep who passed the exams – fuck, he could even go to college if he wanted to. But there's something about him that's, well, it's different, and like, he really can knock people sideways, even my mates who find him a bit wet. I mean he does things what you wouldn't expect him to do, and he does them suddenly, and like when I see that, I know that he's good, and that he understands.

It were him who got hold of the French francs. I mean I'd sort of suggested it, like 'Wouldn't it be a crack if . . .', I'd been the one who'd thought about it and all that, but he was the one who actually gone and done it. He comes round two days ago, and tells me I've got five goes to guess what's in his pocket, and I didn't say 2,000 French francs, because, hell, I weren't expecting that. But that's him, see.

Si's tall, and he's wide, well shouldered, but he don't really have to shave yet. He's got a happy face; big nose, big teeth – that should have had braces like what my dentist gave me – and these really strong eyes, yellow eyes, sort of old fag-stained lampshade-yellow. The only bad thing about Si is his clothes. He wears fucking boring clothes. I mean at times I've got to apologise for them, I've got to tell the people that they're not actually him, that he is actually alive under them, like he's breathing and pushing the shit around, and he's good. And like, he's Jewish too. Well, not a real Yid, he eats bacon and shit, but you know, his family are sort of proud of walking through the desert and surviving all those frog storms, you know, feel part of history, and they have their Friday night family meals with their little hats on, and they sing songs in whatever it is, and he had to learn all that guff for his thirteenth, but it was worth it, you know, with the presents and money and shit, and like I was sort of well proud to be his mate and all.

Me and Si mostly does things just the two of us like, and I reckon he finds some of my mates a bit too fucking loud, but he still gets on with them, shows them respect, and so if they don't want to give it back, well, like fuck them, they're ignorant, because Si and me we got history, we got childhood in common. I mean like we walked to school for years, and even though we didn't see each other in class or nothing, we always walked home together, and I went round his place all the time, and, you know, we built carts, and went out on expeditions, and made huts down in the railway goods yards near the marshes, and like he helped me with work and I helped him with swimming and football and shit, and he didn't care what people said about me, and I didn't care what people said about him, and it were good. I mean even his parents was friendly with me, like I was always welcome, they always wanted to know

4

what I done that day and shit, and like often I'd stay the night on the floor beside his bed, and at about 10.30 his mum would come upstairs with orange squash and biscuits because she knew we were going to be talking for ages, which was good of her, right, and then his dad would come up and tell us stories, you know, stories about Simon White and Ken Jacobs, and that always made us laugh, because his name is Simon Jacobs and mine is Ken White, and they was good stories about ghosts and adventures and shit. I mean, hell, I still go round there, and like we don't get the stories no more, and we don't get orange squash neither, and – I'm not going to lie – that's a bit disappointing really, but they're still glad to see me, they still laugh at my jokes, they still ask me what I'm doing, they still is interested. And fuck it, even if they're just parents, you know, with problems, even after all that, they can still surprise you. Like they drive simple people down to the seaside every year, you know, the really thick ones with flat faces, down to Southend for the fun-fair, and like they even took me once, and bloody hell, they went on ALL the rides, and Si's dad even sat in one of the dodgems and hit the other cars with his black umbrella – well the car Si were in anyway – and he kept shouting 'Tally-Ho!', and we were well embarrassed, but we didn't say nothing, and on the way home he sang some really stupid songs, and it was bloody difficult not to laugh at him and all. So, like these are straight people, but good, and I suppose that's where Si gets it from, that's what makes him different – I mean all his family can shock you. Fuck, Friday night meals round at his place really was different for me, what with the candles and prayers and shit – you were never allowed to blow the candles out neither, they always had to blow themselves out, you know, tradition or something like that. I mean we didn't have nothing like that in our family, we never even used candles – well, not unless the power was cut

5

off. Our meals was over and done with as soon as fucking possible. We talked and shit like that, but at the table we ate, we got it out the way, because me and my brother and sister always rowed when we talked, and you can't row and eat at the same time. You see my family's not like Si's. My family is falling to pieces.

Let's start with my mum. My mum is a fucking tart. She'd spread her legs for a sodding goat and then go and complain that she weren't treated with respect. If I was my dad I'd have booted her out years back, but for some dipshit reason she's got him wrapped. Last year she were away with one of her leg-overs for a two month fuck in Majorca, and you know what my dad said, this is him, 'Well at least she's happy'. He's got a face like candle wax, and all he thinks about is shit like that. If my mum IS here, she's usually pissed or doped up to her eyeballs and all, like if she's not fucking she's pumping up shit, and lecturing me about how dreadful her life is. My mum throws her arms around me about twice a year to tell me that she loves me, and like I believe her, but it don't count for much when you know if you steps back she'll fall flat on her face. My dad is not much better than my mum neither, but at least he's around a bit, at least he tries, like he always tried to talk to me when I was in trouble at school and shit, but his concentration span's not very good, so it weren't much help – hell, I don't think he's even noticed that we've all left home.

Let's put it this way, I won't miss my family, and they won't miss me. Si and me, that's what it is now, like that's what it's always been.

I sorted out my money by working in a hospital, in the stores, delivering food and shit to the kitchens and around the wards: cornflakes, jam, bog paper, you know, and like it was alright, and we had these flat trolleys that took some steering, and I got real sharp with mine, like a huge fucking skateboard, stood on the back free-

6

wheeling down corridors, one foot down to skid the corners, a good laugh, and I saved a load, at least £200 – well dad said I didn't have to pay no rent – but like my boss, right, was fifty-eight, and he didn't approve of me using the trolleys for a laugh. This is him, 'What happens if someone's on crutches, and you comes hurtling round the corner?' And this is me, 'He'll fall over', which is true, but he didn't see the joke. So I got an official warning, and like three weeks later I got the sack, but shit, why shouldn't I have bit of a laugh? I've done other jobs too. I washed cars where Si's dad works, and done a bit of painting and decorating for mates of his mum, even though that one didn't work out too well neither, and they had to get someone else in halfway through, because the paint sort of separated on the walls, like they reckoned I should have wiped the walls before I started painting, but like how was I to know they were covered in grease, I mean shit, it weren't my fault, and like I reckon it looked quite good, specially after I'd put the third coat on, but they didn't like it being all sort of tacky, and wanted it scraped off, but hell, they didn't trust me to do it, did they? I mean there's no pleasing some people. They paid me though, which was right. But like what with that work and a few deals here and there, I've got at least £400 which, fuck me, should see me through, and hell, Si's got loads of money, because he does these magic shows at kids' parties with his kid sister, cutting her in half and shit, making flowers come out of his sleeve, eating razor blades, stuff like that, and he makes a bloody fortune, so we won't never be too short, even if my dosh's not enough.

So tomorrow, we're out of here, like tonight's been our last night, and Si's having grub with his family, and like I've been getting smashed with my mates, and it's been a shit hot night, five of us on the razzle, one hell of a session, starting at the Nag's Head, and like I gets there about seven, and there was all my mates, outside, pints lined up, and spliffs rolled, and we never looked back, party party party right through to about 1.30 when we got back to my place, and like that was shit hot too, until my mum came home.

My mum's smashed out of her head. She won't admit it, but she is. She comes in tonight, my last night, right, and me and my mates are pumping the CD a bit, alright I know that gets up her nose, but we turn it down and she still starts screaming about the neighbours – screaming you notice – and then she begins to lecture us on drinking, her, arseholed, and she's lecturing us on how to hold your drink. She comes in swaying and screaming and can only keep going by leaning against the door. This is her, 'What the fuck do you bastards think you're doing? This is my bloody flat, not some doss house', and then she grabs Alan who's outside the front door chucking up, and drags him towards the stairwell, and he slumps and she falls straight over him, and well, you've got to laugh, so we do, and that's it, back she comes, screaming so the furniture sort of shakes, and the lads have to get out – my last night here and she's booting my mates out – and I get angry, because like she's insulting them, and they've not done nothing, it's her. But she don't see that. This is her, 'Go on, out, all of you, take your stinking breath and get out of my flat!' And this is me, 'Their breath? Their breath?! What about yours? You could start a fire with what's coming out of your throat.' This is her, 'What you saying, you little shit? What you fucking saying?!' And all my mates have gone quiet, you know, they're trying to make it to the door, because they're mates and they don't want to get me in no more shit, but I won't have that because no one talks to my mates like that, and so this is me, 'If you were speaking proper, if you weren't smashed as a fucking koala, I might want to listen to you.' And she comes at me off the door, swinging, but misses, and I have to stop her from falling again, and if I wasn't so

8

narked, it would all be dead embarrassing, but like my mates weren't narked, and they were embarrassed, and so like no way could I get them to stay, which is a right fucker when you think about it. Of course as soon as they'd gone, she passed out. Like typical or what?

She's still there now, face down in a rug, and like I'm in my room, but I can't sleep, because, fuck me, I'm getting out of here – tomorrow. Si and me! We're getting out of it.

Out Of It

I got up at nine and went down to the station for my
passport photo, which I look fucking sexy in, and then
went to the post office to get my passport proper – I
hate post offices, they're always full of old people and
mums with screaming brats who are bored out of their
minds and only want to prove that they exist – and then
it was back home to get my bag and face mum and shit.
The stupid cow's not talking to me. This is me, 'I've got
the passport.' This is her, '............', so I showed the
picture to dad, and he laughed, and this is him, 'You
look like a fucking toilet brush', and this is me, 'Fuck off
Dad', and this is him, 'One look at this and they'll never
let you into their country', and this is me, 'Do you want
any duty frees or what?' and this is him, 'Where's my
tea?' He can be a right dick at times my dad, but like,
he's alright. So I get my bag from my room, and like I
come out to say goodbye, and I go to kiss my mum, and
she looks out the window, so I lick her cheek, hug my
dad – he's laughing – and I'm gone. I mean, stuff her.
Yeah, and someone's bound to do that.

I got to Si's place about eleven, and he was waiting in
a clean Marks & Spencer jumper with a picture of an
elephant on it, and I'm not having it, I'm not travelling
with a bloke who's got a jumper with a fucking elephant
on the front, and I tells him to change it, and he looks a
bit upset, but goes and puts on a tracksuit top, like with

10

a hood, Jesus, from dead Marks and dead Spencer –
only thing they do good is women's knickers, and I don't
wear them. So then his parents sort of kiss us, and wave
goodbye and his mum slips him twenty, and then his
dad slips him thirty, and he must have seen me looking
because he hands me ten too, and this is me, 'Blimey,
Mr Jacobs, you won the pools?', and this is him, 'Yes'.
And he had too, £250, and like we heads out onto
Stamford Hill, and there's a 253 there already and within
ten minutes we're at Manor House and about to hit the
Underground when I hears a car hooting like shit and
it's my brother, and he's driving down to Dartford, and
he reckons that we can get a hitch on the A2, and this is
him, 'But why don't you get the train to Dover, you
thick gits?' and this is me, 'It'll be a crack', and like Si
didn't say nothing, so my brother sort of snorted, and
this is him, 'Bollocks', but he dropped us at Dartford,
and like this is it, this is where it really begins. We're
both nervous, I mean he knows I am, because I'm
itching, walking about, gabbing, and I knows he is,
because he keeps checking if he's brought things, and
we're both dead excited too, and we're laughing a load,
and like it feels like none of this is happening, like it's
sort of impossible that we'll soon be out of the country,
and we keep patting each other, like we're making sure
we're really here, like we don't believe it, and hell for
the first two hours it were fun, even if the cars just went
past and past and past.

It were about four hours later, at about 4.30, that this
bloke stopped, and we were well pleased, because at
last we were away, and we piled into the back of his
Sierra and he drives us ten miles and then turns off for
Sevenoaks. Hell, the stupid thick twat meant to go down
the A20. I mean if we'd have known he was going to
Sevenoaks we'd have never accepted the lift in the first
place. But what you supposed to say to a twat like that?
We don't have to wait long for a second lift though. This

11

old bird in an Astra picks us up, and her car smells of piss, and I'm bloody surprised she picked us up in the first place, because like we could be muggers or anything, but then having told us she's going to the coast she turns off at sodding Strood, and I wish I had been a mugger, because we're stuck where the motorway starts and it's 6.35. Cheers. It's not till 7.45 that an old Mini van pulls up, and we pile in the back, and like the stink of Hope was huge because the bloke's got a big spliff on the go, and he's got good sounds and all, and so it's like a dream, but then after about ten miles we breaks down, and he's not a member of nothing, and it's a crap dream, and we have to walk two miles to the next junction to get another hitch. It's not till 10.35 that the next person pulls up, and they're in a Volkswagen van and all, and like it's full of bloody Aussies and Kiwis listening to INXS, which is shit, I mean, Jesus these people are boring – two of them are P.E. teachers for fuck's sake – but they get us to just outside Dover, leave us, waving as they head to Deal, and Si and me has stopped talking now, we're like numb, and we start the walk down the hill to the Eastern Docks in silence. It takes an hour to get there, and when we arrive it's 12.40. It's taken us twelve hours ten fucking minutes to travel ninety miles. And the next boat's not for five hours. Is life a total shit or what? But we done it.

So we're sat in the bloody ticket office reception lounge place, with nine other bored bastards. There's the fat bloke two plastic bucket seats away mumbling and grumbling in his sleep, a pregnant woman who can't get comfy and who has told everybody why she missed the boat, and it's her husband's fault, and like he's put most of their holiday money into 'Kill the Terrorist' which means I never get to have a go – shithead – and then there's the German couple with their rucksacks and health, and they're asleep around each other, and there's the people who are cleaning, which seems a job done in your sleep and all, and in the corner is a man that they discovered by trying to sweep him up. This man is fucking long, like his body, face, hair, it's all long, and he's covered with newspapers, and asleep underneath the seats, and like when the brush hit him, he threw up an arm to protect his head and caught it between two bucket seats, and then he panics some more and tries to wrench his hand out, and you can see it hurts – which is a laugh – and like all he had to do was turn his fucking arm round, but he didn't and his face is panicking all on it's own, and everyone is thinking he's a complete jerk, because he is, and this is him, with this deep bloody voice, booming like a bass in slow-mo, 'Sorry, sorry, oh oh, ow, shit, sorry', until he gets free, and disappears into some other corner, hoping no one noticed – dickhead – and like this is what we had to put up with. I mean we was stuck with this lot until the sun comes up and we is allowed onto the ship, and like I couldn't believe it because the ship had been there all night doing sweet fuck all, so why the hell hadn't we been allowed on it for a bit of decent kip? I mean, I ask you, it wouldn't have killed no one would it? But like me and Si is alright, we've had a day and night, and it's come to an end, you know, and well, it's not a journey we'll forget, so, you know, we're happy enough, even if we'd've been a lot happier if we hadn't had to hang around with those boring bastards in that crap ticket lounge place.

When the boat finally does leave we're straight into the canteen and stuffing down fried egg, beans, bangers, and shit, with no messing, and then who should come in? Why, if it's not the dickhead, the long bloke, bass in slow-mo. This is me, 'How's your hand?' This is him, 'Oh you were there – I took off quite a lot of skin, actually.' This is me, 'That's what happens when you fight chairs.' And I laughed to Si, and he sort of grinned at me, and chuckled at the man, but he were nice about it, so the man smiled back before he went to get his toast. Si's no good at laughing at people, not even behind their backs, I mean even then he doesn't really put his fucking heart into it. Mind you the crossing makes him laugh. I mean it were well rough, and we don't mind, but all the other fuckers on board does, they were dead miserable, like chucking up all over the place, and is that funny or what? And then when we reach Calais they're all desperate to get off, but they got to be slow about it, and so Si and Me get to walk the gangplank first, and then we reach customs first and all, and this is me, 'Good thing we didn't pack the smack', and this is the customs officials, 'Onheon heon' and then they searched everything, well, of mine, and like it were obvious that I was joking, but they didn't have no sense of humour, and like Si was well good, he just stood there and talked French, and they seemed to like that, but they didn't find nothing, and they didn't seem to like that, but I did, and I was dead glad to get out of there and all, and like then we set up our hitching post on the other side of customs where the cars drive out, and we shoved out our thumbs and start pleading for some wanker to stop, but they all keep going, and like I'm doing everything, laughing, smiling, praying, pleading, but there's not nothing that will stop the fuckers. And then that's it. Our boat's empty, and we're stuck between customs and Calais, and I mean sod this. This is me, 'Sod this, Si.'

And then it happens, like from nowhere, rattling out from the far side of customs, where he's been having his vehicle strip searched, out comes a Volkswagen Combi, and guess who's driving it – the dickhead, Slow-Mo, and he's stopping, his long face looking out of the window at us with a smile, and like what's a bloke meant to do? So we gets in the van and off we go, with Bob Dylan on the stereo, and this time it's my turn to feel sick. Jesus, Bob-fucking-Dylan. The man's dead.

Slow-Mo is going to Germany for a concert. And so

14

are we. Well, not quite, we're getting out at Nancy, and like to start with I got to say I wasn't looking forward to it, but not for long, because it only takes him ten minutes to bring the conversation round to what really interests him. This is him, as we bump across some crap Calais railway line, 'So do you lads smoke?' I look at Si, he looks at me, and I takes out my duty frees and offer him one. This is Slow-Mo, 'No, no, hash.' This is me, 'Fuck yes.' This is him, 'You got any?' Now I'm not a tight bastard, but I'm not going to have some wanker smoking all my gear just because he owns a van. I mean, like, this stuff has got to last me till I get back to England, and fuck I have just got it past a load of thick-fingered Frog customs blokes. So this is me. 'I got a bit. Not much, enough for a couple.' This is him, 'Well roll up then, mine's up my arse, and I can't get it out and drive at the same time.' So I climb over the seat, you know clamber into the back of the van, and pull my stuff out of my arse – shit, great minds, eh? – and I break off a small lump, put the rest of the Half in my bag, and clamber back to the front seat. I roll one of my specials on Slow-Mo's atlas, and light up. A1. Thick smoke rolling down my throat, love it, filling my lungs, spreading air all round my head, and then I pass it to him, and he tokes long and hard, tokes fast, four-five-six, and I'm watching it get smaller and smaller, and my nark is building up inside, because when's he going to stop toking on that? When's he going to pass that thing over? And I'm about to say something because he's almost down to the fucking roach when he passes it across me to Si, and now I'm watching him, and like Si's not a great smoker, he fakes it a bit, holds most of it in his mouth and pretends, and like this is getting up my nose, I mean on one side I've got a fucking glutton and on the other side I've got a fucking waster, and shit, I'm getting pissed off, and then Slow-Mo makes it worse, like Slow-Mo opens his ignorant bloody mouth. This is him, the wanker, 'Not much good, is it?' And I mean like this is good Hope, I got this from Garth, and he's always got the best, and now some wanker in a Volkswagen Combi is telling me my spliff is 'not much good', having smoked most of it, like fuck him, and I start to feel my fist clenching and I'm ready to row, and just as I'm reaching the 'fuck you' stage, he pulls the van to the side and brakes hard, very hard, so I chokes on my seat-belt, and this is him, 'Hell if we're going to get out of it, you'd better use mine.' And he's out of the van, his hand goes down into his crutch and comes back up with an impossibly large bag of grass. And shit, is it good or what? Fuck, my gear IS crap. I mean this wanker has me out of my head with three lugs – even Si's eyes are red. And now I know I'm going to enjoy this trip. This is what travelling should be. Hell, who wants to get out at Nancy anyway? I mean even Bob-fucking-Dylan is making my foot tap. Like is life weird or what?

Midday and we're about halfway, passing pretty near to Reims, and Slow-Mo is not going fast, in fact with every spliff he slows down by at least five miles an hour – sorry, kilometres an hour – and like as we crawl past a brilliant looking café right in the middle of a great flat bit of France, we all want to stop, like meet our first proper foreigners, so we pulls up outside, and a group of old Frogs stop their drivel and watch. This is a back road, a country road, none of this motorway crap, and they're not used to people like us interfering with their daytime routine, like this is something to talk about, and that's what they starts doing as soon as we're past their table and I've said hello in my best French. This is me, 'Bonjour Monsieurs', and this is them, 'Onheon heon, Anglais, onheon, Anglais,' and shit.

So we go in through the door, and everyone stops, turns and looks. Why? We've got two legs haven't we? I look around the place, look them all in the face, and then go and join the others who have pulled up stools at

16

the bar. Si smiles at everyone, and Slow-Mo orders a
bottle of rouge. Now this stuff is rough, I normally drink
lager, but hell, when in Froggy-land, eh? So first
mouthful and I have to fight the fucking stuff. I mean,
Jesus, it's like sandpaper, but wincing, looking at each
other for support, we swallow the bloody shit, and then
laugh a bit and try a second mouthful, which is easier,
and by the end of the bottle it's slipping down a treat,
and we're ordering another. And that's when the local
comedian came and joined us. He wanted to pay for the
bottle, in exchange for taking the piss. I mean we didn't
realise that to start with. To start with we just thought
this was sort of local hospitality, you know, the way
country people is, but then he starts on about roast beef
and shit, and everyone is laughing and they don't realise
that Si has a GCSE in French and understands them, so
that when he talks back they laugh even more, and start
talking Frog with an English accent, but you can see
that some of the wankers are feeling a bit embarrassed,
but not the comedian, not his main audience, they were
still enjoying themselves I reckon, and we were the joke
– you know, you can feel things like that, even in a
foreign language. And it's not good. It's like there's
something wrong with you but you don't know what it
is. I mean you got no chance of understanding the joke
– like, why's we so funny? So I thinks well fuck this I'm
going to beat them at their own game – I'm going to be
funny, and I does it. I have them rolling in their frigging
seats. This is me, 'Onheon, bonjour, je m'appelle,
onheon heon, and toute cette Frog merde', in an English
accent, but I'm feeling a bit angry and all. So then the
barman gives us another bottle, and the comedian goes
round the back of the bar, and starts talking to us in a
stupid high voice, sort of like his bollocks are in his
throat, real high squealing shit, and he's still on at us,
and I'm starting to get dead annoyed because he can't
take no hint, and either he's real thick or asking for it,

17

and then – and this blew the lot of us away – Slow-Mo joins in for the first time, and he does it in the same voice, real high, ball-less high, high as the dickhead comedian, and in fluent Frog, perfect, and the comedian's face drops like a lip burning curry dump. He's narked – this voice is his voice, this is his joke, his big joke, NO ONE can do this voice, this is his. So he lays in heavy at Slow-Mo, and it's obvious he has shit on his face, and the rest of the bar is loving it. Loving it. They come from all corners, all round us, and they're pissing themselves. And Slow-Mo just grabs the comedian's face, pulls it across the bar and kisses both cheeks, shit and all, and this is him, 'Mon frère, mon frère', and the comedian is fucked.

When we left the bar four hours later I am annihilated. I have spent four hours pouring red nightmare down my throat, listening to Slow-Mo and the Frogs, and I have never laughed so much in all my fucking life. Well, that's not quite true, but hell, had I laughed or what? Si sat there, chuckling, throwing in a line from time to time, and I could see he was concentrating like hell, and was suffering from the rouge more than the rest of us because he don't drink that much – sweet wine on Friday and slow pints when he feels he has to – and at one point he dozed off, which got a lot of laughs, but he took it well, and hell he tries, which is what counts, like he don't mind what the rest of the world does, and like you could see they liked him. I tell you what though, I wish I spoke French, I mean all I got is Si's dictionary.

When we gets back in the van, Slow-Mo's not feeling like driving no more, and who can blame him? We're all beyond help. So we drive down to this small wood that's off the road to the left, and we parks like under these trees. Now I've not seen a lot of the countryside, you know, I'm not a great one for trees and parks and crap, I mean they've always been places to play football or tread in dog shit, and so it's weird enough driving through the stuff all day, but now, now we're going to sleep in the bloody place, and I mean, I may be pissed out of my brain, but this ground does not look comfortable, like there's shit everywhere, branches, leaves, plants, grass, insects, hell you can't move for it. But Slow-Mo's not going nowhere, and so I think 'Oh sod it', and we set up camp. Si gets out his tent, and we bung that up, and then we get out the Calor gas thing, make up a cup of tea, and collapse into the mean-shit grass that Slow-Mo lives for, and boy is it good. I mean, my first few lugs, and on top of all the rouge, my head won't stop spinning and swaying, and I have to fight a tight throat, but two lugs more and the grass has won, like hands down, and am I gone or what? Come sundown we're floating, the world has developed a new kind of gravity and it don't involve us.

You ever watched a sunset, I mean, really watched it, seen it go down, like soaking the fucking sky? I mean, shit, it's awesome. And then, oh then the stars, I mean a great big sodding curve of bloody sky, and it's black, not city yellow, black, and the stars, Jesus, the stars, they're just THERE. Hell, no way could we sleep in the tent, it'd be like fucking with a condom on, and so we lay under the trees, and looked up through their real dark shadow, through the branches, up to the stars, and I felt, like, well, like I've never felt in my life. It sort of got my stomach, like I felt part of it. I felt me and the stars was mates, me and the trees, mates, me and the ground below – mates. I know that sounds like wank, but wanking does have its uses, and I mean, hell, that's what it was like. I tell you, I can hack this shit. Like is this what we came here for or what?

19

Carry On

Next morning was no worse neither. Seven o'clock, sun comes through the trees, hitting me full in the face, and whop, I'm awake, straight off, ready. Beside me is Slow-Mo, and he's cross-legged on his sleeping bag, dressed, and rolling up. He nods my way, and this is me, 'Good morning, or what?' and he passes me the spliff. My first lug is joy, like a slap of cold water, and as I'm soaking it up, sort of wide awake but still enjoying sleep, I'm hit by a sudden desperate need, like my body reminds me it exists – one smoke and my arse starts screaming. It's packed in there, and it's got to be emptied. I'm in the middle of a foreign country, the nearest toilet is fucking miles away, and I need a dump. This is Slow-Mo, 'Oh stop grinding. Do it behind a tree.'

Now look, I'm not a wimp, but 'Do it behind a tree?' I mean, shit. Behind a tree? This is him, 'Well you're not doing it in the Combi.' So I'm off in the trees, and like how the fuck do you choose which tree to dump behind? I mean there's thistles and shit everywhere, and hell, what if someone walks past? You got to choose a good spot. So finally I've found my place, I pull down my trousers, squat, and like I tread on a sodding twig, and it twists under my foot and goes straight up my arse, and I leap back up, thinking I've been bitten – well you would, wouldn't you? I mean, Jesus, I freaked. This is me, 'Ya! Jesus! Jesus! Jesus!' And this is Slow-Mo, a

20

voice from nowhere, 'Big one, is it?' Like did he expect me to laugh or what? I squatted more careful second time, but hell, it's not easy to keep yourself from falling over. I ended up, arm out behind me, half twisted around, leaning against the tree, because it were either that or I was going over. But then, and this was weird, when I'd finished, I noticed this sort of breeze, and it's like cooling, and suddenly I'm enjoying it, I mean I felt great, like I'd achieved something. Pathetic, huh? I mean dumping against a tree's not exactly a major achievement, but I tell you, hell, it don't half feel good. There's another thing about dumping in the open too. It don't break. It's like one long coil of the stuff. I never knew we had so much in us. I reckon it's because our toilets back home are so sort of narrow that the shit breaks up into little sections like it does. Slow-Mo's noticed this too, and when Si came back from his morning session, he agreed and all, but he was a bit embarrassed about it.

So, back in the van, then to a cake shop for croissants and black coffee that tastes like melted coal, and within a few spliffs we're on the outskirts of Nancy, and this is it. Decision time. But there's no decision to be made really, and I mean Slow-Mo says we can hang around a bit longer if we want to, but he's going places we're not, so fuck it, we get out the van and say 'au revoir'. Well Si does. This is me, 'See ya'. And we watch him go.

It were weird seeing the van drive off, I mean we'd only been in it for a few hours, but it had become a sort of a home, and Slow-Mo had turned out to be well good, and it weren't likely we was going to find nothing like it second time around, and so we were both feeling a bit sort of sad really. Neither of us was talking that much. We stood around at the roadside a bit, and nothing went past, and like it don't take long to give up hope when you're hitching, and that's what happened, we felt sort of lost. And then Si realises we're standing in front of a

21

railway station – une gare – and he suggests maybe we should get a train. Now back in London I'd not wanted to do that, but out here, sat by the edge of a dusty road, it seemed a whole lot different. So in we go, and get the bad news, next train to the Med is not for bloody ages, but we can get there a bit quicker by doing lots of train swaps. The bloke behind the glass is not much interested in us though, like he thinks every question we ask is some great fucking chore, I mean, it's his job for fuck's sake, and all he can do is spit out answers and look at us like 'Why don't you get out of my life?' So we do. Up his.

Back outside the station we talks about it, and Si don't want to do lots of trains, and neither does I – who wants to look at every station sign, thinking, 'Shit, shit is this our stop? Should we change here?' I mean it's a bollocks way to travel. We don't want to wait till midnight for one straight through neither, so we thinks about it all and decides to try for another hitch, and hell if no one comes good we can always come back for the late train. Like it's still an option. I tell you though, we both felt a bit pissed off about it, well I did. So, we walk out of the town to find the right hitching spot, and fuck me is it hot or what? Like I'm pumping it. I'm dripping. But Si looks worse, he looks like he's had a swim. He's got this tight curly hair right, like a black man, and it's full up, a sort of sponge, so when he touches it, you know, one wrong movement, one mistaken scratch of the head, it's like a bath overflowing. His shirt has changed colour and all, and the rucksack has glued itself to his back. I would've taken the piss, but I didn't have the energy, and he wasn't complaining enough to make it worth my while neither. It takes at least an hour to find a good place to hitch but by the time we does get there we both look such crap that not even a psychopathic Frog would stop for us. I mean, hell, it would be like throwing two buckets of water all over your upholstery.

Seven in the evening, we've cooled down, and we're not talking. We're not doing anything. All we can do is wave a not much interested thumb. Sod it. Si suggests going back for a meal and then the train, and this is me, 'Fish and chips, fish and bloody chips. That's what I want.' And just the words bring back a bit of life. The idea. We're on our feet before you can say 'cod in batter' – which is what we feel like – the bags are straight onto our backs, and we turn like two desperate Siamese twins, and a van comes up the hill, pulls over, the door swings open, and some Frog dork with a stupid red beard and a football for a face is leaning across the passenger seat offering us a lift. Shit – is life a bastard or what? We got in the van. It was a Luton. It felt like home – except the steering wheel was on the wrong side.

Pascal, that's his name. He delivers furniture – meu-bles – we're in a meubles van for fuck's sake, and he's still got deliveries to make. I mean, what's a bloke meant to say? 'Arrêt the van I want to catch le train'? We're stuck with a football on legs. Worse, we're stuck with a Christian football on legs. There are crosses everywhere for fuck's sake. He's even got the Virgin-fucking-Mary hanging from his mirror. Three of her. And there are about twenty badges stuck all over too, all of them with the same sodding picture on, like, some bloke humping a kid around on his back, and then there's these reflector messages. Si says they're things God has said – but hell, God don't speak Frog, does he? These things look more like them stickers you get in pubs, you know, 'You don't have to be as thick as shit to work in here but it helps', or 'Please don't feed the bar staff', or 'No tabs', which probably is something God would say. I mean if Pascal Charlton here really has covered his van with soundbites from God, then boy he must spend his life feeling depressed, like it can't be good for him, and hell, he

23

sure does look depressed, I mean he hasn't smiled once since we got in the cab. That's God for you – wanker.

Si is doing his best to talk to the man, I don't know why, I mean all he's doing is making it more obvious that no one else is talking. I'd join in but it takes me five minutes to get a sentence together, like by the time I've looked up all the words I've forgotten what the first one were anyway. Si and I talk a bit too, in English, but somehow it feels like we're talking behind Bobby Pascal's back, and all of this is boring, uncomfortable, shit. Then after an hour or so we pull up in some small village in the middle of these fucking hills and Bobby leaps out, and like there's nothing else to do, so we leap out as well, and fuck me, in a tiny village in the middle of nowhere there's a meubles shop, not a small one neither, and before you can say 'grab my end' Si is unloading stuff, and after a bit I give him a hand, and we get two chests of drawers and a stack of chairs off the van and into the shop before Bobby's even finished getting the papers signed. He looks up at us, and fuck me he smiles, a great big Froggy grin – like the stitches down the middle of one of them old leather footballs that got soaked in the rain and weigh half a ton – and now Bobby gets ridiculous, he's thanking us loads and loads, laughing and patting us on the back, and I'm sure he's taking the piss, because the meubles manager is laughing too, and flexing his biceps and pointing at me, which I don't like because, well, shit, we've just carried his fucking furniture into his fucking shop, and we're not getting paid or nothing, I mean who the fuck do they think they are? So this is me, 'Well fuck you arsehole' and I'm picking up the chairs and carrying them back to the van, like I want to chuck them through his fucking window, 'You carry the sodding stuff yourself.' And I'm out the door, and chucking the chairs into the van, and Bobby's rushing out and he's all over me, this is him, 'Non, non, non, onheon, mon ami' and shit, all flustered like, like he's worried he's upset me, and I don't know what to fucking do, because this is getting a bit embarrassing and the manager is outside now, and he's taking the chairs, and he's even trying to speak English, all sort of 'You no understand', and this is me, 'I fucking do understand', and this is him 'Non, non, come, come, you drink, drink', and Si has come out and he's grinning at me, and I feel a right prat now, because the manager has got a bottle of pastis out and he's pouring us drinks and they're all going 'cheers' and 'salut' and being so matey it's ridiculous, and I realise I've been a bit of a dick, but I mean like it were understandable.

Bobby was a bit pissed when we got back in the van, and he's sort of relaxed and trying to chat to us, and Si is jawing back, and I reckon I understood a couple of bits they said, so I get Si to translate, like telling me the words, and I say, 'Vie est meilleure après une boisson' and Bobby fucking laughs, looks round at Si, and gives me a football lace grin, and this is me, 'Keep your fucking eyes on the road mate', and he laughs and does a bit of a snake between the white lines and only just misses a chicken that's walked out into the middle of the road and sat down. And all I can say is that the Frogs don't give a stuff about drink driving laws.

Two villages further on and we stop for the last delivery of the night, and when Bobby stops outside this car showroom – that's right, middle of nowhere, a car showroom – out comes this bloke with his arms spread out wide, and Bobby leaps out of the van and the two of them starts hugging and kissing like long-lost brothers, which is exactly what they turns out to be, well not long-lost, but brothers, and then as we unload a small sofa without a back – a sort of bench with cushions – Bobby's brother (must be Jackie) pisses off to serve a customer who's come to check out a crap looking Peugeot, and I look at my watch, and fuck me, it's 8.30. 8.30 and in the middle of nowhere, and the car showroom is open. They're a bit different over here. So I says to Bobby, 'Ouvert, why?' And I points at the shop's 'Ouvert' sign, then to my watch, and shrug, and he doesn't understand a word I've fucking said, thick git, and just sort of grins again, and looks at me seriously, like he wants me to try again, and so Si translates, and Bobby relaxes. That's how I found out about what a real lunch-break is. I mean close at 12.30 and come back at 4.00, now that's good. These Frogs can't be all bad.

So when we've finished carrying the sofa thingy into the showroom, and Bobby's got us a drink, Jackie comes back minus one car – I reckon he knows how to sell, because he's got one of those irritating faces that looks like it likes you even if you don't know it, and so you find your mouth smiling back and you don't know why – and he pushes us out of the shop, locks the doors, and then clambers into the van with us, and suddenly we're going up a dirt track and pulling up outside a big house, not plush, sort of grey concrete with grey tiles on top, but big, and there are lights on, and the door is open, and as we thump into the house there's the noise of loads of kids and, Jesus, a stench of garlic. And that's when I realise what's going on. We're eating here. Oh shit. Frog food, with the Frogs. Not a lot of things put me out in life, but right now, I have to tell you, I was worried. I knew I wasn't going to like the fucking crap they eat, and because I've got some manners, I mean like, it's not easy to turn down someone's food, especially if you're unexpected and they go into over-drive trouble to make sure there's enough for you, like I knew I was going to have to eat some of the shit, and I was not looking forward to it.

Into The Night

I'm still thinking about the food problem when we's pushed into the sitting room, and then I stop. There are kids everywhere. Eight of the little bastards. And they all come running, leaping all over Bobby, and all I want is to get the fuck out of here, out into a wood somewhere, out under the stars, and smoke a lot of drugs. But I'm not going to. I'm going to play with Frog kids. Isn't life wonderful? I mean, shit, do they make a lot of noise or what? Si is in the middle of the floor doing magic tricks with a coin, a handkerchief and a banana, and they're screaming with excitement. Well the young ones, the older ones are sat on the sofa, looking at me, all except the oldest one, and she's on the other side of the room trying to watch television, and I'm trying to watch her. She's got tits like you dream of. I mean they is wonderful, big, jumper-poking beauties, and it's really difficult getting a proper look at them with their father standing in the room, specially when you know that he knows that his daughter's knockers are exactly what a full-blooded Englishman would like to ogle at for at least the whole night, and that if he got half a chance he'd like to do a lot more than that too. So I'm sitting there, fighting a stiffy, trying to pretend that I'm watching Si, and every now and then being distracted by the telly, but this is not easy when you don't understand a word that's being said on the news, and I have to hope that they don't think about that. And then dad comes over, and stands directly between me and the box, and I now know for sure that he knows, so I give him a grin, and he's not grinning back, he's looking furious, and he grabs me by the elbow and is pushing me out of the room and into the hall outside, and turning me so fast that I'm against the wall, and he's lecturing – his breath stinking of the crap they're expecting me to eat – and I know what he's on about. This is him, 'Ma fille!' Fille this, fille that, fille this, fille fucking that – and then he starts to poke me in the shoulder with a stumpy finger and I'm going to rip his fucking head off, his shirt is in my hands, my head is going back to butt, and out the corner of ice-cold red choking anger I suddenly see Bobby with this desperate look on his face and in his arms is the youngest kid, and I don't give a shit, but it does stop me for a second, and like Si is in, between us, pinning me to the wall, and I can't reach the Frog bastard, I can't get at him, and I'm screaming, and this is me, 'Fuck you man, fuck you!' and Si is shouting at me and all, shaking me, and I see his face and it's not happy, and it brings me back, and I can see where I am again, and like I'm breathing proper again, and I hear myself, like this is me, 'I'm sorry, alright. SORRY. Excusez-moi. Right?' Wanker. And I turn away, sort of calming down, and I see the wife coming out the kitchen, and this is what brings me right back, because like I can't believe it, I mean her knockers are even better than the daughter's. Jesus – she's had eight bloody kids and all. And the dad is telling Bobby what happened, and I reckon Bobby's apologising too, because he pushes me to one side and this is him, 'You stop now.' And he points to Jackie, 'Mon brother.' And Bobby looks so sort of upset about it all that I have to tell him I'm sorry again, and then go over to Jackie and shake his hand, and tell him that I'm eighteen and can't help it, and this is me, 'J'ai eighteen' and I hold up 18 fingers, well 10 and then 8, and point to myself and point to my crutch, shrug and grin. And suddenly he has me against the wall again, and I push him away, and this time I'm confused as shit, and Si is there again, thank fuck, and explaining that Jackie thinks I were saying that I'd fucked eighteen women, and I have to laugh, because I wish I had, and I try to explain again, and Si translates, and Bobby and Jackie look at me for a moment, and then they see the joke and begin to laugh, and I say I'm sorry again, and he says he's sorry, and then this is him, 'Mais, no more', and he puts his hand over my eyes, and this is me 'Oui, but no more . . .' and I put my hand over his mouth, '. . . either', and then we are being pushed into the dining room, and he's pouring me a glass of the red crap, which I suppose means I'm forgiven and all's well in the mind of the Frog.

All this excitement of course has taken my mind off the food, and so it's a bit of a surprise to find myself suddenly faced with the fucking stuff. The first load is in a big bowl in the middle of the table, and I'm served first, me, bloody hell, and it's soup, which can't be too bad, but it is, because it's cold. Cold bloody soup. Jesus. It don't taste as bad as I expected though. Well, I don't taste none of it in fact, because I've got this trick where I can squeeze my nose from the inside, like you do when you swim under water, and it means that I don't taste whatever it is I've got to eat, I mean I've used this trick loads of times round at mates' houses, especially when they give you those stews where the meat is not meat but white soggy fat, and like when you're expected to eat sprouts. But then I goes too far, I mean this is me to super-knockers-mum, like a dick, 'Delicious' and suddenly my plate is being refilled. Well, what's a bloke meant to do? I drain my second bowl, and like then I manage to hold off the offers of a third helping, and sit back thinking I've done alright. Which I have, except that I've downed three glasses of wine already and it's

29

gone straight past the soup to my head, and like that's one of the problems with drinking wine, I'm not used to the stuff. I'm a lager man, the amber nectar, so when I get this wine crap to drink, I sort of, well I swig it down, and you don't notice when you're doing that because it don't taste strong or nothing, and like there's something about this crap that Jackie has given us that's not heavy like the other rouge we had out here, I mean this doesn't burn, it's light, it opens your eyes, without you realising it, and before I know it I'm trying to talk French to Bobby. Somewhere out of nowhere I've found all these words, like they must have come from all those Teach Yourself French lessons we got at school. All those tapes they gave me to listen to, those fucking exercises about catching a bus, or asking where the camp site is, all those hours of boring drivel, somewhere, somehow, some things have buried themselves, words, verbs, nouns, that sort of crap, and now, right now, they decide to come back out of hiding, like they weren't there when I really needed them – where were they when I was doing all those assignments, and all those tests and exams? I mean where were they during my orals? Not 'gobble gobble', you know, when you have to talk to your teacher on your own in Frog – the words weren't there then. But now, oh now they all come out, and Si's face, like, it drops. He's never heard nothing like this from me before, and neither have I. But the great thing is, I mean the unbe-fucking-lievable thing is, they seem to understand me. I seem to understand me. I'm not using a lot of words, but I'm using them well, and like I'm telling them about how we travelled down, and things like the hitch we got in the shit Mini van. And this is me, 'Et aprés vingt minutes, la voiture finis, comme ça – erhuh erhuh erhuh – '. And I'm doing sort of juddering impressions, 'Et est necessaire à marche, pour une heure', and I mime trudging, and I looked around the table and they is all watching, and suddenly

I realise this is easy, the Frogs love mime, all that Marcelle Marcelle crap, like they invented it, well not invented it, I mean, fuck, everybody tells you things with their body – like Jackie's fille – I mean even fucking bees tell each other things with their body, so the Frogs didn't invent mime, but they sure as fuck make the most fuss about it. So like when I finish there's a bit of a silence, and then everyone starts talking again and Bobby starts to ask me some questions, and my Frog starts to struggle a bit, because the dick's not using the words I know, but he don't seem to mind, and I manage to find out his mum's name, and where he was born, and I've never heard of it, but he's heard of London, but not Hackney, and then we discover that we're both into football, and he knows about Arsenal but not Tottenham which is a wank, and I know about his team Marseilles, but I tell him he should support a local team, not one just because it's the best, and he laughs, and this is him, 'Mais tu aimes Arsenal' and this is me, 'Non je fucking don't mate. Tottenham, Tottenham,' and I lift both arms up, swaying and sort of chanting 'Tottenham', but not loud or nothing, and he grins and says he's sorry but he hasn't heard of Tottenham. And we're talking, you know, talking.

So I'm feeling pretty sort of relaxed when super-knockers-mum brings in the next course. Hell, if I can talk their language, I can fucking well eat their food, can't I? No I can't. Not if it's mussels. Oh Jesus, mussels in onion water. And Si is going all stupid, he just loves 'Moules Marinières' – that's what it is he says, 'Moules Marinières'. Muscles in piss that's what I say. And the mum is getting all excited, because Si and her's getting on like a fucking house on fire, and the kids are laughing at her and she's laughing at them laughing at her, and Si is given the biggest portion of mussel crap you've ever seen in your life, like piles of the shit, mussels start at his belly button and end up at his tits, a pyramid of the fucking things, and all I can think of is this, 'Dear God, don't don't don't give me a plateful like that'. And God is listening – well he's not, but you know what I mean – because my plate is only piled up to the solar plexus. But it's enough.

Jesus, what do people see in small bits of barely dead rubber with grit in? What's the attraction of eating five-year-old blue-tac? Why, why, why, should anybody in their right fucking mind even consider going down to the seashore to look for a bit of tissue that sucks water in and shits shit out and that's it? I mean, fuck it, I'd've thought Christians shouldn't be serving dangerous food like this to guests. And that's another thing, I mean like they ARE dangerous. They can kill you, mussels. Like if they're dead before you kill them then they kill you. Don't that tell you nothing about the little bastards? Let's get this straight, mussels are weird shit to eat.

I eat mine very slowly. I try a number of different ways. I chew fast, I chew slow, I chew fast and slow, I swallow them straight down, but it doesn't matter how I do it, no siree, once the little fucker hits the back of the throat I can feel the whole thing tighten, like my muscles are contracting in sympathy with their evolutionary predecessor, and I've got that vomiting feeling. All I can do is wash the bastard down. Vin. Glasses and glasses of vin. Until finally the plate is empty, and oh thank God, oh, thank God, it's over, like I've done it – I've eaten every one. Boy, my dad would be impressed. He'd understand what I'd just been through. But super-knockers-mum hasn't got a fucking clue. She's onto me like a Red Cross worker. I've got both hands across my plate, I'm nodding my head 'Oui, oui, delicieux' and then shaking it and I'm patting my stomach, 'Mais non, j'ai full . . . full . . . FULL' and I'm getting desperate. And then Simon, my mate, my best mate, my oldest mate, my best and fucking oldest mate is holding out his plate – ASKING FOR MORE, and she's lost interest in me. She's LEAVING ME ALONE.

He says he knew I didn't want any more, but that he didn't know I was so shook up, and he says that I was certainly looking pale, and this is me, 'Are you surprised?', but the most important thing for him was to get my second helping. That's what he says, but I reckon, somewhere, because of all those years, there was a sort of bell, an alarm, that just sort of let him understand. Hell, he certainly understood that I was pissed.

I sat pretty quiet for quite a while. I mean like I was feeling like crap. I know Jackie looked my way a couple of times, and I remember thinking, 'Oh he's smiling' and trying to smile back, and hoping that I'd managed it, but no one else was taking much notice, and if they were I didn't care. I don't know how long it were until the pudding arrived, but it felt like forever, an eternity, like hell. I am in a stranger's house – I'm in a stranger's country for fuck's sake – and I don't know nothing. I don't know how long the meal goes on for, I don't know where I'm going to sleep, and most important, I don't know WHEN I'm going to sleep. And all that keeps running through my mind is, 'Bed, bed, bed . . .' And it's like looking down a long tunnel because you can see this thing calling to you, telling you to shut your eyes, close down, but somewhere is this other voice, things you've been taught, manners, and Jesus they're the worst little bastards of all. Parents' voices. So I hung in there, until the pudding arrived. But I wish I hadn't.

Pudding was like water-ice, lemon flavoured, sorbet. Now there's nothing that could go wrong with water-ice is there? Bollocks. This water-ice, my water-ice, no one elses – so I discover – was soaked, drenched, swimming, in eau de vie. I'd never had eau de vie before. I didn't even know what it was. But I know what it is now. It's neat fucking alcohol, that's what it is. And this stuff was

98% proof. I have since discovered that Jackie gets it from a mate of his. Well this mate is a total shithead – and so is Jackie. I have discovered quite a lot about the rest of the evening in fact. Simon remembers the lot. The bastard.

Waking Up

Apparently the eau de vie was the last straw. I toppled straight backwards after only three mouthfuls of the decoy water-ice. My chair went with me, we hit the floor, and I rolled half off. And that was that for a few minutes or so. Apparently a row happened. Mrs Jackie was not happy with Mr Jackie, she had watched him filling my glass, encouraging me to knock it back – of course she didn't even think it might be her moules marinières' fucking fault, I mean I'd fooled her there – and I may have been Anglais but I was a guest in her house, etc. etc. Jackie meanwhile was pissing himself laughing. He knew I was a loud-mouthed merde who couldn't hold even half a glass of wine, and that I'd been asking for it, and then he started shouting at his daughter who had got excited because she's just found out that I'd liked her knockers – they all want it – and then he starts shouting at the second from youngest who is feeding cheese to the dog, and then everyone starts shouting, because that's what everyone does once a row looks good, especially in France, and Simon has got me up off the floor with the help of Bobby, and suddenly I throw up, a torrent of mussels and onion pouring out in a burning red wine sauce, but that don't matter by now, because everyone hates the father and is feeling sorry for me. Normally I hate sympathy, but like this time I don't care, because it meant HE was in the shit.

I tell you, all I remember was waking up with the sun blinding me, like I was in a single bed with Simon looking at me, worried.

I didn't join them for breakfast – it would only have been croissant and crap anyway. I felt dreadful. I needed a fry-up. It's a weird thing that. Why is it that fry-ups sort of fill your mind when you're arseholed from the night before? I reckon it must be something to do with all that fat, like I've always imagined the fat sort of filling up the holes, the empty-as-fuck bits, the bits that weep at you on the morning after, weep weep weep in open battle with the other side, the full side, the if-I-look-at-food-I-will-die side, the side that takes the smell of food and turns it into thoughts of vomit, and these two sides mess with each other, screaming yes, screaming no, and whatever you do you'll regret being alive anyway. But if you do get the fry-up, a proper one, no half measures, you will survive the day, you'll make it to lunch, and you won't die, you'll start to feel better quicker, there's no doubt about it. But of course I didn't get a fry-up, I got fuck all.

I don't think they wanted to encourage me to stay around for much longer. Bobby turned up at 10.30 and said he had to be going, this is him, 'You get up, we go. You no get up, we go', and this is me, 'Errrrgh'. By the time I was dressed, Bobby was all agitated like, looking at his watch, sucking his teeth, and then when I was finally done, and hell it had only taken ten minutes, he bundled me down the stairs, past a bloody quick 'au revoir', and I was back in the front of the Luton with my army bag being lobbed up to me. I didn't catch it neither, so it caught me instead, like full in the knob. I tell you, he couldn't have done it better if he'd tried.

I didn't wave as we drove away. Bobby wasn't talking, he was driving, and Si was kind of smiling, and he wasn't trying to talk neither, but he was like making comments, sort of filling the silence, but it weren't like pressure, just gabbing, keeping the driver entertained, keeping him from thinking too much, keeping us together – well someone had to, and it sure as fuck weren't going to be me. You ever slept in the cab of a Luton with a hangover? I have – it's shit. Your head falls forward at the neck, it rolls with every twist and turn, but because you're three-quarters asleep you don't notice until you wake up, like with glue in your eyes and onions in your mouth, and Christ do you know your face has been on your chest or what? It's not just your neck that hurts, it's your shoulders, where the muscles have been at full stretch, taking the strain, and now every time you turn to look it's like someone's stabbing your jugular with a fag – well that's what my neck felt like when I woke up during the third delivery of the morning. I'd slept through the first two, but on this one we were stopping off for lunch and all, and so I thinks, 'Fuck it, I might as well have something to eat', and I helps lug in these couple of drawers to an old biddy's place, and then Bobby takes us to this little café and orders for all of us

  I hate it when people does that, I mean what about what I want, what if I don't like his kind of shit? So I didn't eat much, well not to start with, but after about ten minutes my stomach started to beg for more, and like I had to fill it, so I did wolf a bit, and the food weren't bad, and hell Bobby was a bit more chatty and all. It's obvious that he and Si are best mates now, like a morning's work has done them good, and that feels a bit odd because it's a bit like being left out, you know, like I missed something, which I have, and so I tries to join in too, and because my Frog is shit again that's not easy, but I got to give it to them, because they sees I'm trying my best, and they were both patient, looking kind of keen when I tried to say things, helping out, but I knew that nothing was quite what they were talking about, but hell at least it was close, and I mean Si was laughing – I always make him do that – and Bobby was joining in

too, so by the end of the meal I reckon they'd remembered I was back with them. My head was clearing up
and all, grub and vin doing the necessary, and hell last
night was something I still didn't know much about, so I
was starting to feel pretty relaxed again by the time we
gets back to the van, and it were good to be part of a
threesome again – not a fucky fucky threesome, part of
a team, you know – and we head back out onto the road,
and the sun is shining and Si starts telling me all about
Jackie and the eau de vie and like he was embarrassed
at the time but now he's seen the funny side, and he's
shaking his head and sighing with a laugh as he remembers it, and even Bobby laughs and says his niece is
always getting into trouble like that, and so we're
working well, hitting the meubles shops, and humping
the gear real fast in and then straight back out, and on,
so that Bobby is like way ahead of himself and dead
pleased at it all. He's even put one of my tapes on, and
like he thinks it's dreadful, but laughs a lot about it, and
gets Si to translate the lyrics, and I reckon that they
shocked him a bit, because he tut-tutted at some of
them, and the windows are wound down, and the wind
is pulling at my face, and trees are everywhere, and
Bobby throws this thing round all the corners, and like
I'm telling you, this job is good.

And then, at about nine o'clock that night, we're
coming down a road from the hills, and suddenly,
without any warning, suddenly there in front of us is the
sea, the Med, and it's a shock, like we weren't expecting
it half so quick, and Bobby hangs a right, and we heads
toward this beach and he pulls up, and this is him, 'C'est
tout pour le jour, maintenant nous mangeons ici', and
we're in the car park, and there is the sea, like yo, the
fucking sea, and the sand, FUCKING SEA and FUCKING
SAND, like that simple. I mean all you got to do is see it
to be knocked over with this sort of excitement and this
sort of amazement, because I'm telling you, it's so

fucking big. It just goes on and on. I suppose it's like
any big bit of water, I mean if you suddenly find yourself
by a great big patch of the stuff, it's pumping, stomach
thrilling, brain lifting, and hell, you're buzzing, like this
fucker is big and you really are small – that's what I felt
like anyways, and Si was the same. He stood there all
quiet looking out at it, and then sort of turned, and I
heard him gasp, and the sun was sinking behind us,
going down behind the hills we'd just come out of, and
you should have seen his face, it was like magic, and I
went and stood beside him, and this is me, 'It's repeated
tomorrow' and he laughed but he kept looking because
he didn't agree, this was his sunset, and then it had
gone, and he snapped out of it, and we got excited
again, because we'd gone and done it, we'd reached the
unknown, and it was shit hot. But like, then Bobby is
getting out of the van, towel at the ready, and he's going
to have a swim, and he's sort of encouraging us to join
him, and Si's grabbing his stuff and changing before I've
even thought about it, and of course all his stuff is at the
top of his bag, and mine is at the bottom of mine, and so
I've got to empty the whole fucking thing to get at them,
and like all of this when I'm not even much of a
swimmer, I mean I can swim and shit, but I'm not a
'Let's go down Clissold Swimming Baths' type – like it's
too much chlorine and too much body bumping shit –
but hell, this was something else. I mean I've seen
waves a few times – Margate, Clacton, Hastings – but
somehow they didn't seem inviting like these ones did,
like these were shouting at you to dive in, and so I'm
feeling a bit of a cripple, what with them waiting and
all, and so I tell them to get in there without me, but
they sort of want to go in together, and so we does, like
they wait, and I strip down as quick as I can, and then
the three of us, whiter than the sand mind, start
running, laughing and shouting and running and whoop-
ing down to the frothing white crap, and 'doof' we splat

into the stuff, legs kicking, arms swinging, and I can tell you, shit, it were WONDERFUL.

I didn't want to get out, I wanted to float and spin and turn and do those dolphin sort of leaps, and dive under, holding my breath, and grab Si's legs and heave him over, coming up laughing, with him fighting back, but not being much good at it, but trying because this felt so fucking free, and it's so simple, and hell, who cares if salt water does your eyes in, because like this is the best bloody womb I've ever been in.

And then after about twenty minutes Si was on his way to join Bobby drying back on the beach and I was starting to feel a bit cold, so I swim towards the beach till my stomach grounded, and I rolled round and sat up, the sea still washing over my legs like air round a car in one of those wind tunnel ads, and I shouted to them, against the noise of the sea, like at the top of my voice, and this is me, 'Can you get pissed on sea water?' Because hell, I felt off my trolley after all that adrenalin – like is this a big game or what? And this is me, 'Alright, you can pull the plug out now.'

Back on the beach, we dressed, locked up the Luton, and headed up the sand towards the restaurant at the end, and there, under this sort of bamboo roof, we ordered grub. Now I don't like fish, but Bobby sort of went on and on, and Si was up for it, so I felt I was going to look like a dildo, and I said yes. YES. Three letters – but boy can they change your life. This fish, right, still had its eye and everything. Skin, bones, tail, fins, and this eye – this white pusy horrible eye staring straight at ME. What d'ya do? Oh fuck – you try and eat it, don't you? Eat and pray.

Si knew what to do, the wanker. Don't ask me how, but he just sort of peeled off the skin, and then sectioned the fucker. No bones. Nothing. So I copied him, and it didn't work. My fish looked like a rubbish bag after the cats have got at it. But, and this is the really weird bit,

40

the fish, the bits of white stuff I managed to salvage, they were gorgeous. I mean, like, they made the cod from 'Our Plaice' seem like tasteless pulp – and I like a bit of cod. This stuff was delicious. And by the time I turned the fish over I'd started getting the hang of it, and by the fourth section, apart from one bone that got impaled in the roof of my mouth, I was real impressed by my technique, and like the other two didn't say a thing neither, nothing, they just ate, drank, and yabbed, like I didn't feel a wanker at all, and now, well now, hell, I might even try poisson again. And that's another thing, I always thought poisson meant poison, but it don't, it means fish, like that explains why I didn't understand half of that oral what I failed. I tried to tell that to Bobby, but he didn't get it.

So when the grub is gone, we're all real happy, and Bobby whips out a pack of cards, and says like 'jeux' and we play this game where you get the pack between three, give some cards to the person next to you, and then try and win tricks, but you have to make sure they got no hearts in, or the queen of spades, and is it fun or what? I mean, like, the sea is pounding – it don't stop, does it? – and the stars are all up there, and we're having a bloody riot. Hell, Si's dictionary is red hot I'm talking so much. Shuffling, dealing, talking, drinking, playing. Come midnight we're all in sodding heaven.

I tell you, if you get the chance, do it. Take a mate, get the hell out of the shit you're in now, and do this. You might even win. I did. D'you get that? I won. I WON. And like you got to remember loads of cards too.

So about 12.30 the Frog who runs this place starts to stack chairs – like unsubtle or what? – and we realise we should get out of there, but well, fuck it. About 1.30 the Frog is staring at us. We're the last. And I don't get this because we've got to pay loads of bloody dosh for the meal, and it's a gorgeous bloody night, and we're having a bloody good time in his café, so why doesn't he take his fucking eyes and look somewhere else? I mean I'm getting pissed off with all this looking, and so this is me 'Oi, monsieur, un autre bottle de vin', and like he shakes his head, and points to his watch, and this is him, 'Vous allez', and I don't know why, but this really got my balls, because who's he fucking think he is? And so I get up, and I go over really close, and this is me, 'Un autre bottle de vin, s'il vous plaît.' And like I can feel myself going cold, and that's always a sign, and I reckon we've earned another bottle, and I certainly don't want to go, so why the hell should this stupid greased back Frog kick us out? And all I can see is his face, and like into this suddenly comes a hand on my shoulder and it's Bobby, and he's laughing, and I don't see nothing funny, but he's holding a wad of cash, and he's passing it to this other Frog, and this makes the Frog step back, move away, which he weren't going to do before, like when we were eyeballing, and he goes to the cash register, and totals up our bill, and Bobby pushes me back gentle like, and Si is pulling my arm, and looking a bit worried. Then Bobby's at the cash register with the other Frog and like I don't know what he says, but he has this bloke laughing, and then fuck me, he comes over with a large bottle of brandy, sits down at the table, and ruffles my hair, and this is him, 'If you can't beat them, join them, no?' and I mean what do you say to that, like he's ruffled my hair which is not on, but he's sat down with a bottle of brandy which definitely fucking is, and like Si's face is begging me to shut up, so I just accept the drink, because hell, that's all I wanted in the first place, and Bobby deals the Frog in. Good thing too.

About 2.30, I'm rich. We've put money on points, and hell, I don't know if I'm lucky or what, but hell I'm rich. Si's poor, but fuck what's that matter – I'll lend him cent francs if he gets desperate.

3.00 the cards is put away, the Frog is our best mate and dead pissed off that we won't be back, and like when he kisses Bobby I was serious worried he was coming for me and all, but I had my hand out well in front of me, and he took the hint, and we said our 'au revoirs' and then headed back to the van, like singing, and Bobby laughs because he knows 'Sur Le Pont D'Avignon' too, and hell, are we rat-arsed or what?

Bobby is sleeping in the van of course, while me and Si gets out our sleeping bags, stretch out on the beach, roll a spliff, and yo, what a fucking day, all being wrapped up in Hope. We're lying there, a three skinner, a sort of orange beacon to pleasure, burning between my fingers, sucking between my lips, and this smoke, my first real smoke of the day – boy have I missed you, boy have I been thinking about you – the first proper hashish hug, the shoosh of smoke, running through my gob, sweet like a first hit of coffee, running down the throat with a stroke like needles, stretching into my lungs, and like they widen, I can feel it sliding from those little sacks of air, passing through them, into my blood, and the blood gets bigger, it sort of expands, and It's going through me, sailing past my nerves, my muscles, my tendons, riding past, arms outstretched, and they go 'yeah', telling the next one along what to expect, as the hashish hug heads up, sort of like a saxophone towards my brain, and I can feel it coming, and then wow, my head is filling too, and all I want to do is laugh, because this great bloody feeling is taking seconds, and I know I deserve it, I know it's what I need, I know this is right, with the stars doing their star shit above me, and the waves doing their rolling dumping shit twenty metres from my feet, and my best mate doing his chit chat about the fucking day shit just an armstretch away. Yup. This is how the world should be. It shouldn't be all that thump thump thump shit, that filling you with crap shit, that 'you got to do this, you got to do that' guilt shit, it should be this. I mean as we lie here on the comfiest bed you can ever bloody sleep on, as we settle in the sand, I realise what the dead have been getting to me about for all those years – they're stuck in shit, and they're terrified I won't be, that I'll find the answer that they haven't – and now all those dicks cemented in their own crap lives will be freaking, because this is it, this is what life is meant to be, I mean it really is this fucking simple. You don't need to put all that time and bloody effort into making yourself dead, you don't need to sweat day night day for the dosh to buy your clothes, your home, your grub. All you got to do is get the fuck out of it. And Si and me is lying there talking about this, talking about us, this, each other, the way people make all this sound, like to have this you got to have worked all year, as if it's some reward for being a good little citizen, like 'You've done everything you were told to, you've worked hard, and now here it is, your turn to choose. Look at these brochures, watch these programmes, lust after these prizes. Yes, now it's your turn, and you get to choose.' Bollocks. They've spent all year salivating, hating the people on the travel shows, green with loathing at the jammy bastards on the expenses paid extravaganzas around the world. Well, well, where's the fucking camera now, eh? This is not a reward. This has just been taken. Seen Wanted Taken, and it's not hurting a single fucking person, and yet the way the dead go on, you'd think this sort of wandering was a bigger sin than fucking a nun in a betting shop. And like Si and me, we can see why people is frightened, like they're scared of leaving what they know, not taking their home with them, doing things not a lot of dead friends have done before, but what we don't understand is why they don't try. Give it some fucking welly, open up, go for it, I mean hell everyone wants to get out. Everyone wants to be free of all the shit. I mean that's obvious, so why don't they just do it?

But like this is where Si don't agree with me. He reckons some people stay at home because they like

44

staying at home. They think they're free there. But I reckons they just don't see that they've been suckered. And like I'm trying to get him to realise this, when he asks me a question that throws me right out. What he wants to know is why I lose my temper like I does? I am shouting at him a bit, because like he just don't see what I mean, and that's not like us, and it feels weird, and so I reckon that's why he's asked the question, so I tell him that it's because it's like he's not listening, but he pushes that aside, it's not what he meant, he weren't asking about him and me, he were asking about me and other people, and like he's asked me this before, because he don't really understand it because I never really lose my rag with him, and hell it's not an easy question, it's like trying to explain why you laugh, and all I can tell him is, this is me, 'I'm as good as anyone else, and if they don't see that then you got to make them.' And Si understands that, but he don't understand how hitting people makes them see you're as good as them. And this is me, 'You're not a fighter mate', and he has to agree with that, but still he reckons I make life harder for myself. But like that's Si, I mean that's why he's such a good mate, like he listens, and he makes you think, even if you do end up proving to yourself you're right.

And Si and me sits gabbing like this till the sky starts to change, till it takes on this glow like a city has at night, a red orange yellow sort of load of light, and it starts spreading up from the far end of the sea like London is marching up the hill on the other side – and it spreads, spreads until the first sharp burst of real orange comes up, brighter, brighter, bang yellow, bright white yellow, as the sun rises and we can't help giving screams because shit, you ever seen the sun rise up out of the sea? It takes your brain away. And then it hit me, like really hit me, I mean when the first man realised, when his brain actually understood, that this huge ball of heat, this sort of life-saving light, was going to come

45

back day after day, had to come back day after day if he was going to keep going, well, hell, that's when he would've gone down on both knees and said 'Thanks mate' to the big fucker in the sky, and there, that was it, that was Religion. It began with the first person who understood the rising sun. And like this got me really going inside, because it's Eleven when you understand something most people don't, I mean shit, probably most people doesn't even think about things like that anyway, but I does, I mean it's important – not Important like it's going to save the planet or nothing – but it means you know why things are. Like, if you realise why people started religion, well, then you realise why people's still doing it, and that helps, because you can make them see what a shit-arsed con it is. Like, if you can make them see why they need it, well then they'll start to feel a bit stupid doing it, and then they'll stop, and well, then, hell, think of all the problems that would sort out, and Si lists a load of them, and I roll another spliff, and it's a beauty, it's the best, like it's the last one and the first one of the day, and as we lug on it and settle down to a bit of sleep, all that keeps going through my head is words, like lyrics, sort of a rhythm, like running me into dreams, and it keeps on going, like – relax, turn your back on what you're told to think, forget the bollocks, you don't have to do it, you don't need to believe them, you don't need to be loaded, because look at me, like what's this then? What am I doing? I'm not loaded, I've got fuck nothing, nothing, all I got is a thumb, all I got is a thumb and a bag, all I got is a thumb and a bag and some clothes, a thumb a bag some clothes and a mate, and that's all, and it's the bees-fucking-knees, better than anything you've got, because this is the way it should be, because this is the way it is, because this is so bloody obvious, and fuck it, because this – it's totally fucking free.

Another World

Si and me were woken up at 8.00 by a copper poking us
with his foot, and he was dead pissed off, and so were
we. I mean, what a bloody dreadful way to have to wake
up. I felt like shit and all, you know, what with having
been dealing with the world's problems all night, but
what you meant to do when a copper's kicking you
awake? Shit, you wake up, don't you? Specially when
you discover it's illegal to sleep on the beach, and like
you're surrounded by spliff butts. Oh wow, what a
fucking dreadful pair of sinners we is. This is him
'Onheon, heon, Anglais, Anglais, onheon', but like as he
starts to get real stroppy Bobby appears out of the van
and the copper starts to row with him instead, and like
it's obvious that he's just trying to save his ugly fucking
face now, because he's not going to nick us when we've
been working with another Frog, who's saying we're
alright, and are moving on and stuff, and so he gives us
a good finger wagging and pisses off. I wave goodbye to
the fascist dead brain, and then we stumbles over to the
bar, to have some crap breakfast, before heading back to
the van, and that sort of sad bit. We're about to lose our
meubles. Bobby's going left along the coast and we
wants to go right. He's told us about this real cheap
camp site ten miles or so down the road, though, you
know, and he says it's an alright place, and so we reckon
well, hell, he's done us good so far, let's trust him now,

47

and so we're standing by the van saying our 'au revoirs' and his football face is looking sad, and Si even kisses him on both cheeks, which cracks me up, but I'm not having any of that and like me sticking my hand out cracks Bobby up, and then he gets in behind the wheel and he heads off up the road, and his white rear disappearing with a hoot of the horn and an arm waving out of the window, and hell, I got to say it, he weren't bad for a Frog.

So here we are at the side of the road, and it's back to our thumbs. We take it in turns, half an hour or so each, but it don't make no difference, no one's stopping anyway. Wankers, the lot of them – just because they've got cars and we haven't.

The road is bloody straight, the sun is bloody hot, and you'd think we were bloody pissed off, but we weren't, I mean it didn't seem that bad really. Hell it weren't raining, and like the heat is different, it's sort of clean, like you sweat and shit, but it doesn't get inside you and make you feel heavy. So we're happy, even if we haven't moved an inch. Hell, even Si has started dancing to try and get cars to notice, like he must be having a good time to do that.

We've been there six hours when a white Luton van pulls up and a football looks out, and grins, like huge. This is me, 'Bobby, fuck me, Bobby, you wanker', and this is him, 'Ken, you is a wanker also.' And I pissed myself. Like I said, he's not bad for a Frog.

So Bobby drives us the ten miles up the road, hangs a left in the middle of Sainte Maxime, trundles up this hill, and after about a mile he drops us off outside this camp site. This is him, 'Vous restez ici. C'est bon', and this is me, 'Et tu es bon, mate, aussi', and he gives that grin that I'm already missing, and the Luton chucks a 'U'ey and disappears for a second time, horn hooting and arm waving.

The camp site looks pretty good and all. It's full of

48

trees and shit, and the bloke who runs it, you know, Le Patron, he takes us down to this patch, and this is him, 'Ici', and that's it, he turns and he's gone, like he's a right rude shitface. Mind you if you're that ugly, you have to be pissed off with life. This bloke, right, must have had people playing golf on his face for bloody years, it's so fucking pock-marked you could test drive tanks on it, it looks like the moon for God's sake, and his nose, right, looks like someone's been jumping on it full time, it's spread all over the fucking place, I mean talk about flat, Jesus, it takes up half his fucking face. His ears are like plasticine that's been left in the sun, and his hair, well, he's got fuck all, fuck all on his head that is, most of it has emigrated south, and boy has it found his body fertile or what? It's crawling over his fucking collar for Christ's sake – like hasn't no one told him? Mind you, when he breathes you understand why no one would talk to him – like his gums have gone, his teeth are black, and he must eat garlic, onion, and dog shit by the van load. It's like having a sewer breathe on you. His body smells too, like a crutch five days after a serious fucking. This is a man you don't want to spend time with. In fact this is the sort of man who makes you dead grateful when he says 'Ici', and then pisses off.

So we've set up our tent, we've spread out our shit, bought some crap from the camp site shop, and now we're cooling it. Frankfurters, Vache qui Rit, French loaf and a tomato – fucking heaven. Sat outside the tent gabbing, watching the world shit by. Good.

Our next tent neighbours are bloody geordies, and like I don't get on with them, but these two, they're not too bad. One of them even made me laugh. This is him, 'Worra you got there? Dick in a loaf?' and then he passes the spliff. Now is that one fuck of a way to make friends or what? His name's Ralph, he's got stubble for hair and sunburn like you've never seen – I mean hell, Ralph don't understand the sun – the blisters are all over his bloody shoulders, and they're big shoulders too, I mean this bloke is built, like his chest is twice the size of mine, and I'm not exactly small, but I reckon he's alright, even if he has got a stupid fucking name. His mate's name is Don, and he's got this tight curly hair and a bright red peeling face, and he's one of those wiry bastards, small, like one muscle stretched over really thin bones, the sort you knows will fight real dirty, and I reckon he's not bad neither, even though he don't talk much.

So Si, me, Ralph and Don, we're knocking back the rouge, lugging on the Hope, and hell this is good. These two is working out here, flogging ice creams on the beach, and they reckons we could do that too, but I don't know. I mean who wants to be servants to the Frogs, eh? But they start talking about the slimline tonics with their knockers out to the sun, and how you can ogle them from behind your shades and no one notices because you're working and people always looks down their noses at the sweating bastards of life. So Si and me is thinking that maybe we might do a bit of this ice cream selling shit, but in the end reckons, what the fuck, we'll give it a day to run about our brains. Let's check out the knockers as free people first, eh?

By midnight we're all well gone, and Ralph suddenly starts talking quiet to Don, and then he's grinning at us, and this is him 'Wanna take some serious drugs?' and like, fuck, they didn't have to ask, well they didn't have to ask me, Si's face looks a bit nervous when he sees me standing up straight away saying let's go, but he does follow us, even if he is a couple of strides behind. Now I'm expecting to jump into a car and head into town but Don just pisses himself when I says this, and this is him, 'Nah', and we walk to the far side of the camp site, and he knocks on some tent's tent-pole – one of those big family size tents, you know, with an extension out front – and this is Ralph, 'Stay out here a minute', and then the tent unzips and a hand opens the flap and they go in, and Si and me is left standing under the trees in the moonlight, and like I can see he's worried. So this is me, 'You don't have to do nothing mate', because I reckons taking drugs is up to you, I mean it's stupid to force people, specially with good drugs, because they cost and shit, and if you don't really want to do them you're not going to be relaxed neither and so you're not going to enjoy them and that'll be a waste, and like I know that a lot of my mates back home reckon that's a dumb-arse attitude, I mean they think it's dead funny to hit people with the stuff when they don't know what's happening, but bastards my dickhead parents call friends once did that to my sister and she fucking freaked, and it were dreadful, the worst thing I ever saw happening to her, and hell it put her right off drugs and all, which is not a surprise, but is a pity because she's missing loads, even if she does reckon she's healthier because of it. That's what she gabs anyway, 'I'm healthier', but I don't reckon that's right because like with all the shit that comes out of cars, and all the shit they bungs in water and that sort of crap, well hell, we're all rotting away on the inside, so why not enjoy it, I mean like at least you got a healthy mind, and that's got to be good for the body. Si knows all this, because we've talked about this sort of shit, and hell I'm used to him saying no, but this time there's this glint in his eyes, a sort of 'I want to go for it' glint, and he says he wants to do it, and he sounds determined like, and I reckon that that's alright and all. After a few minutes of hanging around though we is both getting a bit impatient, sort of pacing, and then without no warning the tent unzips again, and out comes – wait for it – out comes a fucking German. Jesus! I'm about to take drugs with a fucking Kraut! He speaks English mind, so it's not too bad, and there's two other people in the tent, a couple of Dutch dick-houses, and they're out their fucking trees already, like one of them is holding this bit of rug and she's turning it round and round and round and staring at it with this huge fucking grin all over her chops, and the other one is moving this fag backwards and forwards in front of her face, and like her eyes are really wide, staring, and she's sighing now and again. Ralph tells me this is Paula and Anna, and this is me, 'Paula the Anna one', and Si laughs, and so does the Kraut, and I can see he's spacing too, but he holds out his hand and it's big, and his name is Michael and this is him, because Ralph's told him about us, 'You're velcome in my tent', and this is me, 'Cheers mate', but I have to struggle not to mention two world wars and the 1966 World Cup.

Michael's got a shit hot sound system too, I mean like it's turned down, because a tent's not got good insulation, but shit is the sound clean or what? And so are his drugs. He promises us. And so does Ralph. This is him, 'Away man, this stuff's clean.' And I'm telling you, he's right and all. It's a mickey mouse sheet, £sd. And it's not a bad price neither. And like this is a shock too, because hell I'm in the middle of Frog, and like I definitely weren't expecting stuff like this out here, and then when it turns up it don't cost loads neither, and I can't help it, like I'm excited, I'm in the middle of a camp site, and I'm about to take a cheap trip to heaven, and my best mate's coming too. Hell, I couldn't ask for nothing more.

I'm still watching Si, mind, I mean I'm not worried, but like as I said, I know he's not done stuff like this before, because he always kept away from the real party, you know, watched listened laughed, enjoyed it all second hand, but now he's going to go down a tunnel that's going to shake him all over, and I want to make sure he's approaching the tunnel the right way, not fighting or forcing, but arms open, because like if he hits it wrong, he'll slide, like it'll turn into a hole, and falling down there is for life. But as soon as he'd dropped the

52

tab, he relaxed, like he smiled at me, and gave me the wink, which looked kind of cute, because he always looks a bit awkward when he does something he thinks might be cool, and I laughed and ruffled his hair, and he ruffled mine back, and so I knew he was alright, and I relaxes too.

So we've dropped the tabs, and they only cost fifty francs, which is ridiculously cheap, and we're sitting in the tent lugging on spliff and waiting, because it takes about an hour for hallucinogenics to hit, and I'm feeling pretty gone, and like Si looks totally gone, but we're fighting the alcohol and dope and hanging in there for the acid kick, and Don and Ralph are taking turns being real funny, sort of entertaining Paula, Anna, and Adolf with the games and shit that always MAKE a tripper's trip – lighting matches, juggling, walking on the spot, dancing, stroking the tripper's arms, writing messages with fags in the air, talking with water in their mouths, that kind of thing – and then after about forty-five minutes of Don's doing all this shit, while I'm rolling yet another spliff, Ralph says the word 'Breast'. Now, I can't actually remember what he was going on about at the time, but that don't matter, because the important word was definitely 'Breast'. It started Simon off.

'Breast', and Si sniggers. So this is me 'Breast', and he's giggling. 'Bosom', and he's laughing, laughing like it's everything, and then every time he seems to have it under control 'Breast' 'Bosom' 'Tit' 'Knockers' 'Bazoomers', it don't matter how you say them, they set him off again, and he can't do nothing about it, he can't stop. Simon can't stop laughing and it's fucking funny, like he looks so goddam innocent. Like there's this big bloke, and he's out of control, and loving it. And so are we.

Now, of course, after about ten minutes of him giggling the rest of us get caught in our own personal rushes, the world changes, and I mean changes. Anything that moves leaves a trail to mark its route, every sound echoes in your head, every movement is floating, every colour is another colour, every object comes alive. The fag between my fingers becomes a little man swinging a pick-axe – not nasty mind – the camp bed beneath me is rippling with water, the floor is ankle-deep feathers, the zip is a full scale fucking orchestra, and every time Si stops laughing someone just says 'Breast' and the air moves again with all that happy crap. This is tripping, this is time sort of squashed up and stretched out, this is senses discovering that the world's not what they thought it was, this is dead good, and you want it to go on forever.

I don't know what time it was that Ralph and I left the tent, and I can't remember why we wanted to leave neither, like there will have been a reason, but I do know I couldn't stop rubbing his stubble head, and that we floated through the camp site and out onto the road and that we were dead excited about going down into the town. Ralph and me, best mates, best mate you could ever fucking hope for, and as we step onto the road we step onto a conveyor belt, and our legs are moving but we're not walking, it's everything else that's on the move, I mean it's gliding by, trees, the sort of dark lines of houses, telegraph poles, the lot, and all we're doing is padding like a cat into a carpet, and then quite suddenly the sea has joined us, has slid up towards us, and we are padding in sand, like blancmange, and we got to lie down on this shit, we got to sink into this stuff. So we does.

Flat on my back in blancmange – Yo! Above me is the moon and it's big, perfect round, shining straight down on me, me in my own world, me, part of the planet, and this cloud comes from nowhere, slides in front of the moon, and light spills around its edges, bright white light, and suddenly in the middle of the cloud is a face, like I know this face, a face that has always looked down on me, this is the face of that wanker, God, but right

54

now, he's smiling, telling me that I am good, this is good, everything is good, and it always will be, and what can I tell you, I'm so fucking happy – I'm telling it like it is – I start crying, wet warm tears – ME! And I turn to Ralph who's lying beside me and this is me, 'Look, look', but Ralph has gone, gone, and I roll my head from left to right, and he's nowhere, just me, on an empty beach, and like I feel this small fist in my gut, a fear, but it's not growing yet, because I look back up and God is still there and I can hear him and this is him, 'It's alright, it's OK, the world is good, and nothing can change', and I start to laugh, happy joyous sort of laugh, and slowly God slides away, slips away, and I'm looking at the moon again, and I can't help it, like I have to think of Le Patron, and I laugh again, silently, inside, feeling what a laugh is like without the noise.

And somewhere deep in my head there's this splashing, above the roll of the sea, a splashing, and a voice, and it's taking its time to come up, but it's building, growing, and then I recognise it – Ralph. And the fist thumps me, full, hard, spread, and I'm staggering to my feet, panic smashed into me, panic like you don't know, and I'm running down to the sea, running, but the sand is stopping me, and like this is fear, because I can't see nothing, and all I know is this voice, screaming, screaming, screaming, and then I hit the water, and it's like 2000 volts that jerk my feet away from me, knock me back, and I'm over and I can't see this stuff that's swallowing me, and as I stand I feel it suddenly drop away and I'm under, sinking, my arms up above me, and I know this creature, it is Hate, and it wants me, and my legs kick, my arms clamber, but there is nothing to hold, everything is slipping through my fingers, and as I breathe it thrusts its arm down my throat grabbing at my lungs, knocking life out of me, smashing me with so much fucking agony that my eyes are bulging, bursting, and suddenly I'm hit by something so fucking hard that my head is spun, and this stuff is scratching at me, tearing at my skin and I grab it, pull it and it's sliding but I CAN hold, I CAN move, pulling myself up, along, and suddenly I'm being dragged back, my legs, useless against the grip, and oh God, hate has me, throwing me up, and thumping me down hard, twisting me, pulling me back, playing with me, as it wrenches me over, jerks me along, scraping its claws across my body, and I'm rolled again and my face is hit by cold, then rolled back into the warmth that smothers me, grates me, chokes me, and then round again, and my mouth is gasping and grabs some air, grabs again and again my arms still dragging and cold air is sweeping over me and as I pull again I feel the hate backing away, running over my legs, teasing me with its power, and I know I've escaped, I know it has let me go, but I can't stop the shivering the shaking the choking coughing retching, and I'm covered by this fucking stuff, filling my eyes my ears my nose my mouth my throat, this stuff that's sticking to me scrubbing at me splintering into me, and I'm shaking my head trying to rub this fucking stuff off me but all it does is bite, each bit pricking at me and oh Jesus Christ Jesus fucking Christ I'm so fucking confused. And then I see two feet, two feet, in front of me, and there's this voice, and this is it, 'What you been doing you stupid cunt?' and this face comes down, burnt, blistered, hairless, and it blows up like a balloon as it comes closer, and I know this is hate, and it has walked around me, has stopped its games, has stood in front of me, and I'm desperate, I'm scrambling in terror, scrambling between knees and hands and feet, scrambling to get away, and all I can hear is this laughing, laughing, and the voice, calling, 'Ken, Ken', and I know it knows my name, it knows me, and this is worse, worse, Jesus, and I'm moving now, stumbling away, and the voice is following me, coming as if from inside me, and this is it, louder and louder, and I'm trying to push it away, 'It's me you bastard, it's Ralph, Ralph', and the name runs around my head, and it is like another world dawning on me, a sort of revelation slowly rising out of mist, settling into a shape I recognise, and suddenly I stop, stop, as the name comes out of the past. Ralph. Ralph!

And do I feel a dick or what?

Up and Down

I'm sitting on the sand as Ralph comes over, and I'm still shaking, shaking like a vibrator, and he arrives, and this is him, 'Fuck or what mate, you alright?'

And then I remember, as his face turns purple, I remember, I've dropped a tab, and it comes back to me, and suddenly I feel this sort of control coming back to me, and I remember what's been going on, I remember where I am, and this is me, 'I thought you were drowning.' And he laughs, friendly like, and this is him, 'No, not me.'

It took a while, but everything did calm down and after sitting looking around for a few minutes with him sort of talking about what he'd been doing and me not really listening, we were able to head back into town and stare at all the lights, and the fear were gone. But Jesus, it had been like the worst.

We got back to the tent as the sun was coming up and by now I was happily tripping again, like I'd forgotten all the shit, and me and Ralph were having a good time, and as we unzipped the tent and went into the others' world it were obvious that so were they. Si – and this is the total fucking truth – Si was still laughing, and it were easy to see why. Paula was doing handstands in the middle of the tent stark bollock naked. I mean no one had to say nothing to Si, he just had to look. Hell, it cracked me up and all. I mean heavy breasts wobbling upside down – now is that weird or what? Don was helping Paula with her handstands and all, and it were obvious that they was good mates now because his hands sure weren't standing, they were all over her, and she was loving it. Meanwhile Adolf and Anna were on one of the beds, fully dressed, playing backgammon. Now I've not seen backgammon played much before, but sure as fuck it's not meant to be played this slowly is it? Hell, you got to grin. But what got me most was what Si had been doing while we were gone – apart from laughing. Si's main interest was this stack of cigarette butts, a sort of house of cigarette butts, like he's been building this fucking thing for over three hours, and he was dead excited by it, you could just see it, I mean when we got back the first thing he wanted to know was if we'd bought any butts with us because he'd been all over the camp site collecting the buggers but he'd got them all now, and the place was clean, and he still needed some for the chimney and an extension out into the garden. He was so fucking proud it were great. This had been his trip – wandering around the camp site cleaning it up, then building a house and laughing. Shit, you got to give it to him – good or what?

Of course because they were all so busy it did feel a bit odd coming back to this place, you know, so much had happened to us, and so much had happened here that there were this sort of gap between them and us, and like you didn't want to interrupt no one or nothing. So I sat myself down and started rolling a spliff, and Ralph got hold of some paper and starts to draw pictures, and it really sort of surprised me because they were fucking weird, aliens you know, fantasy and stuff, but they were shit hot and all, and hell, I was well impressed, and so was Si, but he wasn't going to hang around to see how they came out or nothing, because he'd got too many other things on his brain, you know, and he's got to get out there again, butt hunting. So I'm left, me and my spliff, and I decides to go for a wander round the camp site and all, and out I goes, but I don't get far, because there's this tree outside, and it starts talking to me, you know, saying things like 'Climb me', and so I has to, and up I goes, and have I got a view or what, like right out over the town and shit, and I'm up there talking to the branches, who are bloody friendly, and there's all these cocks crowing out in the valley, you know, not like in the movies, not sort of clean crowing, but crap crowing, starting off all enthusiastic and then sort of dying off halfway through like they got sore throats, or had a rough night, and you got to laugh, which I do, and I tell you I don't want to come down neither, I'm happy among all these leaves and shit, and so I stay up here with the wind blowing a bit, and the tree chatting, listening to what I got to say about the world, and stupid as it sounds I'm having a bloody good time, and then Le Patron arrives and blows the whole fucking thing. He's not happy. Fuck, the tree's happy, I'm happy, but he's not happy, and he wants me down. Now this is a problem. I'm over twenty-five feet up in the air, and even though I'm tripping I knows I can't fly, and like this is one of those weird ones where it was a piece of piss getting up here, but how the hell do you climb down? Of course by now Le Patron is shouting at me to get down, and I'm shouting at him to piss off – because if he hadn't mentioned getting down I wouldn't have started thinking about it and realised it weren't on, and like hell, I don't want him to know that I don't know how to get down neither. But I can't have sounded too convincing, and he starts getting quite stroppy really, calling me 'stupide' and 'idiot', and shit like that, and if I wasn't stuck up here I'd've floored the arsehole, and fuck it I reckon he's doing more to wake the camp site than all the half-hearted cocks in Frogland, and so I tells him to 'fermez la bouche', but this just makes him even louder, like this is his place and he obviously reckons he can wake who he likes, and he does, because soon people is coming out of the tents to have a look, and they're a bit pissed off at being woken, but as soon as they see me up the tree some of them start laughing and then they all join in, and this sort of makes it harder for Le Patron to be so angry because I'm not looking like a trouble-maker now, just an Anglais berk, and so by the time a ladder has been brought and I'm climbing down he's already heading back to his office, shaking his head and muttering but no longer interested, and the crowd gives a round of applause and sort of slap their foreign hands on my back, and they feel real heavy, and then everyone has gone back to bed, and the only person left looking at me is Si, and he wants to know if there were any butts up there.

The acid kick was starting to die away for me now, you know, and my eyes felt locked open, and the rest of my body was sort of aching all over, like it had been playing football for a week without telling me, and so I left Si to finish his trip on his own and headed back to our tent. He didn't seem to give a stuff, which was a bit of a relief really, and so I tried to sleep but it was only a half-hearted success, and like when Si appeared a couple of hours later, looking the colour of all the balls on a pool table, the two of us lay there moaning about the heat, tossing and turning, sort of sleeping, dozing off, and then waking, and the trip was still part there, but part gone, and finally at about midday both of us gave up on sleep and decided to get the fuck out of the sweat box the sun had turned our tent into, and see if lying on the beach was any easier.

Of course before you lie on a beach you got to get there, and this was like hell, I mean our bodies were like Action Man's, a fucking fantasy of muscle, every joint had to be moved by hand, and to make it worse my lungs felt like they'd spent a week stood behind a 253 and all, like they were tight, pulling across the chest, and breathing was exhausting, and so it took bloody hours to get there, well one hour, and then when we did the place was packed. I mean hell, this was a Saturday OK, but it was only June and you couldn't move an inch, I mean the sand had completing disappeared under bodies and it took us about twenty minutes to find a space, and that was half in the shade and all, under these wooden steps that led down to the beach. But as soon as you lie down, who gives a shit, eh? What really got me though, was that after about ten minutes there was Ralph and Don, and they were working, don't ask me how, but they were. And this is Ralph, 'So you wanna job?'

What's a man meant to say? Well, we said yes. And they told us to meet them in this small café across the road, opposite the steps we were under, and then they were off. Si and I must have slept then, because suddenly it was about 3.30 and like I was dead glad we were in the shade, because we'd have looked like carrots if we hadn't've been. Even though we were in the shade we were dead hot though, and so we wanders down for a swim, and I got there and last night came back, sort of flooding over me, and fuck it, I couldn't believe it, I mean I'd nearly drowned in a foot of water – well almost, because about a couple of metres in there was this shelf where it dropped away and that was what I'd gone down, but I hadn't been down there long – all that scrambling and choking and rolling had been in ONE FUCKING FOOT of water. Jesus, it makes you think, don't it?

Death is bloody easy. You don't need to learn how to do it or nothing. Si and me spends a bit of time talking about this, you know, because his trip had been bloody different to mine, and he'd not even thought about something bad happening to me, I mean he'd hardly even noticed that we'd left the tent, but we had, and I'd nearly not come back, I'd nearly died! I mean shit, you can just be gone, like GONE, and that's it.

I've never really thought about it before, because, well, you know, I never known anyone who's died or nothing, well a couple of grandparents, and I was still young. And like, as Si said – what would my parents have done? I mean Jesus, would that have been a shock or what? Like Si reckons it was a bit dumb to go to the beach on that stuff, but like I wasn't to know that was going to happen was I? He says it was thick though, but what the fuck does he know? This is me, 'What d'you know, fuckface?' And he just looked at me, didn't laugh or nothing, and this sort of hurt look snuck across his face, and like the stupid dick had taken it all wrong. So we stopped talking about death, and I didn't go for much of a swim, you know, walked out a few feet, and then walked back again. It woke me up a bit though.

It's a weird thought that, you know, what parents must feel like if their kid snuffs it, I mean like as parents you must sort of expect to die first, and if you don't, you know, if you find yourself at your kid's funeral, fuck, it must feel like you've failed or something. Mind you, most parents have failed, just by having the snot-rag. Shit, how many people do you know who would be better off not born? Must be millions in Africa alone, you know, shit, they're gonna die miserable anyway, they're not going to have lived much – so what was the fucking point? Hell, half the people I grew up with hardly had anything to smile about, I mean those dorks wouldn't have missed a fucking thing. It would've made the class sizes smaller and all. I might even have learned something.

So, end of the day, Si and me is sat in the café waiting for Ralph and Don, watching the street go by, and like, even if our brains are still not all there, these cafés is good, not like a local or nothing, but still good, and it feels smart being in the open drinking pastis and checking out the Frogs' legs, arses, knockers, faces, all that kind of stuff, you know, all in swimming costumes, well, if you can call them that, because Jesus some of the costumes are so bloody small it's like a bit of string covering the clit, and that's it, that's the lot. And what I want to know is, isn't it painful getting rid of all those pubes? Because they must have to do it every fucking day, I mean like you're not going to tell me the Frogs aren't normally hairy, I mean hell, they've got sodding hedges of the stuff under their arms. And that don't make sense, like why are they so worried about the stuff between their legs and not the armpit shit? I don't know.

So Ralph and Don come walking down the road and they're carrying these cooler boxes, and Ralph's got a tray round his neck, for doughnuts and shit, and Don's got this sort of orange backpack with tubes sticking out which is for drinks and shit, and they both look knackered, but they're grinning, and Don slaps Si on the back, and this is him, 'Away lads', and so I get up and walk away, but it don't get a laugh, and so I pretend I was going to get some drinks, which isn't too clever because Si and I just bought one already, and I end up buying them one, and as I'm coming back, they're all leaving so I'm feeling even more of a wanker, but follow them anyway. We all go round the corner and there's this van parked in this car park, a big yellow Peugeot version of a transit really, and there are about ten people hanging around this van, all of them carrying cooler boxes and trays and drink backpacks and shit, and there's this bloke in the van taking the stuff from the people, and he looks a right dead fascist twat. He's nagging them, telling them they've done bollocks and stuff, and taking their money from them, counting how much stuff they've got left and giving them back their commission for the day, and these poor sods who have spent all day slogging away on the beach in boiling hot sun, all sort of mumble and grumble when they count their takings, but you can see that no way are they going to argue with the twat in the van. And the joke is the twat's name turns out to be Dick, which is just about right, and so he's not twat in the van but Dick in the van, and like he doesn't laugh when he hears me saying this to Si, but turns to Don, and this is him, 'And who may I ask is this man, stood with three pastis' in his hands?' He's all stuck up his own arse, you know, a voice like Queen fucking Victoria, only not so high – in fact it's one of those really deep fuckers that vibrates around a whopper of an Adam's apple that sticks out like the Guinness logo – and I hate him already. So this is me, 'Ken, and I want a job. Cheers.' And this is him, 'My, you're not very good at interview technique, are you?' Dick. So Si sort of glares at me a bit, and then goes over and shakes hands with Dick the Dick and starts talking, and hell I don't know how he got sharp, but after five minutes he's got the upper-class wanker smiling and nodding, and we've got the job on trial – even if Dick the Dick looks at me like I'm a fried breakfast he's just dropped on the stairs – and we got to be down here in the car park the next morning at ten. So it's not worked out too bad, but I tell you, I know I'm not going to like working with the man in the van, and he's not going to like working with me neither.

After Dick the Dick had gone, me and the lads wandered back up to the camp site – stopping at the supermarché for some of the red crap, and baguettes and cheese and tomatoes and shit – and like they're looking even more knackered than we are, so we all sit down outside our tents, and hell, there's not a lot of gabbing going on, so I just lie back and watch the camp site while I chew on bread and cheese, and this is good, specially with the rouge thinning the blood, and like after an hour of this I'm me again, sort of feeling a bit more like a human, and hell it's only taken the day, but even feeling real shit like I has it's been a good day, and that's what this travelling is about I reckon.

65

About five tents up from us there's this Bar-B-Q being set up, and a few of the ice cream sellers are getting things together, and like I've been watching them and there's been loads of laughter and shit, and you can hardly miss this lot, because they got voices like young versions of Dick the Dick, all back of the nose crap, and like Don comes out with only one thing when I mentions them, and this is him, 'Cambridge', and it turns out they're all at university there, some of them training to be teachers and shit, some of them doing degrees in being really important, and they look like they like being them, which I don't understand because I'd fucking hate it. There are a couple of them who don't look as bad though, and so I mention it to Si but he ain't moving and so I decides to join them, to sort of introduce myself, and so over I goes, and say hello and offer a few frankfurters, and the bloke doing the barbecue is alright. His name is Dexter and he's from Luton, which isn't his fault, and he says thanks for the stuff and offers me a drink, and just as I've finished my first glass this snooty cow comes over, this is her, accusing like, 'Who are you?' so I tells her, and this is her, 'No one asked you to come to our barbecue, did they?' and this is me, 'No, but I'm here', and this is her, 'Well go away then', and like this cow has got money all over her, her voice is fucking dripping in the stuff, and, you know, she's all pretty pretty with a frilly fucking shirt on, and what she needs is a good shafting. Then like Si appears and I reckon he saw this mooer was getting my goat, and he starts talking to her about flogging ice creams and shit, asking her about it sort of thing, telling her we're starting tomorrow, and she looks at mc like she's swallowed battery acid, and this is her, 'I can't imagine he'll be too successful', and I want to kill the upper-class shit bucket, but I just say, this is me, 'You only got a cucumber for company, or what?', and I turns away and goes back to Dexter who's a brother and no way is going to give no shit, and I can feel

66

her eyes staring into my back, like she's just got what I meant, and I tell you, it feels good. Dumb cow.

Dexter grins at me, and we get on with gabbing. Out of the corner of my eye I suddenly notice that Si is still talking to Catherine – that's the snooty slag's name – and she's sort of smiling at him a bit, even though it looks like she wants to go and all, but she's still there, and I reckon she's sort of in shock, because someone's given her the lip she deserves, and then the two of them go over and she introduces Si to the rest of her mates who are sitting in a sort of circle playing charades, and a few of them look my way, and so I look back, just sort of smile and nod, but no way are they going to ask me over, not that I give a shit, because me and Dexter is going to have a spliff once the meat's cooked. And this is me, looking at the students, 'What chance of cooking some meat in one of them then?' and he sort of smiles, and this is him, 'I gave up trying after half an hour, mate.' And this is me, 'Don't blame you. You'd probably have choked on all the fucking plums', and he chuckles, friendly like, and this is him, 'They're not too bad.'

After the meal, me, Dexter and this other bloke, Steve – who is obviously a mate of Dexter's, and comes from Wales and whose dad worked down the mines – we goes off and has a spliff and like they give me hints about the job, and like they're not bad these two, and then as we're going back to the rest of them we bump into Adolf and his Dutchies, and I invites them to the party and over they come, and Adolf has got his guitar, and we sit down and start singing and strumming and shit, and then Adolf goes off and comes back with some joss sticks and like I knew he was a bit of a hippy but, well, you got to laugh. So he's lit one up – rose, I think it was – and we're just about to do another Beatles number, which are crap but at least everyone knows the words, and over comes Catherine and she's pink in the face and she's furious, and this is me, 'Don't you like the

Beatles then?' and she ignores me and says to Adolf, 'Do you really have to play that thing here? No one asked you did they? No they didn't.' And Adolf, who's a quiet sort of bloke, just looks a bit upset, but I'm really pissed off, because what the fuck is going on inside her head? I tell you, this is what her attitude is, 'I'm number one, I'm me, you're nothing but a pile of irritation, and you have your place but it is not my place, where I am is not where you should because you are dirt to filthy up my life, and I have this right because I am wonderful, and I have control over my life and you do not because you have achieved nothing, and I already have qualifications and can ride a horse, and my friends would laugh at someone like you because you are common and I am not, and you go out with girls who wear bicycle shorts and running shoes and they are common too, and so you should not come near me because I am not common, I am ME, and daddy has told me what people like you are like and I have seen it too when you are coming out of public houses, and I went to a proper school and you did not, and I have money and you do not, and . . .' – this is what I saw scurrying behind her brain, hidden from her – '. . . if I chose to come here and you chose to come here what does that say about me?' And this is what I can see in that pathetic little face, terror that she might be the same as us, and so she's got to prove she's not, she's got to prove she's better, and so I'm up, like fast, my face right up to hers, eyeballing, and this is me, 'Do you fucking think you rule this planet or something? Do you seriously think you is so fucking important?!' And she pushes me aside and grabs hold of the joss stick, I mean bloody hell – the joss stick? – and she throws it onto the ground, and starts to stamp on it, like some spoilt little kid who deserves a good thumping, and this is her, 'Get out, go on, get out, all of you!' And now everyone has stopped yabbing and they're all staring at her doing this sort of Highland fling on the joss stick, and this is me, 'You're a rude cow, who is making a total prat of herself.' And she stops stamping and on the turn slaps me right across the face, like real hard, flat palm – crack! And by now Adolf has got up and he's going because he don't want a row like this, but I'm really fucked off, like I'm cold, red blind with fucking anger and I push this upper-class bitch back and back until she thumps against a tree, and I've got my fist up against her face and I'm telling her, this is me, 'You should learn a few fucking manners you dumb-arsed thick-brained snotty little shit, you should fucking learn that if you hit someone they're sodding well likely to rip your dead shit face off your pathetic little upper-class arsehole shoulders . . .' and she's crying now, sobbing and I'm feeling good, good, because the cow deserves it, and this is her, 'It was our party, our party', and this is me, 'No, it fucking wasn't. This is a camp site you dumb ignorant shit, people goes where they like here, you understand me?!' and like I'm really threatening her, and I can feel my right hand strong, choking her, and it feels good because this bitch has got it all, and she knows nothing, she's just living on other people's misery, and she don't want to see none of it, nothing ugly, nothing real, she just wants to have a NICE TIME, well she's not having it now, not after what she just done to Adolf, and I know I'm making her sob more, but the fear's good for her . . . And then someone's pulling me off her, pulling me round, and I swing, hitting them in the face, sliding off the jaw, my fist thumping into their shoulder, and Dexter staggers backwards knocking into Simon who's coming on too and behind them running toward us with great heavy breathing is Le Patron, and I bend down to Dexter, and this is me, shouting, 'Shit mate, shit, shit, I didn't know it was you', and I'm helping him up when the Le Patron arrives and Si is desperately trying to calm him down, but Le Patron's not having none of it because this is his little Catherine,

69

this is the cutey he's been ogling for weeks, this is the orifice he wants to fill with his stench-ridden cock, and that's it, he's not listening to no arguments. He wants me out, or he's calling the wankers in blue – the ones with the guns.

Fuck them, that's what I say, fuck the lot of them.

And like then when we're frog-marched back to the tent, Don and Ralph are there, hiding their spliff, and like grinning, and this is Ralph, 'Good party, mate?' and this is Don, 'Try the camp site over the road', and both of them is laughing and Le Patron screams at them that it's not funny, and then starts shouting at us to get the tent out of there, and then starts shouting at Ralph and Don to get their tent out of there and all, and on and on about disparu and allez, until we've got everything in some sort of a pile, and like Ralph and Don's not laughing no more, and Si is not talking neither, and we heave this mess onto our backs and head out of there, feeling the eyes watching us, the statues who have just had their evening's entertainment, and the four of us is walking through the gates, leaving the fucking dump, crossing the road, and on to the next place. And I'm telling you, I look at the lads, and there's an atmosphere.

Starting Out

Typical, huh? Ken is excluded. Now, was I asking for that? Course I bloody wasn't, it was her, she was asking for it – hell, she NEEDED it. Like, it weren't my fault, I didn't start it, I was just having a good time, we all was, but she had to come along and ruin it, and I hate it when people does that, break things up because of their bloody problems, specially when their problem's not a problem at all, but just something bloody stupid. I mean it's hardly surprising I lost my rag, is it? I says some of this to the lads, but it don't really help much, like they need a bit more time, and so I reckons the best thing to do is shut up. So I does.

The camp site over the road is a bit different, it's sunk sort of ten feet below the road level, and is a big field really. We find a spot easy enough and all, and it turns out Les Patrons of this place think Le Patron of the old place is as much of a wanker as we does, and so by the time we got our tents up Don and Ralph aren't too pissed off no more, and even though Don makes a few off comments Ralph knows the score, he knows life's not worth getting uptight about, specially when it turns out this place is a few francs cheaper and a couple of tents down from us is four Swedish bints with love-me knockers, and because hell in the end they reckon that little stuck-up Catherine needed a good seeing to and all. Si though really is quiet, I mean I know him, and it's like he's more than embarrassed, and if he hadn't been my mate for so long I might even think he was being a bit of a fucking wimp. He just puts up the tent and goes to sleep, ignoring me, like he's sulking, and I reckon that at least he should talk to me about it – I mean she was the one who started it – but no way am I going to force him, I'm not going to put my head in his face if he don't want it, if he's not interested, well, tough shit, know what I mean? So I go and have a few drinks with Ralph instead, and I reckon we're going to like this camp site and all, because the two of us sort of sat outside the tent and at least three people stopped for a gab, and Ralph only knew one of them, and the others were just sort of passing, but wanted to be a bit friendly, and they was asking what we was doing here, and they lugged on a bit of spliff, and hell one of them had some Hope himself and all, and then they sat down with us, and it was like a good party, and we hadn't been expecting it neither. Then Don came out of his tent and he wasn't pissed off at all no more, and I felt lots better and all, because the people here is well funny, and shit one of them even supports Tottenham, and like it turns out the two of us have been at loads of the same games, and we reckon we must've even travelled on the same bus to a couple of the away ones, and like it makes you bloody think, don't it?

I got back to the tent about two, and Si was flat out, so I had a goodnight spliff, and there I am, lying in my sleeping bag, and it suddenly hits me that I've only been gone for six days, and like so much has happened already, and I'd never have thought all of this would have gone on, I mean fuck, is life weird or what? And my head is sort of full with everything, and like it's sliding around all over the place, and I don't know what'll happen next, and I'm running all these ideas and slipping into dreams, and then sleep drops without me knowing, like jumping from the high board. Blackout sort of thing.

The next morning, the seventh morning, I was woken by Ralph, and it was time to start work. Si was already up and out, and he'd had a shower and shit, and when I rolled over to groan at the day, I put my face right into the middle of his wet towel, and it was like a kick start, because I hate wet things belonging to other people, like it's wet with THEIR body fluids, and it was fucking cold and all, and I was out that tent drinking Don's coffee and lugging Ralph's spliff within thirty seconds. Did I need that or what? Back came life, and last night – the lads told me to forget it – and then the three of us got stuff ready for the day, like munching on yesterday's bread, and we was ready to go, but Si still hadn't turned up. Now I weren't all that worried but I did sort of wonder what was up, because he's reliable, you know, and so I wanted to hang around for him, but Ralph and Don said we couldn't wait, so I left a note on the tent, and this was it, 'Gone. Hurry up', and then we went.

It took about fifteen minutes to walk down to the car park and when we arrives Si's already there, and he comes over, all smiles and shit, and saying he were sorry he hadn't let us know where he were, and like then he smiles over at the stuck-ups who are there and all, and they smile back, and the bitch is there too – she's turned her back, mind, haughty like – and I don't get it, because I mean, like, has he been with them or what? And Si sort of gets all conciliatory now, trying to explain sort of thing, but you can see he's a bit worried, because that's exactly what the wally has gone and done, he went over to say a sort of sorry to the nerds on the other side of the road, and like he's talking fast now, so I can't get a word in, but I don't know if I want to get a word in anyway because I don't know what to think of him. So he goes on about having to work with the nerds, and not wanting to be at war, and how they're not all bad, and

73

he knows I must reckon he's being a bit of a prick, because he knows I reckon it was her fucking fault and he knows that I must reckon that all he's doing is making them feel they was right, and that shits like that always feels they is right anyway, and that I reckon they reckon God gave them everything because they deserved it, and that I reckon that's bollocks and the reason life's shit for everybody else, because like they're selfish and greedy, and pleased with themselves – which makes it even worse, but like Si knows that's what I reckon, he understands that, but he reckons he's 'made things better', and when he's finished, all I can say is this, this is me, 'You can make things better?' because he's gone on so long I've had difficulty following, and like I've got a real heavy head so I can't be bothered to argue anyway. I mean, the only person I want to talk to is Dexter, because he's going to have a well sore jaw this morning – my knuckles hurt like hell – and it weren't nothing to do with him. So I tell Si he can do what he fucking likes, and I go over to Dexter.

Dexter meets me halfway, and I pat his chin, show him my knuckles, and sort of half laugh, and this is me, 'I didn't realise', and this is him, 'It's alright mate, I understand', and I know he does because he's a brother and they got to take loads of shit, you know, they're used to it, and so we're standing there gabbing about it, and he's telling me not to worry, and that he reckons the stuck-ups will come round, and I got to say it, I mean I don't see what he sees in them, like what's he doing with them in the first place? And while he's talking I'm thinking, and I still don't understand it, because he must feel he's a sort of token, like so they can prove to themselves that they're not racist or nothing, but then again I suppose that's better than being shat on, I mean at least you feel welcome, but if you is the token aren't you being shat on anyway just by being it? Aren't you only welcome because you're differ-

74

ent, and not because of who you are, or what you do or because you come from Luton – because, hell, none of the stuck-ups come from there, I mean shit, they'd probably never even GO there (well, neither would I, but you know what I mean)? And then it suddenly sort of hits me, like Si's a Yid, and even though he don't practise or nothing he's always sort of had to fight it, like it's made him feel a bit different, and you know dorks have always taken the piss because he's had half his knob chopped off, and in the showers at football I've had to stand up for him loads of times, you know, telling the wankers who are giving him the You-a-Yid grief that he does eat bacon, and shit like that, so they laugh and forget they want to pick on him, and like thinking about all that makes me reckon that maybe Si wants to be accepted by the stuck-ups and all, just like Dexter does, because it'd sort of make him feel that he's got some-where – but hell, that somewhere seems more like solitary confinement to me. And I look across at Si, and I got to grin, because a mate's a mate, and you don't back away from them, and like Si did promise he didn't say I was in the wrong, you know, just that we was sorry things had got out of hand, and hell what's it bloody matter eh? I mean, I can live with what he done, even if he should have told me first. And like I'm feeling pretty good about all this, when suddenly I realise that Dexter has sort of finished talking and he's looking at me like he's just asked me a question, and shit, I don't know what the fuck it was.

So I'm standing there like a berk, wishing I hadn't had those spliffs, stammering about, going on 'Well I'm not sure', and from behind me comes the cavalry, Ralph comes up and saves my brain, and this is him, 'Eleven o'clock and still no sign of Dick', and it takes me a moment to get it, and by then Ralph's off again about Dick the Dick, saying he'll turn up moaning about problems at the base, and that it's the usual story, because if we're late then we just get the sack, and like that's no surprise because all bosses reckon we're liars and they're saints, and that we need threats to keep us working while they need their problems understood, which is bollocks and is all to do with power not teamwork like they go on about – on and on about. And of course Ralph's right, because when Dick the Dick does pull up, he leaps out the van like a posing walrus, and starts moaning about the 'dreadful delays' back at base – which by the looks of him means he overslept – and then he starts to boss us around like we're plankton.

Si and me is last to get our cooler boxes, and in them is all this dry ice, and about fifty ice creams – chocolate, vanilla, orange and lemon – and we got to call them 'Chocolat' 'Vanille' 'Orange' and 'Citron', and I tell Si I'll call them 'Chocolat, Vanille, Orange and Renault', and Ralph says that's an old fucking joke but laughs anyway, and then I get given a tray full of doughnuts, 'beignets' is the Frog name, and there are 'pomme beignets' with apple in, and ordinary ones with sugar on, and they don't look too bad, and then Dick the Dick tells me and Si to get into the van with him and he'll drop us off at this beach that he wants us to do – it's a couple of miles out of town. Typical, or what? So in we get, and Dick the Dick tells us to count up our stock careful because everything has to add up at the end of the day, and then he asks us if we've got change, and Si has, but I haven't, so Dick the Dick gives me some francs, and makes a note of it – he does this while we are driving, just to show how clever he is – and then when we get to the beach, and this is him, 'Right, out you get, and I'll be back here at 3.00 for refills, and here at 6.00 to pick you up. Alright? Now then, listen carefully, because this is the one bit of advice that I will give you – shout your lungs out, let the punters know you are there.' So that's what we does. All day long.

And what a fucking day. Eight hours we're expected

to do, eight hours of up and down this hot bloody sand, up the beach, turn around, down the beach, up the beach down the beach, each run taking about half an hour, and like this is ridiculous so I reckons the wankers can come to me, and I set myself in the middle of the beach and start shouting. By about 2.00, I've eaten loads of ice creams and sold five, and Si has only eaten one and has sold forty-two, and like it don't seem fair, and every time he walks past, he makes me feel I'm just lazy, but that can't be the problem, because hell, I've been shouting my lungs out, haven't I? I've been sat out in the sun all the time, haven't I? Hell, I've walked about a bit, you know, I'm knackered. So what I reckon is it's because he speaks Frog. I mean it's not like he's loads prettier or nothing, I mean he's a bit prettier, but that's not a reason to buy a beignet. You don't sort of think, 'He's a bit of alright, I'll buy his doughnuts.' Then again, maybe you does. Whatever way it is, I reckon they're bastards because we're selling the same things, and like hell, I'm shouting louder than he is and all.

By the time Dick the Dick turns up for a refill it's clear that I'm crap at this and that Si's not. Dick the Dick doesn't help neither, he looks at my box, looks at my takings, and this is him, 'You must have eaten a lot', and this is me 'Yeah, so what?' and this is him, 'You owe me eighty francs', and this is me, 'That's bollocks that is. I don't have to pay for what I eat.' And I'm telling you, in his eyes was victory, like he was loving it, his voice was dancing with joy, and I felt his superiority, this is it, 'Oh yes you do, young man', and I loathed him, hated him, and somewhere I heard my anger shouting at me 'Show the fucker, show the fucker', and it was hot anger, like indignant, embarrassed, and like there was only one way to win. So for the rest of the afternoon I worked like shit. I 'paraded my wares', I sang about them, I danced about them, I done the fucking works, and guess what? The Frogs stare at me like I'm an Englishman desperate to sell ice creams, and ignore me – I reckon they are born senile out here. But the Krauts and the Dutchies and the Anglais, they're different, they love it, they sort of think 'Hello, here's a berk', and the Huns reckon they must reward this much effort, and the Dutch think the English are so much fun, and the Brits feels sorry for me, and so come the end of the day I've emptied my box and borrowed a few from Si and all. And most important, I've come up with a strategy – I'm going to play the Englishman. I shall roll up my trousers, put a knotted handkerchief on my head and carry this umbrella I found. Si is pissing himself, and I don't blame him – I look shit hot.

Dick the Dick is unimpressed. He looks at my empty box, he works out my commission, and this is him 'Right then, young man, your commission equals exactly what you have eaten. So that leaves . . .' and he picks up his snotty little notepad, 'the twenty francs change that I gave you this morning.' And he grins and takes everything I've got. I am standing there with an empty hand. Zilch, fuck all, zero, nothing. I've not made a bleeding sausage. Out of all that sweat, slog, and fucking idiotic behaviour, not a single fucking bean. Shit. But the Dick in the Van seems so happy about this I don't say a word. I just take the money from Si for the ice creams he gave me to sell, and this is me, 'Drive on James.' And Dick the Dick's face drops, only slightly, but I'm telling you, it drops, and like now I have to grin, because I know I can do it, and the deep throat is going to know it and all. He's not going to sack me. You wait and see.

Si has made about 150 francs from his day, and he's dead pleased and so he buys us the bread, cheese, frankfurters and rouge for the night, which is pretty good of him, I reckon, and then we head back up to the camp site where Ralph and Don are already chatting up the Swedish groin-aches. We get our supper ready and then go and join them, and like one of the Swedes is

78

giving me the eye and she is fucking gorgeous, with these huge blue eyes and this dead short blonde crop, and sit up tits, and I reckons I'm in there, but then she asks, this is her, 'Why you have a handkerchief on your head?' and laughs, and I come back dead quick with, this is me, 'National Costume', but my mouth is full and so it comes out as 'Nashchernul Chostroom', and I spit a load of food out, and she looks disgusted, and I know I've blown it. I try to get it back, but it's no good because she don't like Hope neither, so me and Si decides to get an early night, because like our legs is knackered and all, and we fall into the tent, and I roll up this spliff that is fucking huge, and even Si has a go, and like this one does us in, like the two of us are totally gone, and I says to Si, 'The top of my brain is floating in the clouds like a sparrow shit shot from a sore sphincter into the updraught of a passing seven four seven', and I start laughing, 'Try saying that in one breath', and I say it again, this is me, in one breath, 'The top of my brain is floating in the clouds like a sparrow shit shot from a sore sphincter into the updraught of a passing seven four seven – try saying that in one breath'. And Si tries, and cracks up halfway through, and I don't know how long we went on for but eventually Ralph came over and told us we was insane wankers and we should shut the fuck up, and this made us laugh even more. And then I heard it, the buzzing, that dentist drill beside your ear, and we both knew that a mosquito had snuck into our tent, and we both knew it had to die. It was a brief battle. It lost. I caught it on Si's shoulder with its mouth full. What is it with mosquitoes, what is it that turns them on? I mean who in their right frigging mind wants to eat blood? Si says it's the female who sucks the blood, and that seems about right, like women have been doing that ever since they sent us out to hunt. 'Here you go dear, bleed me dry.' That's why they have periods I reckon – it's sort of overflow. And then from somewhere

79

outside comes Ralph's voice again, and it's sort of singing, and this is him, 'There was a vampire called Mabel, whose periods was very unstable, at the height of the moon, with the aid of a spoon, she'd drink herself under the table.' And I pissed myself. Of course Si didn't get it. But he will.

In There

Day two on the beach was loads better. I took down a
bottle of Coke so that I didn't have to eat all of my own
stock, and I limits myself to only eating two glaces, and
that's not bad, specially because I had one too many in
my box today anyway, and so with a lot of marching up
and down, I've got rid of nearly eighty ice creams and
about twenty beignets, and I'm over 160 francs richer.
Dick the Dick says nothing, so I just grins, and this is
me, 'Sorry Dick.' But like I know I can do it now, and
even though it's exhausting, as the days sort of go by it
does get easier. And hell the job does have perks, like
half these leg-spreaders down on the beach are topless,
and they love it when you ogle. I mean you can see it,
they turn over just as you're passing, or sort of arch their
backs, or run down to the sea straight in front of you,
bounce bounce bounce, and there's no way they don't
know you're having a damn good look, and there's no
way I can stop myself neither, you know, like sometimes
I remember all that feminist sexist crap we got at school,
equal opportunities and shit, and still I can't stop myself
ogling, even when I try, and like in the end I reckons
the only equal opportunies I'm good at is that I'll give
all of them equal opportunity to sit on my cock. See,
there's another thing, people is always going on about
what turns men on and shit, and all I can say is that it is
Women. Big ones, small ones, in-between ones – you

81

know, big on top, small down below or small on top and big down below – hell, I don't care a stuff, women are women, and I want to shaft the lot of them. Mates of mine are always going on about the slags in the Sun, but I'm telling you they're just one type of knicker dropper, the type you don't get your hands on much, and I don't give a shit what anyone says, they're not like that first thing in the morning because all women I've seen can't hide the fact that they droop, sag, crease, and shake, and they've all got to talk and all. Hell, women are women, and a photo is only something to help you wank, so it's a lie, and hell, if you says a lie is what you want to have, you sure as fuck is going to be disappointed. I tells my mates this, but I don't think they get it. They go on about firm tits, pert tits, upright and downright tits, tits here, tits there, tits-every-fucking-where, and like I'm not saying they're wrong, but it's the way they say it, like they've got to prove something, like proving they're not poofs, proving they're real men, but they're not talking about the tits I normally see but about ones that the slappers probably haven't got, and at times I reckon they go on about it so much they really is bend-over merchants. I mean look at the statistics – what is it? One in five? Fuck, I got more than five mates.

Anyway, there's this one knob's nightmare down on the beach who makes me burst my rolled-up trousers. She's this gorgeous Frog girl who's out with her mum, and oh my God, she's to die for, like she looks up at me from these huge half-down eyes, and like she's all dark, and I want her, and I know her mum knows, and is ignoring it, like she's almost proud, and the girl gets up whenever I comes by, and she walks in front of me, and looks at me like I'm edible, and her breasts are there, centimetres from my hands, and like sometimes she stops me and asks me in this hushed voice – that sprints straight to my groin – for one of my glaces, and then while I'm fumbling for her change she always starts to

82

eat the ice cream, right there, in front of my face, and
you knows what I'm thinking, and she knows what I'm
thinking, but I can't do nothing about it, because I can't
think of nothing to say, like my brain just empties, and
so we sort of part, and she goes back to lie down, and I
go off, and she watches me all the way down the beach,
watches me, and when I say beach, she's not on sand,
she and her mum are out on this stretch of rocks all on
their own, and it's between two beaches that I go
between, so I can't help it, I mean I got to go past loads
of times every day, and I can see her from a good
hundred metres away, and as I walk closer I know she's
watching me, and like I am desperate, but not once does
she come down without her fucking mother, so there's
never a real chance, not even when she bumps into me
swimming. And like this goes on for over a week, day in
day out, and the two of us never gets it together, but we
both know that that's all we want to do, but at the same
time, I mean hell, I reckon we both knows that it's not
going to happen. Course that don't help, like that don't
stop the fantasies does it? This is mine, at night, this is
what I dreams, not once, not twice, but three bloody
times.

It's a Sunday morning and I come over the rocks and
she's not there, and I know what's happened, I know
her holiday is over and she has left and like I can't tell
you, it's miserable, like the biggest fucking let down of
all time, and I'm even depressed in my sleep, and the
next hundred yards down the beach is like a vacuum, is
like Hell, and then as I reach these big rocks that start
the next beach it all changes, the sun comes out, and I
see her, lying alone, between two large flat boulders,
and my groin leaps straight into my brain. There she is
looking up like she does, and she's asking me for 'une
glace', and as I bend down my hand touches her leg and
her hand touches mine, and oh God, she pulls me down,
She pulls Me to her, and our mouths hit like skuds, all

over, her great big lips drowning mine, and my knob is screaming, and her breasts are so big, so firm, so aaarrrgggh, like, WHO MADE THIS WOMAN? And then I feel her hand on my erection and she is moving me up and down and guiding one hand down to her knickers, and I can feel her hair, like it's knitting between my fingers, and I know it's going to happen, I know this is real, every dream I ever had is coming true, and this is not excitement this is heaven opening up the gates, and I've slid off her cacks, and she's ripped off mine, and she's taken a dollop of spit and she's smearing my knob, and the helmet is filling up, expanding, and I can feel, bigger and bigger, and suddenly I'm kneeling and she's got her legs apart like they're pointing the way and my knob is moving towards her . . . is moving towards her . . . is moving towards her, and it touches, it touches the skin, and the skin is slowly peeling apart, the moistness is welcoming me, and then, like why? Why? Suddenly from nowhere there is a voice, a voice, a fucking voice, screaming out 'Cacahuètes', and it is coming closer, and both of us hear it, and this is the wrong moment, this is the WRONG MOMENT, it's fucking dreadful, and we got to try and stop, but we try to go on, like we have to, but it's that bloody peanut salesman, like he's on his way, and it's no good, we know it, we both know it, but I don't care I don't care, and I'm still sliding in, like the first five millimetres are almost in, but her hands are on my chest and she's pushing me back, sort of gasping 'Non' 'Non', and I'm gasping 'Oui' 'Oui', but it's no good, it's no bloody good, and suddenly we are sitting up straight and the peanut man is stopping in front of us, to display his wares, and like they are the biggest bloody peanuts you've ever seen in your life, and he's standing there, chatting to us, and we're still stark bollock naked, and he hasn't even noticed, and like he's Danish, he's always friendly, he's always relaxed, he's got plenty of time, and I know it, and the moment is passing, like a storm cloud is passing in front of the sun, and now coming down the beach is the shouts of the mother, and it's like she's pulling her away from me, like she's being dragged back by this wire, and she's going, looking at me, staring at me, like reality all over her face, and suddenly the bloody Dane is gone and all, and I'm left there like a full sponge waiting for someone, anyone, to pick me up, and squeeze. But that don't happen. I'm back at the end of the beach and I'm walking, and this time there is no one there, no one nowhere, and it's like walking into a black hole, like walking into God's real big joke. And it's all over, and I'm telling you, it ruined my bloody night. Ruined it. Well it would, wouldn't it?

Of course she isn't the only person I saw regular, I mean there's people who waits for me now, and grin when I turn up, and I've even got quite a lot of Frogs who buy from me, and that always feels like major success. So I'm making regular money, and even Dick the Dick occasionally seems to think I'm not a total wanker – which is funny, because the more I see of him the more I know he's one – and like Si is doing good too, and he's moved to a different beach and all, which is a bit of a shame but like he said he weren't given much choice so there's not a lot we can do about it, and anyway it don't matter too much because we're both doing alright out of this, specially now we've worked out these scams. Oh yes, the Scams. Lovely things they are. The scams mean we make almost serious money, and for fuck's sake, it caps the whole thing off and all, like half of us ice creams sellers is ripping the company off left right and centre, right under Dick the Dick's nose, and he sees none of it, and like that's amazing because he spends so much time looking down his nose you'd reckon he could see the lot. Mind you, he's looking down from so high up – him being related to God and all, and having a special calling in life to make people feel thick

85

– that I suppose it's not that surprising, and hell he's got a load of nostril hair in the way and all, like two tassels in search of garden shears, and that can't help, and neither can the fact that most people think he's an escaped fucking looney sadist with a miserable brain to live in and so can't wait for the chance to rub his face right in it.

So then, scam one for smearing Dick the Dick's face with shit, and for feathering our own nests, is this – hell, it's so simple it makes you want to dance. The van pulls up and about ten ice cream sellers grab the boxes – which are all individually numbered because we ask for different numbers of ice creams like according to what goes well on our own patch – and as soon as we've got our box we take out a couple of ice creams and give them to a mate, then we goes over to Dick the Dick and says we're two short, and so he double-checks, sees we're right and gives us two more ice creams from the spares box. Now two ice creams is no big deal you'd think, but look at it this way – we get 10% of sales, so if you nick two extras it's the same as selling twenty more ice creams. Good eh? But like what gets me is that three or four of us can get away with it every day – I mean, can't he see? We rotate who actually tells Dick the Dick they're short of gear, because we know you got to vary it a bit or even Dick the Dick'd get suspicious. We split the profits and all, like working in a team, and like my team is Ralph, Don, Si, and sometimes Dexter and Steve, and there are other teams at other pick-up points, you know, doing similar sorts of things. Sometimes Si gets a bit guilty about it and all, you know, a bit righteous, but it don't usually last long. Anyway, scam one pretty much guarantees an extra thirty francs a day. We got to keep this hidden from the stuck-ups though because I wouldn't even trust them with my deodorant stick, like give them half a chance to lick arse and they'd do the dirty straight off. But it's not too much of a problem, because most of the time we avoids each other like the plague.

Scam two for making Dick the Dick look like a dick – nick ice creams from the spares box while he's not looking. This can involve a decoy, or it can be a spur of the moment thing, but like you can't always get away with it. Scam two is good for about ten to twenty francs a day spread out over the week, if you're lucky.

Scam three for making Dick the Dick look like the brain-deadest boss in Europe – buy your own ice creams. You got to be careful here, because you can't let the numbers you're selling for the company fall off too much – this is the same for all the scams of course – and you got to make sure that you don't send none of your home-bought ice creams back to the factory with your end of day returns. Ralph did that, but thank fuck he only sent back the one, and like next morning he went straight up to Dick the Dick and told him he'd left one of his own ice creams in his box yesterday, and did the Dick have it because it was his mid-morning snack, and if they hadn't sent it back to him then it was like they'd got a freebie off him and so he should have an extra from the spares box, and like Dick the Dick was dead confused because Ralph looked so serious, and he sort of said OK, and Ralph announced it was a Cornetto he was after and took the biggest one there. I reckon that was a one-off though. Scam three can bring in as much as you're willing to risk, let's say thirty francs a day.

Scam four is just plain illegal. Buy beers and flog them to carefully selected punters. This is shit hot, because the punters usually then offer you a beer from your own load, and so you gets paid to drink your own beer, which is why it's shit hot I reckon, and a good way to get talking to people and all. I met this one couple and he's a photographer and she's a model, and he's fucking hysterical and she's fucking gorgeous, and they was out here for a couple of weeks, and they had underwater cameras and the lot, and like they weren't working or nothing, you know it was a honeymoon, and hell I even got myself asked out with them a couple of times, once to lunch and like later that night when they took me for a meal. And we had a shit hot time, like they got this huge wanker wagon – you know, a Range Rover type thing – and we went to this well smart restaurant, and I even had to have moules with them, and this time they was a bit better, I mean I only got about ten of the buggers, and then later that night I even went back to their room and got them stoned, and then at about 3.00 in the morning she got into bed, and it were obvious she wanted to get some sleep, which is fair enough, but there wasn't a spare bed for me or nothing and so of course he had to drive me back to the camp site, and like even though I didn't see them again on the beach, was that a good fucking day or what? I did see them driving through town a couple of times mind, but they didn't see me, and like I was a bit pissed off because I'd bought them beers and all, but it weren't that important because I found other punters who wanted them. Anyway, scam four was worth about twenty francs a day.

The last scam, but not the least, is the most enjoyable. It's when the people packing the boxes back at the freezer depot makes mistakes and put extra beignets and glaces and shit in your box. All you got to do is make sure Dick the Dick don't notice – which's not difficult. This one is like Christmas Day, like it only happens rare, but fuck, does it make you happy or what? Scam five was probably worth about thirty francs a week.

Put all the scams together and I reckon I'm adding 100 to 150 francs to my takings every day so that I'm earning at least 250 francs minimum, and when you think the camp site only costs sixty francs and the food and drink about fifty francs, and Adolf's Hope is dead cheap, I'm putting away about a hundred francs a day, which fuck, is not bad. I mean living out here can be well cheap if you want it to be, specially if you live on pain, Vache qui Rit, frankfurters, and rouge. Mind you we've moved on from frankfurters, we've got into saucissons, and some of them is just like neat garlic and shit, and I never liked garlic before, but these things are dead good, especially the dark red ones which make your arse sting when you shit the next morning, and like I had twenty-two of these the other night, and I must've stunk like a Turk, you know head turning time, because even a couple of the punters on the beach sort of grimaced when I asked what sort of glace they wanted.

That's another good thing, I'm learning Frog out here. I mean at school it took me a year to work out the difference between j'ai and je – because I wasn't listening – but now, fuck, I can do whole sentences without even thinking, like I know what I want to say already. Say I want to buy some bread, I don't think, 'I want some bread please' and then translate it, I just think 'Je veux une baguette s'il vous plaît', and like the Froggies laugh at you because you're Anglais and your accent is crap, but they like it because at least you're trying. They're a bit like that, the Frogs, they think they're special so they like it if you try to be like them. Mind you, they get off on laughing at people and all, because I mean, have they got a sicko sense of humour or what? Like when we was hitching, loads of them would stop, wait till you got to their car – you know, after you've walked fifty metres up the road to get to them – and then they'd drive off, pissing themselves and waving, like they expected you to enjoy the joke too. I mean that's just fucking mean, that is. They often laugh at us on the beach and all, because we're working so hard and they're not, which I reckon is a bit shitty too, and you should see how they treat the lookie lookie men who come over from Africa with stuff to sell on les plages, I mean the Frogs treat them like they're dog shit they've just trod in. I tell you if I was a lookie lookie man I'd go straight back to Africa, I wouldn't want to be anywhere near half the Frogs if I was them, I mean they're so fucking racist – you know, down their knob time. Anyway, I reckon I got the Frogs sussed, and I've got a pretty slick patter on the beach and all. This is me, 'Des glaces, beignets aux pommes, des glaces, chocolat, vanille, orange, citron, Renault, Rover, Rolls Royce, Rolls Royce! Hashish, COCAinE! CRACK! Des glaces, des glaces! HerOIN! ECstasy! Beignets aux pommes, des glaces! Marriage licenses! Divorces done trés vite! Des glaces, des glaces! Condoms! ProsTITutes! DAMes DE LA NUIT! HEROIN!', all of it said sort of clipped, but rolling off the tongue, and it makes the punters piss themselves, and I mean, fuck, is that good for business or what? It must be, because, hell, right now I've saved up at least 2000 francs.

Life on the camp site is pretty good too, and even if the Swedish tarts have only come good for Don, I'm having a fucking ferocious time. Every night's a bloody party, you know, we all sit around outside the tents – and it's getting to be a good bunch down there now – and we drink and sing and smoke, and laugh loads, and sometimes we goes into town and all, wander about off our faces, moving traffic signs and shit, and like we play these fucking hysterical drinking games – they always make Si look a right berk – and even with all this partying we've still not heard a single fucking complaint from no one. Now is this how life should be or what? Of course Si usually needs a bit of encouragement to get going at night, because like he weren't used to it, but fuck, he's getting used to it now, you know, and even though sometimes he finds it a bit difficult to keep up with the gabbing, you know misses the jokes and shit, and like because his jokes are always so dead simple the others don't even realise they are jokes, I sort of find myself pissing myself on my own, but I'm used to that.

I mean it's always a been a bit like that, and maybe it's because he's different with me, you know, we talk about loads of shit, and when he's with the lads he can be a bit sort of quiet, staring off type of thing so it looks like he's not really listening, and I suppose if you didn't know we was all having such a shit hot time you could reckon he was bored or something, but I know he's not, and I mean he keeps saying he's happy, and I believe him because he does look it, and the fact that he goes off for walks from time to time is normal and all, you know he probably just feels like a break every now and again, you know, to get his head together, and hell lots of people does that. Like my dad does it all the time, so I don't see why Si has to be embarrassed about it, but at times he is, like last night he was gone until one in the morning, and he didn't really want to talk to me about it when he got back, you know, he just sort of grinned a lot, and said he'd gone to take some photos of the bars in town, but like when I checked his camera this morning he'd only taken about six or seven shots so there can't have been a lot worth shooting, and I don't really give a stuff, but it would be good if he told me what he was up to without me having to sort of ask, you know, just told me if he wanted a bit of time to himself. But I'm not that bothered, because life is good and the only thing that is missing is some love-valleys. A few of them does pass through the camp site now and again, which is good, but I tell you I've still not had a shag yet, and that feels a bit unfair because I reckons I deserve one – I'm still suffering from unfulfilled dreams of a grope behind the rocks – and I mean hell, it's not easy to wank here neither, not when you're sharing a tent, and specially when you're sharing a tent with Si. In fact I got so desperate I had to have one in the camp site shower – dear God, let the noise of the water be loud enough – and shit did the earth move or what? Jesus, the spunk started travelling from my feet, shaking

91

me all the way, and it didn't bloody stop until it hit the shower head. I felt like I'd been hit with a huge sponge baseball bat. Doof. I came out of there a different bloke though, sort of lighter, with a grin the size of a melon. Problem is, you have to leave it for a couple of weeks or you don't get nothing like it the next time. Ralph does it every night according to Don, he grinds into his lilo, all muffled grunting and stuff. Don likes doing it in the sea according to Ralph, but he got caught by this bloke out snorkelling the other day so he's sort of lost his confidence a bit. Si does it when I'm out the tent I reckon, because I've checked his sleeping bag and there's definitely stains in it. He says they're from a bottle of suntan lotion he spilt, but I reckon that's just a cover-up. Ralph reckons Si's having wet dreams, but if he is they're bloody quiet ones, because he don't wake me.

The real problem is this though, you got so many pictures stored up from the day – big hips, no hips, flat bums, stuck out could-balance-a-pint-of-lager-on-them bums, short bums, long bums, hard stomachs, soft stomachs, big bap nips, small chocolate button nips, aggressive mounds, moulded lips, thick thighs, pencil legs, hair down to the waist, hair starting at the waist, Nazi crops, black hair, red hair, skin like unripe banana flesh, skin like over-ripe bananas – you got the lot, and, you know, it's all part of a day's work, all of it wobbling and bending and stretching and bouncing right there in front of you, and like with all this sun too, I mean fuck, does it make a man horny or what? So you'll understand, right, that not getting it is well frustrating, especially when you see some of the poser wankers who go thrusting around in their skin-tight briefs thinking they're studs. And I mean, hell, do these copper-coloured Frogs know how to pose or what? They spend the whole bloody day messing around with some young bint in the sea, posing at such a fucking volume that they know no one's not going to see what they've got hold of and what you haven't. I mean it's enough to make you, well, I don't know, jealous, I suppose. And the worst part of their fucking game is that they treat people like us ice cream sellers like shit. All we can do, right, is to try to ignore them, because like if you do have a row it blows the sales for the day – I'm not kidding you. One day this poser dork starts to walk along the beach behind me copying my patter, taking the piss, all for this little group of over-ripe wankers, and so I turned around and hit him in the nuts with my cooler box, and like it felt fucking great, but for the rest of the day no one bought a frigging thing because they was all so shit scared of me. So now, if some third-rate brain does that copying shit – which they does – I just starts doing my stuff more, copying them copying me, and everyone thinks 'Well he's alright then', and start laughing at the poser instead, and sometimes it even helps sales, which I mean almost makes it more fun than hitting them in the nuts, but is more of a private sort of victory, because you have to swallow fucking loads of pride, and have to fight feeling the cold anger and wait for the reward, and then sometimes you don't get the reward, so you wish you had hit them in the nuts, because that is guaranteed and immediate – they go down, you feel better. I don't reckon my style with posers is as good as Si's though, because he just turns round, goes up to them, and starts selling, and then when the poser walks away Si follows, just keeps going until he's over with the poser's mates, and the mates, because they're Frogs, love seeing their mate being wound up, and so they buy ice creams from Si just to rub it in, and that of course is shit hot. I can't do that because my Frog is not as good as his, you know, he can understand the insults and use them to his advantage, and I'd just stand there looking confused and that'd play straight into their miserable tight fucking hands. The knobheads. So what I reckons is that he can deal with it his way and I will deal with it my way, and like what's it matter? Because, hell, we both got this job bloody well sussed. And nothing is going to change that.

On Time

What me and Ralph reckon is that it's time to really party. I mean I know we get smashed every bloody night, and sometimes I don't know how we ever makes it down to the beach in the morning, but what we need is something a bit different. And so we decides to get it. Ralph and me has sorted out this night down at this disco, and the place is only about half an hour away and it's meant to be shit hot, because all the ones round here are a total fucking rip-off and play European dead music, and like everyone's coming along from our site, because fuck this is going to be a taut night, and everyone does come too and all, about twelve of us, right, you know, Si, and sellers and shit, and we all get there about eight and like the place doesn't even get going until at least eleven. So we all meets in this bar and start drinking, knocking them back, playing left hand drinking, you know, touch the glass with your right hand and you got to down it in one, and we're all gone, well-fucking-spaced, and I've got this smart trick which is to ask people what the time is, and this is me, 'What's the time?' and like they all wear their watches on their left wrist, so they all put their glass into their right hand to check the time, and voilà, this is everyone, 'Down in One, Down in One, Down in One', and people are not half fucking stupid, because loads of the fuckers fall for it, and I don't get why, I mean, Jesus, Si

fell for it twice! And then he went and fell for this next
one a couple of times and all, and this is a piece of piss –
all I does is wait till someone's got a full glass, then I go
and knock it so the beer goes all over their hand and
they put the glass in the dry hand so they can shake the
wet hand, and half of them sort of lift the dry hand with
the pint up in the air so they look like they just made an
offside decision, and half of that lot then make a stupid
noise, like 'Woooo' or shit like that, and then they see
what they has gone and done and this is them, 'You
bastards', and this is us, 'Down in one, Down in One,
Down In One', and like it's amazing how many fuckers
fall for that one too.

So, you can imagine, most of the people is real blasted
come eleven, when we hits the disco – Si is even trying
to sing a filthy song – and I'm one of the few who can
see single because no fucker's caught me out, and like
I'm dead pleased too, because I can stand, and it's a well
active disco and dancing with the Frogs can be a load of
wank, I mean they're all over the fucking shop waving
their arms and shit, sort of jiving bollocks. But like
tonight I'm feeling good, moving well, and even the
Frogs move out the way, make space for me on the
floor, and so everything is going shit hot, and hell, I've
even got this dripping Danish duchess making moves
towards me, and I'm so fucking together I'm playing it
cool, but not too cool, and hell this is it, this is the night,
and I know it, I can feel it, and the excitement is there!
I'm going to warm my cock, I'm going to house the
homeless, and like the blood's already flowing just at the
thought of it, and not even Ralph throwing up on the
lighting board is going to ruin my evening, nothing can,
hell I've already got my hands on her tits, my tongue
down her throat, and her warm little fingers massaging
my flies, and this evening is going places!

Or it was.

At about 1.30 a group of Anglais wander in, not many,

five or so, and I don't pay much attention to it, because like I'm well in already, and my dark-haired little beaver is oozing for me, and fuck, why should five Anglais be a problem? I'll tell you why. One of them heads for Si, one of them pulls him real close, one of them is real quick, real familiar, and it is Her. It's the snotty, joss stick hating, ego elephant. It's Catherine. It's the stuck-up shit face who deserves to be dead, and he's snogging her, my best mate is snogging HER, and like he's not vomiting or nothing. And then it hits me. That's what he's been up to at nights. He's been up her. He's been shagging the upper-class bitch, and like what the fuck am I meant to do now? And she's sort of pulling away, and hell, I could laugh, because she's not pleased with him, she's not happy that he's pawing her, that he can hardly string two words together, that my left hand drinking has left him a lurching, pickled, head dead drunk, but like that's not the point, that's NOT THE FUCKING POINT! And right now I'm well pissed off, more than that, I'm sort of beyond anger, I'm unhinged, and not even a Danish pastry is going to melt that blizzard. FUCK HIM! FUCK FUCK FUCK HIM!! You do not do this to me!! And so I'm over there and I'm shouting, like screaming, I'm screaming at him, I'm screaming at her, and Si looks shocked, almost terrified, confused, lost, like his bowels have gone, like he's the nearly dead man and I'm the half-starved vulture waiting to start dinner, he's out of control, he's all over the fucking place, and I'm glad, victory rises two fingers up, I can see this littleness about him, he looks small, pathetic, and I feel this sort of warmth, and I realise I'm sweating, that the people around are watching, silent among all this shit music, and I'm breathing hard, and that's good, and I reckon he's feeling like the dump that he is, and it's being witnessed. And sweety sweety Catherine's not looking happy neither, this surprise meeting has turned blood colour, and all she can think of doing is running,

97

getting back to the paradise of her ignorant fucking pride, and like she drags him, suddenly starts pulling, shoving her way to the door with the stumbling traitor stretched out behind her, trailing like a bag of training balls, and before I can kill either of them I'm standing by an empty bloody space. Before you can say 'What school did you go to?' she's out of there, faster than I am. But I'm not giving up, fuck no, I'm not giving up that easy, I want to hear them bleed, and like I give chase, and I'm into that car park as soon as I can get those fucking Frog bastards out of my way, but all I get to see is Si's nodding head disappearing in the back of a Golf GTI, down the road, crammed among the up-there dog piles, NEXT TO HER, next to that head that is going on, giving a fucking lecture, and I can tell you – you can hear it.

And what about me? What am I?

I'm the problem left behind, that's what I am. Shit. SHIT. SHIT!

Inside

I stayed in the car park for about ten minutes, hit the nearest door with my fist, and wished I hadn't, and oh fuck, I don't know how to tell you what was going on in my head, like Jesus, I'm empty, hollow, my guts have been stuffed with blue-eyed fucking fury, and it's shoved out anything good, so I feel lost, like a stranger, and I don't know where the fuck I am. I'm totally fucking miserable. He's my best mate, and he don't understand. He's my best mate, and he's conned me, he's lied, he's deceived, he's shat on me. He's put twelve years in a box, turned on it's head, like suddenly all of it was a waste, suddenly none of it meant nothing, jack-shit. Bollocks. How could he do it to me? He was my mate. Like I'd do anything for him. Fuck it, he was my BEST MATE!

That's when I started drinking. And that's it. I don't know what the fuck happened after that. All I know is that I felt more miserable than a bitch being stuck by the pack, like I'd been screwed worse than I knew could happen.

You want poetry?

My soul was castrated.

Outside And In

So at six in the morning I wake up on something metal with ridges all down it, something cold and bloody hard, and I don't know what the hell it is – drink's a bloody weird get-out clause – all I sort of realise is that I'm being woken out of the drunk sleep of the half dead by something hitting me, like repeated half punches all over, something is piling up on me, burying me like a pyramid of rubbish, a tomb of waste, and I'm not waking fast, I'm waking confused, and it's bloody dark under here, and my head is sort of thick without feeling, like it's been closed up for the season, and I've got to clean it out, but my head doesn't even know what the fuck is going on, so how do you start? All I can tell it is what it knows already, that it's dark under here, and it's getting darker, heavier, trapping me more and more, smothering, and that it's taking too much fucking effort to move, like I'm pushing against the world, and it don't want to let me free. I'm too lost to even panic, I'm too fucked to even think, I don't have hope or nothing like that, all I got is breathing and my senses sort of coming back to me, but I haven't realised it yet, and so my legs are trying to stand on their own, and like something is holding me down, like I'm tied down by some sheet or something, and then suddenly I feel a movement, like the sheet slipping out from my sides, and all this shit is falling away from me, and I'm getting up, rising up, with this thing still draped all over me, still dragging me down, and there's this thumping, like things dropping, and I'm feeling lighter but still in the dark, and from somewhere I hear this scream, and I don't know what's going on, and there's these feet running and voices shouting, and I feel my arm getting free, and as this thing that's wrapped around me falls away, I hear the shouting turning into laughing, and suddenly there's this bright light and it's sort of blinding, and I'm looking out of a tunnel and there's faces at the end, staring at me, pointing, like mocking, and I'm really confused now, because I can see that I'm standing up in the back of a van with cardboard packing boxes all around me and there's this tarpaulin wrapped all round me, sort of hooked on at my belt, and I recognise some of those faces, and it's sort of like being reborn or dying, or some shit like that, and I recognise the voices too, they're English, and this is them, 'It's Ken. It's the bloke from Sainte Maxime', and I'm thinking 'What? What?' and then I'm making my way down the inside of the van, and my mouth feels dry and my head's regretting coming back, and I step out onto this concrete floor in the middle of this corrugated warehouse, and it's like stepping onto a new planet, and there's hands helping me, and this is them, 'Watcha mate, have a good night, did you?' And my mouth is grinning, but I don't know why. And then I see all these cooler boxes stacked up, and these beignet trays, and these drinks machines, and deep freezes, and suddenly it's like someone has explained the plot, because I know where this is, I'm in the depot! But I still don't know why. I mean, how the fuck did I end up in Dick the Dick's van? And so this is me, 'How the fuck did I get here?!' And then one of the faces tells me that the van were borrowed by some of the sellers, and all I can reckon is that I must've fallen in when they left the disco, and they can't have noticed or nothing, or if they did they couldn't wake me when it

101

got back to the depot, like they must've looked at me and thought 'Stuff this for a game of soldiers', and left me there.

My brain is scrambling with all this, trying to remember if I'm right, and then – and this is the really weird bit – the boss appears, a Frog, who I've never seen before, and he's shouting at the workers to get on with it, and then he sees me, and he looks a bit shocked, because I must've been a right sight, and this is him, 'Who is thees?', and the workers explain and he grins and laughs, and then puts his arm around me, like I'm welcome or something, and this is him, 'Well, then, Monsieur Ken, you come to us from nowhere at just the right moment', and this is me, 'What?' and this is him, 'Do you want a job?' and this is me, 'What?' and this is him, 'I know, I know, you work on the beaches already, but what I am thinking is that maybe you want to work here.' And this is me, 'What, here?' and this is him, 'Si' and this is me, 'Blimey', and then he looks at me, waiting for an answer. And I think, like last night comes back to me, and I remember how Simon fucking Jacobs shat on me, and inside I can't help myself, this sort of huge pleasure explodes, a two-fingered Up Yours, a victory that will show him what it's like when there's no trust, when your mate don't stand by you, when your mate drops you in it, leaves you on your own, and this is me, 'How much do you pay then?' And this is him, 'Two hundred francs a day, plus free tent. You work from 5.30 to 9.30 am. C'est tout.' And this is not just a victory, this is a bleeding triumph, and so this is me, 'You've got a bloody deal mate.' And this is him, 'Good, then go with that fille there and help fill the drinks machines.' And that was it, within ten minutes of waking up, I've got a new bloody job and it's going to be a piece of piss. It turns out it's a good bloody thing and all, because when I looks in my bum-bag I discover I've spent all my money at the fucking disco. Like over two hundred quid! Jesus. I told you those Frog places was a rip-off.

But right now, I don't give a donkey shlong about it. The fille I'm working with is a total penis thriller, I mean I'm telling you, she is Completely Frigging Alright. I could look at her for a long time, and I could do everything else and all, and like she's got a well filthy sense of humour and a gob like a rubbish cart, and if it weren't for the fact that her name was Stella she'd be just about perfect. So like the two of us is working dead good together – I mean it's always easy to work with someone who's enjoying themselves, and both of us is doing that – and by the time Dick the Dick arrives to pick up the van for the deliveries, the drinks is all ready, ahead of schedule, and us two is helping to pack the ice cream boxes, and you can see that the Frog boss is dead pleased with his new employee. But Dick the Dick isn't. His jaw falls open, and this is him, 'What the fuck? You don't want to give him a job, he's a berk', and then the clouds part and the hand of my Frog boss descends, and this is him, 'Is he, mon ami? He works very well for a berk.' And Dick the Dick knows he can't talk no more, and this is me, shaking my new boss' hand, 'Well merci, Monsieur, that's bloody nice of you', and he rubs my head, and like this usually drives me up the wall, but this time it drives Dick the Dick up there, and this is the Frog, 'And my name, my young friend, is not Monsieur, it is Albert', and this is me, 'What's your wife called? Victoria?', and Albert sort of laughs, and this is him, 'Actually it is Elizabeth. Another queen, I think.' And I reckon Albert is going to be a good bloke to work for, even if he is a funny looker, even if he does have a moustache like one of those Second World War chappies, a bald patch spreading from the front, and a pigtail trailing halfway down his back, I mean none of this exactly helps him, you know, it don't look dreadful or nothing, it's just that he's a short-arse and all, and so having long hair makes him look even shorter, and that's not helped neither by the fact that he's one of those shorties who's tried to make up for it by getting wider down at the gym, I mean he looks like an ageing Frog trendy who hasn't got it quite right really, but at least that means he wants to be liked. Dick the Dick doesn't care about being liked of course, and to prove it he's decided to ignore me, which is no problem, you know, I can handle that, because I can look through him, dead easy, and that's fun and all, just like it's fun calling him DICK. What gets me is that he don't change his name. Maybe he's like one of those medieval blokes who went round whipping themselves, maybe he reckons his name is a sort of punishment for his guilty deeds, and so I reckon I should give him a hand, and this is me, 'Dick, I've put all the drinks in the van, Dick, and Dick, are they where you want them? Because if they're not, DICK, I can always move them for you, DICK.' And like Stella pisses herself, and he just gets in the van, slams the door and then tries to reverse too quick and stalls the bloody thing. Stella's laughing so much I put my arm round her shoulder, and this is me, 'Mind if I call you Artois', and this is her, 'Why not? Everyone else does.' It's a right bummer that – when a joke turns out to be so old it's already rotting.

Artois and me headed back to the camp site after that, and it's just round the back of the depot, walking distance sort of thing, and this is her, 'If you want to pick up your stuff I can get hold of a bike for you', and I'm well pleased to hear that, because fuck I love riding those things, and this is me, 'Yeah. Can you get it for this evening? Because then I can tell my mates what's going on', and this is her, 'Oh don't worry, Dick the Dick will do that, he thinks he's a fucking newsreader'. And I reckon she's right and all. But I still want to tell Ralph and Don and people myself, like, it's manners, you know?

104

The new camp site turns out to be shit hot, I mean it's got a dead cheap restaurant, clean showers, unblocked toilets, and there's even this caravan we can use. This caravan is where Artois sleeps with a couple of other bints who works in the depot called Ruth and Maureen, and they're alive, but they're not Artois. I'm in a tent next to the caravan on my own, and next to me is another tent with these two blokes in who work with us and all, and they're called Tony and Sidney. Artois says they're bendy boys, but I try to think, 'Well, that'll cut down on the competition', because I can see they're her mates, and it's obvious I shouldn't say nothing if I want to win this one – which I does. When we got back to the new site I was sort of expecting a bit of a party, you know, what with finishing work and all, but it turns out the wimps want to crash instead, and so to start with I was a bit disappointed, but when I got into my tent that all changed because my hangover came back for a visit and all I wanted was to escape the bugger.

About midday I'm woken up by this thumping noise and at first I'm not sure where I am, but when it comes back to me I'm well pleased, and I'm out the tent dead quick, and outside is Artois and Maureen putting up a big sign, and laughing and shit, and the sign says 'Cumalot, Home of the Hound Stable', and this sets me off and all, and the three of us settles down to a few beers and a bloody good gab – you know, what's your history kind of shit – and I'm telling you this really is a piece of piss, like A-fucking-1. Shit, we even have lunch in this camp site restaurant, and I get to have a steak and it's dirt cheap because I work at the depot, and because Artois flirts dreadful with the bloke who works there, and because it's horse, and they tell me this on my second mouthful and I can see they want me to gag or something, but what I reckon is, horses got to die and I got to eat, and 'meat is meat'. Artois laughs dirty at this, agreeing with me, and I got to grin, because I'm telling you I'm going to enjoy this one.

We spend the afternoon down on the beach, and the girls is topless and stuff and at one point I can't get out the sea because I've got a stiffy, like I'm anchored to the spot – well that's what I tell Artois – and she just cackles and goes, this is her, 'Glad to hear it. Maybe we can do something about it later, eh?' And this is me, inside my head, 'Oh yes, yes yes yes, please God, YES!' And this is Maureen, 'Or was you thinking about Tony?' and Tony comes over and puts his hand on my shoulder, and we're both up to our waists and this is him, 'I don't want to disappoint you dear, but I'm taken', and I have to fight a sort of shiver that runs through me, but I know I got to play this cool because they're mates of my life-saver, so this is me, 'I don't believe in destroying beautiful relationships'. And they all laughs, even the poofs, and like he takes his hand away, and I relax, and hell it was close but not as bad as it could have been, but then he goes and dives through my legs, and I mean what's a bloke supposed to do? I leapt away and shouted fuck off. And like what gets me is when they push themselves on you, because some of the ones I've met on their own, like my uncle, they're not too bad, so if they don't try and touch me I don't want to beat the shit out of them. I mean, it's difficult. You sort of hate them for doing what they does, but hell it's not like they're doing it to make life easier for themselves, now is it? I mean there must be nothing they can do about it. The few I've met, you'd've thought they was quite normal until they told you, and hell, they got to breathe and eat and shit, so they can't be that different, even if I don't understand why they'd rather have a skid-mark arse on their knob instead of a wet quim like surrounding them. I mean if it's a toss up between the death-ridden stink or the gorgeous stench, or hard and hairy skin or the soft and giving stuff, fuck, I know what I'd rather have. When I think about it I feel sort of sorry for them really, missing out on that. And like it can't be easy neither, being hated. And that's strange and all because I said I hate them and I would kill any of them that tried it on, but I know what it's like to be hated, I mean I've suffered, and it's shit, and like, well, I reckon . . . I reckon I got to think about that some more.

When we got back from the beach I sort of found an excuse to go into the caravan, you know, I asked if they got any aftersun – which meant Artois had to rub it in and all – and we was being well dirty, and hell Maureen was being even dirtier, which is what she's like, and I'm half ignoring her, because, you know, friends of a valley you're going to plant can be a right pain unless you sort them out early, and I'm sort of trying to make it clear to Artois that we should go out somewhere private tonight, and she's laughing, and this is her, 'But I've got you that bike. You said you were going to see your mates', and this is me, inside my head, 'Shit, shit, shit', because I'd forgotten about that, and I need my gear, and I don't want her to think I'm not grateful about the bike or nothing, so I know I have to go, but this is me, 'Oh that won't take long', and this is her, 'We'll see shall we?' And she finishes rubbing the aftersun in and slaps my back, sort of quite hard, so it stings, and she giggles, suggestive like, and oh boy, I can't wait. I mean, did her fingers know what they was doing on my back or what? And she's holding my stare, eye to eye, and there's that shivering in my gut again, and I tell you I'm not going to spend long with the lads that's for fucking sure.

The bike turned out to be pretty crap, one of them Honda C70's, but hell, it's better than nothing, so I get on the thing, start it up and head off with Artois giving me a tit-shaking wave, and like I can't get her out of my head. Hell, I'm halfway back to my old camp site when I realise I'm about to see Si again, I mean this is going to be a difficult bloody thing to do, specially because it's a bit weird now, what with me having a new job and something moist to look forward to, and like if he hadn't've been such a total two-faced selfish shit then I would never have got off my head and passed out in the van, and nothing would've changed. I mean him treating me like scum has sort of done me a favour really, but I'm not going to tell him that, I mean I can't, not after what he done to me, not after all that betrayal and shit, and so now half of me is still ready to explode, and half of me don't give a stuff, and I reckons probably the best thing to do is ignore him, just tell the others what's happened. But as soon as I've decided that, I find these sentences coming into my head, things I wanted to say to him at the disco, things I've practised, like 'Call yourself a mate? Does a mate start chasing after a bit of skirt who's hit the mate's mate in the face, and like a crap bit of skirt at that, a stuck-up la-di-dah queen, who's not even got manners – a dickhouse who thinks she owns the fucking planet, and gets us kicked off our camp site?! No. No, a mate, a MATE stands by a MATE, he sticks up for him, he watches his back – he can be trusted. Trusted. But you're not worthy of trust, not now, you've blown that, fucked with it and killed it, you've dumped all of it, because you dumped on me.' And I'm real pleased with that line, 'You've dumped ALL of it, because you dumped on me.' And I'm feeling a bit excited about saying that one, and I'm repeating it as I drive into the camp site, and ride down the track to the tents. 'You've DUMPED all of it, because you DUMPED on ME.' 'YOU'VE dumped all of it, because YOU DUMPED ON ME.' 'YOU'VE DUMPED all of it, because you dumped on ME.' 'YOU'VE DUMPED ALL OF IT, because YOU DUMPED ON ME.' 'You've dumped all of it, because you dumped on me.' And I pull up outside our tent, and he's not there.

Shit. Like all that – wasted.

Ralph and Don are there though, and this is them, 'Oh here he comes. Landed on your feet, didn't you?' and they sit there, laughing a bit, and I'm suddenly well happy to see them, and that's a bit of a surprise, and I starts to tell them what happened, and it's well good, and, this is the really weird bit, because like when I'm telling them I suddenly WANTS Si to be there, like I know he'd love this story, and it's not normal – the story's not normal, and not having Si there's not normal – and that makes me a bit depressed, because all of this is a bit confusing. I mean I wants to tell him because he'll like it, and I want to tell him to rub his face in it, like I'm glad he's not there and I'm pissed off he's not there, I miss him and I never want to see him again – now is that weird or what? Mind you, Ralph and Don is enjoying themselves, because well fuck it, the story's dead good, and when I tell them about Artois they do a lot of tongue clicking and nudging and 'Oh yeah', and this is me, 'And like she's waiting for me now, and I'm telling you lads, she's dripping for it, I mean crying out to be done.' And this is Ralph, 'She gorrany friends?' and this is me, 'One for each of you', and I laugh, 'But you're welcome to them', and this is Ralph, 'Canines?' and this is me, 'Howlers, mate, one of them is round and the other is long, and that's it, but hell, they'd probably do you.' And like we laugh some more, and they forces me to have a couple of spliffs, and then I'm out of there, because I want to get away now, because of Si and shit, and hell, because I really does want to get back to Artois, you know, my balls are groaning just at the thought of it.

The lads shout encouragement at me as I drive away, and I shout back, 'See you when I got the energy', and I'm away, down the road, to Her, and hell you can even make a C70 go quick when you have to, like I'm leaning it into bends, throwing the thing about, and it's well good – except when I goes round a roundabout the wrong way because the Frogs drive on the wrong side of the road, and almost get myself killed, with them all hooting and shouting and shit – and like by the time I pull up outside the caravan I've forgotten all about Si, I'm panting, desperate, all I can think about is Artois and me, Artois and Me, Doing IT.

I'm knocking on the door and opening it at the same time, I'm up those steps without stopping, and this is me, 'I told you I wouldn't be long', and Maureen looks up at me, and this is her, 'Oh good.' And I looks around, and that's it. Maureen. No one else. And it's like a vacuum cleaner has sucked out my navel, like a sudden space in my gut, and it's more than disappointment, it's a feeling of failure, like wasted hope, and this is me, sinking, 'Where's Artois?' And this is her, 'She's out.' And this is me, going under again, 'Oh, when will she be back then?' And this is Maureen, 'In the morning, I should think,' and she stands up and waddles over to me like an over-stuffed sheep, and this is her, carrying on, 'She's out with her fella from the restaurant.' And my face falls, I can feel it, it just drops, dragged down to the floor, and this is her, 'Didn't you know?' And she's real close now, 'And Ruth's out too', and I can feel her breath as she looks up at me from that round face, small round eyes sort of sunk somewhere in flesh, 'So it's just you and me', and she couldn't be standing any closer now, and her thick stumpy fingers are unbuttoning my flies, and I don't know what the fuck to do, I mean – what the hell's going on? It's like everything's fallen down on top of me. I need what she's got real bad, but it's not what I WANTED, and I don't know what to do. Should I push her off? Should I pick my clothes up off the floor? Should I push her off, pick up my clothes, get up from the bed? Should I push her off, pick up my clothes, get up from the bed and go? But she is well soft, and she is real warm, and by God she knows what she's doing, and I mean, hell, if I don't look at her too hard she is sort of quite attractive, and shit, her bum does feel great in my hands, and she is real wet and warm inside, and does she want me or what? So, fuck it, what the hell!

Leftovers

I woke up at about 4.30 and she was half wrapped around me, and it was a bit of a shock to start with, because hell she really does look big, and I'm not sure what people is going to say when they find out, but at least, you know – I'm thinking this as I gets dressed and go back to my tent – at least none of my mates are on the camp site, and I feel sort of embarrassed just thinking about that, because, boy would they take the piss, and I mean is that dumb or what? Shit, you're embarrassed and they're jealous – that's really sensible – even having the idea in my head is ruining my morning. I don't know what I'm going to say to her neither, I don't feel relaxed about it no more. Jesus, I'm worrying about all this because we've Done It. It's pathetic. I thought sex was meant to be fun – and it is. It's the after bit that's crap, it's the fact that girls go all weird once It's happened, get all clingy and stuff, and I mean that's what the problem is, I don't know what she's expecting to happen now.

In the end I walked over to the depot early, and waited. I wish I hadn't. I wish I'd walked over with her.

Work itself weren't too bad, you know, I managed to sort of keep my distance a bit, which I reckoned was the best thing to do, and weren't difficult or nothing because we was both busy and didn't have to do any jobs together or nothing, and even though I did sort of feel her looking

112

at me from time to time I made sure I didn't look her way, you know in case I caught her eye, because that would've been well embarrassing for both of us. It meant I had to walk the long way round a couple of times, and then Tony asked me what's up, so I walked straight past her you know, quickly, with a sort of smile. And then bang on nine everything were done, and I can get out of there, and I'm gone, on my way, and as I walk back to the camp site I reckon I've pulled it off pretty well, you know I've chatted with Artois a bit – and like even though it weren't the same I still wouldn't complain – and I've got all my work done, and I got out of there like well quick, and so when I'm back in my tent, and I can hear their voices coming back to the caravan, I'm feeling well safe, I'm on my sleeping bag and I'm dozing off quite nice. And then I hears the zip. Unzipping. Shit, shit, shit – do I pretend I'm flat out or what? Go away! But Maureen's having none of it. This is her, 'Stop pretending you're asleep, you wanker', and this is me, 'What? What?' all sleepy like, 'Oh, it's you Maureen.' And this is her, 'So have I got the fucking plague or something?' And this is me, 'What you talking about, love?' And this is her, 'Listen, you dick, just because I'm fat doesn't mean I'm thick. You're worried sick that people will think there's something wrong with you because you fucked a porker, well you didn't, alright? I fucked you, and if you're so fucking arrogant that you think a night's fumbling with you is going to turn me into some lovesick girlie then you are a turd. Get it? Maybe I don't want people to know I fucked you, eh? Like, you're not exactly Adonis yourself. So, dork, get over your big bad ignorant self, grow up, and just be a bit more bloody sussed! Alright?' And I'm just staring at her as she does up the zip, and suddenly I'm alone in the tent again, and I have to tell you, I felt a right bloody berk, and like there was no way I was getting back to sleep neither, because I've got my pride, and I mean what the hell was I meant to do now? I'm living next to the woman, I work with her every day, I want to fuck her friend, hell, I had to recover my face or I could have screwed things up in a big way.

Not that this was the first thing I thought of. The first thing I thought was 'Me, Arrogant?' But then I sort of realised that you could see it like that if you was on the receiving end, because I had sort of ignored her, which probably does feel like arrogance I suppose, so what I decided was that I should go and say sorry, but when I got outside the caravan the curtains was shut, and that threw me because I didn't want to wake them all up or nothing, I didn't want to make a scene, and so I hung around for a couple of minutes trying to hear if they was awake in there, but I couldn't hear nothing. It was a right pain, and then I started to feel that people were looking at me hanging about, that I might have been noticed, you know, and I must look a bit sort of stupid, lost like, so I went and picked up a newspaper from the table outside the tent – so people would think I'd had a reason for coming out in the first place – and went back inside, and tried to sleep. But I couldn't. Not even a spliff and a wank did the job. I mean I must've laid there for a good hour before I passed out, and I spent most of it not enjoying being me. Shit, is life weird or what?

I woke up late in the afternoon, and sort of like straight off felt embarrassed again. This is fucking stupid, so I went straight out to face Maureen, but she wasn't there, she was at the beach, and I was stuck with Ruth, who obviously knew what had gone on, because she sort of cold shouldered me a bit, you know, answered questions, but that was it and like it weren't worth the hassle, right, so I went back out and got myself a beer from the restaurant, and even this was a pain now, because I had to buy it from the wanker who's fucking Artois.

I checked him out proper this time, and I don't know what she sees in him, because, alright, he's tall, and sort

114

of sporty looking, you know, muscled and shit, and dark-haired, blue-eyed, and with one fuck of a tan, but he just looks like a poser to me, and this is him, 'You like my bike?' And it took me a bit by surprise that – like no one had told me Artois had got it from him – and because she had it made things even worse because now I've got to thank the bastard, and this is me, 'Yeah, it's alright. Cheers.' And I take my beer, and I hate him.

By my third beer he's come out and sat at the table next to me and this is him, 'I learning English', and this is me, stubbing out a fag, 'I done that already', and like the total fuck-face laughs, and then keeps talking to me, I mean he wants to be friendly, and he don't take no hints that I'm not interested, he keeps asking questions, and then he buys me a beer, fuck him, and I can't shake him off! So this is me, 'What's "fuck off" in Frog?', and he tells me. Jesus, that were meant to be a boot in his gob, but no, he don't get it, not this man, he starts teaching me Frog instead, all the dirty stuff, and no way is he going to give up, no way is he going away, shit, he's not even going to give me an excuse to floor him – no, he's going to be interesting, he's going to be good company! I mean, what's a man meant to do?

By about six we is almost having a good time, and even though I still hate the dick, you got to admit it, the bloke is not bad, I mean he's even funny, and filthy, and a bit sick, and like we ARE having a good time, and this is bloody confusing, specially when Artois and Maureen come back from the beach, and Artois sort of blanks me and gives the Frog a huge fucking tongue-bash, and I know she's rubbing my face in it, but to make it worse so does the Frog! Suddenly it hits me, she's told him about me wanting to do her, and the complete and utter Frog snot-rag sort of stops her snogging him, he sort of glances over her shoulder – at me – and then he pulls back, like he's embarrassed or something, and this is the worst, this is NICE, this is humiliating, and on top of having to eat this shit, Maureen's still there and all, and you know I want to talk to her, but I can't, because I can't take my eyes off Artois, because, well, she's got that effect, and like I'm half furious and half squirming, and it's bloody dreadful. Hell, I'm almost glad when the Frog takes Artois back into the bar because at least I can concentrate on saying sorry to Maureen. This is me, 'Sorry.' And this is her, 'And so you fucking should be, you dick.' And this is me, 'Yeah, yeah, I know, but like you know how it is.' And this is her, 'No. Tell me.' And that's the shittiest thing she could've said, because now I've got to explain, and I'm no good at it, and she just looks at me digging my grave, going on about how difficult it can be with girls, and how they can go all soppy and shit, and how it's really tricky working out what's going on in their heads, and how they can use all these emotions on you, and sort of make you feel guilty, and how bloody difficult it is to know what to do, and on and on, and she doesn't give me no help. Nothing. It was hell. I reckon the only reason I got away with it was that I sort of agreed that I must seem arrogant, and rude, and that it must have looked like I hadn't enjoyed myself, when I had, because she's well good in the sack, and after I'd said this, you know after about five minutes of me scrambling about, she just shook her head slowly sort of thing, and this is her, 'Get us a beer, and shut up.' And like that was it. I mean that was it. Jesus!

She's alright, Maureen, I reckon. Hell, we even did it a couple more times, but it wasn't the same, wasn't as good, you know, and we both sort of realised and it just drifted to a stop, but we was still mates, and hell that was easy too, and like I'm impressed with her, I really am. It's a pity she's not Artois really.

Maureen and me didn't do nothing that night mind. I was feeling knackered, sort of relieved too, but knackered, and I hit my sleeping bag like it was safe, home, my place, and as I started to drift, as the goodnight spliff

116

licked my wounds, I kept wanting Si to be there, I wanted to ask him what he reckoned, because you don't need to boast to him, and he makes it seem less important, like more simple, and as I stub the spliff out, I can hear him saying 'You done the right thing, you said sorry.' And I miss the fucker, I mean, why didn't he just tell me what was going on with the stuck-up shit-tosser? I'd've understood. And as I fall asleep I knows I've got to go and see him, and this makes me feel like comfy inside, like something's sorted, because I knows I'm going to make something happen, and it'll be good, it'll be me and Si, and I reckon I hit sleep with a grin on.

The End

I didn't wake with a grin on. I woke suddenly. It was 5.25, and I had five minutes to get to work. Shit. I hate that. And like to make it worse, when I got to the depot Albert weren't there and neither were the van, so I'd rushed for fuck all, I mean all there was was the girls and the poofs, and they didn't know what the fuck were going on neither, so we all got stuck in because what else were we meant to do, and like there was a bit of laughing about and stuff, but we still got on with it, until when no one had appeared an hour later, we're starting to wonder what's happening again, like had the van had a puncture? Or had Dick the Dick got pissed last night? Or was Albert sacking him? Shit like that, and it sort of made us feel sort of half-hearted about the work, because maybe we shouldn't be doing it at all, and there was no one there to tell us what to do, and that weren't normal, but then we thought 'What the fuck, they'll have to pay us if we do the work, whatever's happened', and we got on, until about 8.30, when we were starting to get sort of worried, like this thought was there, like hearing footsteps following you in the street, and I don't know why, but suddenly we all started thinking something nasty has gone on, someone was dead – Dick the Dick hopefully – or the company had folded or some shit like that. So by nine we still hadn't got everything ready, because we were too busy talking about what to do, and there was still no sign of Albert, Dick the Dick, or the van and then finally Maureen says she'll go and find out what's going on, and we can all finish the work, and that makes sense, so we get on with it, sort of thinking about what Maureen's finding out, and then we're finished, everything is packed, everything is ready, everything is waiting for a van, and it's still not there, like all this work we done was a waste of time. So I roll a spliff, take a beignet and wander out the front of the depot to soak up a bit of early morning sun.

I'd just lit up and taken the first full lug when the yellow van swings around the corner and makes my heart do one of them jumps, and I'm desperately trying to stub the spliff out and hide it, and I've bent the bloody thing and pulled out the roach, and like the van rumbles past me, and all I can see is Maureen up front, pissing herself laughing. Bitch – she could've hooted or something. I go back inside, and she gets out the driver's side and shouts across at me that I'm on overtime, and this is her, 'Let's get this van loaded.' So we does. It turns out that the phone is out of order, that Albert has reversed straight into Dick the Dick and the bloke is now in hospital having tests – I have never laughed so much in all my life – and that me and Maureen has got to do the ice cream run this morning, and that's a bit of a pisser, but hell, I reckon should be a crack and all, because I'll get to see Si, which is good, and I'll get to finish the spliff as well, which is bloody good.

We weren't too late getting out on the road, and I knew most of the drop off points for a lot of the sellers, and we had this map too, so we managed to be pretty efficient, like in and out with fuck all fuss. Of course there were a lot of laughter about Dick the Dick, and a lot of happy people trying to pretend they was worried for him, but none of them was any good at it. Let's face it, he was not missed. We reckoned we were a bloody good team and all, and it were great to see people's faces when we pulled up, like they were uncertain, and so we had to take charge straight off, and it were well good, you know, it felt like we were something a bit different, it felt more than just being Anglais living and working in Frog, I mean it was weird, because we were mobile it gave us this extra important feeling, like we were DOING something, like we were in control, and we were. I mean, hell, did I boss Ralph and Don about or what. Not serious mind – fun.

Si was the one who looked most shocked though, he looked dead embarrassed, and got Maureen to check his two boxes, and he only sort of came up to me when he was ready to go – well, I'd been busy till then – and he said he was well sorry about what had happened, and I said I'd see him down on the beach later then, and he sort of smiled a bit nervously, and then me and Maureen had to go, because we had a schedule to keep, and as we drove away, I watched him in the mirror, and like he was staring after us, and I felt sort of good about it, because I reckoned we has broken the ice, and maybe if he really was sorry I could get him a job at the depot and all. I mentioned this to Maureen, sort of told her about what had happened, and she reckons I'm whistling in the wind – whatever that means – but I don't give a shit, because we can all fuck up, even a mate, and like Si and me we go back a long way, and this is the first time we've had trouble, so maybe he's learned, and maybe I should give him a chance, and like I think about this all the way up to the next drop off point, and I reckon that it's not going to be too bad.

We finished the run about 12.30, and because it was lunch-time I got Maureen to drop me off at Si's beach. I'd not been to it before, and like it was on the other side of Sainte Maxime, and it wasn't as long as my one, but boy was it packed, like loads of the fuckers all over the bloody place, and there he was. Si, stood right

120

there, among them all, flogging to Frogs, and he was handing over two beignets, and then taking a couple of vanille out of his cooler box, and I got this well warm feeling, like I was happy to see him, and with him not seeing me it was like safe, and it sort of rushed through me, and I wasn't angry no more, I was sort of chuffed, and so I shouted across to the old fucker, and it felt like I had a carrot in my throat, and he didn't hear me, and so I walked across towards him, and he looked up. He didn't grin like I expected, he didn't get excited, he just glanced either way, and sort of half smiled, and like I reckoned then that he was still feeling guilty, like he hadn't got over it like I had, and suddenly he was hurrying over to me, and I was laughing a bit when he reached me, because I was glad he was hurrying and because he didn't half look funny stumbling over with a beignet tray and an ice cream box, and when we met – in just about the only small bit of empty sand – I go to put my arm round his shoulder, and he just sits, slumps down onto the sand and pulls me down next to him, and I could see he was not relaxed, and this is me, 'You been working too hard, mate', and he had, because he looked terrible. And like then I saw Her – the snake-shit – and she was like frozen in time, stood about fifty metres down the beach, not moving a muscle, just staring, and Si hadn't seen her, he was talking, telling me that he was really sorry that it had all happened but that he was still seeing 'Catherine', and that he was sure we would get on if we had a chance, and that he was really hooked on her, Ken, and that he felt dreadful about her messing up our friendship, and that that's the last thing he would want, and how he wants us to try again, but that he's still got to bring her round, because she still feels a little wary of me, even though he's told her what a great bloke I am, and that if I could give him a little time, he's sure he could bring her round, and like he's really sorry, and then he sees where my eyes are, and follows them, sees

121

Catherine staring at us, and now it's his turn to freeze, for a fraction of a second, and I can hear him mutter 'Shit', and I have to agree. This is me, 'Yeah', and she turns and marches away.

Then I realise, like a door I never noticed before suddenly opens – he's been sharing her beach for weeks now, he's been seeing her every fucking day, he's not just been sneaking out in the evenings, he's been sneaking out morning, lunch-time and afternoon and all, and he wants to go to her now, he wants me to leave, to make his life easy, to save him the dirty work, and I am unwanted, all over his fucking eyes this pathetic guilt-ridden 'Go away', and it's so fucking easy to understand why, like I can hear her huff from halfway down the beach. And I don't know what to do, like I've not arrived back yet, I don't know what to fucking say, I don't know if I'm angry, humiliated, shocked, miserable, sad, sorry for him, or the lot, and all I can hear is this, 'Why the fuck don't he dump her?' inside my head, like over and over – dump her dump her dump her, and so this is me, 'Dump her, Si', and he's shaking his head, and he can't give her up for me, I see it, he hasn't got the fucking guts, like he's going to turn his back on me again, he's going to her for the third fucking time, and I feel the cold, rising up like unstoppable, and he sees it too, and he's stood up, and I'm up too, and suddenly a figure steps in, a figure touching Simon's shoulder, asking for something, and they are in my way, they are between him and me, and I'm dragging her back, I'm dragging Catherine back, and I'm hurling her to the ground, and I'm at Simon reaching for his head, trying to grip it, to scream at him, to butt sense into that dying brain, and like the beignet tray is between us, blocking my way, and I can hear him screaming at me, and suddenly these hands are on me and three people are turning me, and like the first punch lands from around a stranger's shoulder and then another and I'm pinned to the ground

122

and these Frogs are screaming at me, screaming and pointing to this woman lying next to me, pointing to their sister, and I've never seen her before in my life, and one of the Frogs spits at me, and then they are gone, and I'm alone on the sand, and I feel the heads turning away, and Si is saying sorry, and going, and all I can do is close my eyes, and hate.

When I finally stood up, Si was a speck down the beach, and with her. And then I realised something else, and as I walked back to the road, head down, legs still trembling, it ran about my brain, and seemed to make everything even worse. They had one cooler box each. Si had two cooler boxes this morning. Si had filled hers, he'd been doing the proper dogsbody thing. Jesus, the fucker, if he wasn't such a wimp she'd have been at the pick-up this morning, and I wouldn't have got my hopes up, and none of this shit would have happened. None of it.

Of course he was there at the pick up that evening, but we didn't speak to each other. All there was was shit.

Somewhere Else

The next couple of weeks has been sort of quiet, specially because it has rained loads, and because Dick the Dick turned up with only a broken rib, and because I didn't really feel much good. We've been getting up, working a bit, having a kip, then over to the bar, drinking a bit, smoking loads of Hope, and like I reckon it's been good being with girls right now, because like it's different, because they know how to have a good time and shit, but it's a different good time. I mean they slag people off and shit, and they talk dirty, but it's less sort of one person has a go and then it's someone else's turn, it's more like, and this sounds stupid, it's more like a team, sort of they knock themselves and the others sort of lift them up, but with blokes you knock each other and lift yourself up, with blokes it's like banter, a game, but with girls there's more sort of talking, and it's weird because it's sort of difficult but it's good too, and I reckon I'm not bad at it, I mean they don't have to change for me or shit, and it's easy because you don't have to think of funny things all the time, I mean they want to listen to things about you that hurt, but they don't laugh or nothing. Hell, they're not even nasty to me about Si, they're sort of supportive, encouraging, and I find myself saying things without expecting it, I mean I wasn't expecting that I could say what I said, and I reckon I surprised them and all, because they start taking my side, they make me feel that maybe he might come round, that when it's over with her, he'll come back with his tail between his legs, and this makes me feel stronger than him, better than him, and like being with girls is good. Of course I know a lot of girls in England, at school and shit, and my sister's mates, and I spent loads of time with them, but that were more sort of blokes and girls, and we were like two groups sort of thing, not me on my own with them, and that's the difference I reckon, because, well, on our own we behave totally different, and it feels like these girls are sort of treating me like I'm a girl, because I'm sort of watching them relaxed, themselves – and I like it. Mind you we still flirt a bit, and mess around and shit, and I still fuck up from time to time, and they scream at me, and hit me and shit, but that's good too. It all is. Well, most of it, like I'm still desperate to fuck Artois, but that seems about as likely as me growing tits – which I'm not in case you was wondering. They did put make-up on me one night, but that was a joke, you know, it don't mean nothing.

It was a week after I started the loading job that I suddenly realised I'd been missing something, like I couldn't believe why I hadn't thought of it earlier – Scams. Is this the perfect place for them, or what? Hell, I'm filling the cooler boxes, the drinks machines, the beignet trays, and I know what number box goes to which person, and shit, a few extras here and there, and I can give the lads Christmas every day. So that's what I starts doing. For the first few days I don't do nothing for Si, but then I reckons it would sort of prove what I reckon, show him how you stand by a mate, and so I does it for him and all. The thing is, right, should I be giving the lads extra for free or should I go and see them to arrange a percentage sort of thing? I mean I'm onto a good thing here, I can save the same sort of money without having to do half the work they is, so should I

125

leave it up to them to offer? They're not thick, they're going to suss what's going on, and it's a bit sick giving them something without them asking and expecting something in return, so what I reckons is that I'll leave it up until the next time I see them, and then see how it goes, and until then I'll just enjoy thinking about the look on their faces, and I mean hell, it sort of makes me feel important and all.

The reason I've not been over to see them already is that things here have sort of taken up my time. After me and Maureen finished our stuff I found myself sort of, well, not busy at nights, back to the fist, and it didn't look like Artois was going to get anywhere neither, so without really thinking about it, well, things sort of got going with Ruth, didn't they.

Ruth is a bit like a pencil really, like bony, you know, and she don't like the sun too much either, so often she stays back on the site in the afternoons, and one day, well I was feeling like shit, and we was here together, and she wants to play nurse. Well, I'm not going to complain am I? I mean girls like doing shit like that, and I really was feeling crook. My bowels had gone, and I had this summer cold thing – you know, when your head fills up with snot – and I was aching all over, like I was seventy, my joints all sort of knackered, exhausted even by lying down, and I don't know how I got through work, and I'd had one of those aches at the back of the nose and all, you know, the sort of ache that only sneezing helps, and so there I am in the tent, sneezing and moaning, and staggering up to go off for a dump – well, more of a splash really – and I am not a happy man, I'm desperate, and then Ruth brings me a cup of tea, and things get different. She feeds me vitamin pills, and mixes me up a Beecham's Powders with hot lemon and honey – which tasted like shit, but she insisted would do me good – and then moved me into the caravan and sort of sat beside me, reading and glancing

126

over the top of the paper and stuff, you know, reading bits out to me, and I'd sort of get it together to talk now and again, but then I'd feel exhausted and have to stop, and she didn't complain or nothing, I mean she kept doing this for me for three days, and like is this the way to be ill or what? I'd crawl into work, going through it, I don't know how, sort of blank, silent, like a machine, not even having the energy to deal with Dick the Dick's sarky concern, and then when it was over, and I was back at the caravan, Ruth would take over, and it was great, because at home it was my dad who did stuff like that, and he meant well but he was a bit clumsy with it, and sort of forgot what time I should get my medicines and would cook me a great big meal when all I wanted was a bowl of tomato soup, or a bowl of tomato soup when I wanted a great big meal, and like he always got me Lucozade when I hated the fucking stuff, and my sister would help sometimes and all, sort of sit with me a bit, but she'd get bored bloody quickly and naff off, so I mean what Ruth was doing was like, well, like I'd only seen on TV and, shit, I was dead grateful, specially after a few days when I was starting to feel good again but she wouldn't let me get up yet. This is her, 'No, no. You just rest for one more afternoon, it can't do you any harm. I'll roll that joint for you.' I mean, who was I to argue?

Now, I don't know what it is about getting better but the first thing to recover always seems to be the dick, like it's an indicator, the blood gets healthy again or something and it has to practise, and I don't know about you, but I definitely feels dead horny when I'm on the way back. Now Ruth is quite an innocent girl I reckon, I mean she sometimes has to have things explained by the others, and even though she's quick to latch on she can be a bit shocked by it all, you know, and so like when she's making sure that I'm comfy in bed, and suddenly comes face to face with my flesh and blood

127

mast, well, I mean she definitely is a bit shocked. This is her, 'Oh. Oh', and this is me, 'You must be making me better', and she sits down again, slightly red in the face sort of thing. But I can see her keep looking over the top of her paper, glancing at my crutch, and I reckon she was a bit excited, so this is me, 'Do you want to touch it?', and this is her, 'What?', and this is me, 'It wants you.' And she doesn't say nothing. So I sort of pursues it, 'Go on. Why not, eh? Bet you it's just what I need', and she's not sure, but I keep going, and after twenty minutes or so she's sitting nervous at the side of my bed, and I've taken her hand and sort of guided it under the sheet, and I'm using it to stroke my knob, which is aching hard by now, and then I pull back the sheet and pull her up so she's sitting on top of me, and my bulb is pushing up against her knickers, desperate to break through, and she's still not sure, but I'm like talking her round, and sliding her stuff off, and this is her, 'I've not done this a lot', and this is me, 'That don't matter, I don't mind', and she's sort of moaning, wanting it, I can see, but like a bit frightened too, and that makes me harder, and I see her choose, like give in, I see her decide, in herself, and she sinks onto me, and we do it, and hell she may be a bit of skin and bone, a bit hard on the outside, but she's soft on the inside – well, a bit dry to start with – and I reckon it's gone real well, but then when we've finished she gets off me, and hurries outside, and I mean that's a bit confusing, and when she comes back ten minutes later I can see she's been crying, and that's not nice, like I don't see why she should be doing that, because it was only a bit of fun. And then this is her, sort of quiet, embarrassed, 'I'm not on the Pill or anything', and this is me, reassuring her sort of thing, 'Oh that's alright, don't worry about it, it were lovely, come here, come on', and I get her to lie down beside me, and as I'm dozing off I think I can feel her crying again, sort of shaking a bit, and trying to catch her breath, quiet like. I mean, weird or what?

When I woke a couple of hours later she's sat back beside the bed looking at me, and she's all washed and scrubbed and wearing this frock I've not seen before, and this is her, 'Did you, you know, did you have a good time?' And like I grin a huge fucking grin, and this is me, 'Oh yeah, bloody marvellous.' And I reckon everything's OK again, and I pull her over and give her a great big wet kiss, and she holds onto me real tight, and fuck, she really is a bag of bones.

She's a bit clingy all night really, like when the others get back, and it's sort of embarrassing, but after what went on with Maureen I'm going to be friendly, you know, even though it's not like I'd want to do anything more than that, you know, because we're adults and shit, but like when I go back to my own bed that night, well, the tent opens and it's her, and she's expecting to sleep with me, and really I don't want that, but shit, I can hardly kick her out, so I play the 'I'm still not feeling good' line and go straight to sleep, or pretend to, because I mean it's bloody difficult to sleep with someone beside you who feels like a cross between a coiled spring and an ironing board, and like what I don't get is what is she doing here when it's so fucking obvious that she don't want to be here? Does she think she's signed some sort of contract with me or something? I mean did my knob put its name to something without telling me? And like I'm thinking this and sort of laughing to myself as I fall asleep. I tell you though, the next morning, when I woke up, Ruth was still lying in exactly the same position, staring at me, and I sort of half opened my eyes to check it out, and she gives me this nervous smile, and I mumble, pretending I'm only half waking, turn over, and fake sleep again. Hell, I do it for half an hour, right up to 5.20, and she's still not got up, so I think 'Fuck', and wake up. This is her, 'Did you sleep

well?', and this is me, 'Yeah, alright. What about you?'
And this is her, 'It's not very comfy in here, is it?' and
this is me, in my head, 'Too bloody right it's not', but
instead I says, this is me, 'Suppose we'd better get to
work then', and I'm up and out of there faster than a
squirrel up a tree.

I'll give her one thing – she walks bloody quick when
she wants to, I mean, hell, I was going flat out to the
depot and still she kept up with me. It were like having
a living shadow, so I tell you, walking into that place felt
like a relief, like you feel after a shower, when you've
left all the sweat behind you, you're free of all the
muggy, clingy gunge, you know, that makes you feel
sticky. I mean, suddenly I was relaxed, that's it, relaxed,
and the way Ruth got stuck into her work I reckon she
felt the same too, though one time, when I turned round
to get a bag of ice, it looked like she was crying on
Maureen's shoulder, so I turned back pretty quickly and
got on with Artois, but she must've seen too, because
this is her, 'What did you go and do that for?' and this is
me, 'What?', and this is Artois, 'She can't handle it', and
this is me, 'She started it. I didn't force her or nothing',
and Artois put down the machine she was filling, looked
at me sort of like real sick of me, and this is her,
'Arseholes, the lot of you', and she walks off, and I'm
left to do the rest of the drinks machines myself. I hate
the way women do that, putting all men together, like
saying we're all the same, I mean they're always doing
it, and I reckon it's bloody unfair. How was I to know
Ruth would end up being a blubber? I mean, yeah she's
a bit wet at times, but you never can tell what they'll be
like until after you've done it, can you?

The next couple of days was pretty shitty really
because the gang of three decided to ignore me, and if
it weren't for Tony and Sidney I'd've had no one to talk
to at all, and even they was a bit off, being half girls
themselves, and so in the end I found myself in the

restaurant talking to the Frog, Antoine, Artois' bit, and he was alright, he shrugged his shoulders and just said, this is him, 'Ah, women', and like I had to agree.

The second night I was starting to get a bit pissed off though with all the cold shoulder, I mean it were worse than being shouted at, and so I sort of confronted Ruth, you know, to try and find out what the fuck was going on, because I didn't really understand what the problem was, and it was ruining everything. She was dead calm, like gritting her teeth, and she hardly says a word, just sort of looking between me and the floor – but spending most time on the floor – and this is me, 'I didn't hurt you or nothing, we had a bunk up, like you and me, so what's the problem? Like why've I got to be frozen out? I mean, have I ignored you or something? No. I've been a fucking gent. Haven't I?' And she says nothing, just fingers her hanky, and this makes it worse, and I find myself shouting, and Ruth isn't calm no more, like tears shudder up her, and she's off, crying, and Maureen comes running into the caravan, and I'm kicked out – which makes me even angrier, I've had enough, I storm out the camp site. And as I go I hear Ruth sobbing in the background, and I'm thinking, 'Jesus, she's pathetic', and I'm thinking 'Good' too, because I reckon the bitch deserves it now, I mean she's made my life a misery, and I keep walking, following the road, and then I realise I'm heading to the beach, and I walk and I walk, and in my head I'm slagging them all off, all the way, I'm slagging the slags, wishing I'd said loads of stuff, and like after about an hour I find myself in this bar, and I'm still wishing, in a bar beside the sea, and I buy myself a big pastis, and then another, and I'm feeling well miserable, and then I realise where I am. This is the place where me and Bobby and Si played cards that night, this was the first beach we slept on, and this makes me feel worse, because like so much has happened since then, so much has changed, and I'm here

131

on my own, alone, and none of it's my fault, I've done nothing wrong, and it'd all seemed so easy then, and I sort of wish it was a few weeks back, I wish we were playing cards, and like I'm thinking about Si, and his parents, and my family and shit, you know, home and all, and it seems such a fucking long way away, and here I am, and it's like I feel myself shrinking, smaller and smaller, like I'm this dot, this mark, and if I was wiped out, who'd fucking notice? Who'd fucking care? And like I reckon if I was a girl I'd be crying now, because I can feel this swelling behind my eyes, but nothing's coming out, and I stare down into the glass, staring through the maker's name, and then I realise it's empty and go and get another. I drink that, stare out at the sea, drink and stare, and I've got no thoughts, only this feeling of being tiny, nothing, no one, unimportant shit, and like I don't think about hope much because it's bollocks, but I feel like I've got no hope, and that's what keeps going through my head as I drink pastis after pastis, 'No hope, no hope, no hope', and it's dreadful. And then, suddenly, when I'm feeling totally fucking useless, I get this thing that builds up inside my stomach, and it takes a moment to recognise it, and then I realise it's pleasure, like I'm sort of enjoying being this depressed, and for a few seconds it sort of cheers me up, and I look round at all the faces in the bar, but they all seem so happy I feel the walls of misery fucking well collapse on me again, and I have to get out of there, leave them, so I swallow my drink and go down to the beach, lie on my back and look up at the stars. And I'm desperate to escape, and they seem to offer so much, but at the same time they remind me, they remind me that I'm trapped on a piss small shitty fucking planet and what can I do about it? Nothing.

I must've stared up at the stars for hours, thinking about other planets up there, other people lying on their backs, staring up at our star, and there must be thousands of people lying on thousands of beaches on thousands of planets, and all those people feeling small, tiny, against it all, and like what's the fucking point? That's what we're all thinking, 'What's the fucking point?', but in different languages, and I hear myself chuckle, like a stranger, from nowhere, and I reckon the only point is that we don't want to know what the point is, we don't want to face the fact that we're all small and fucking useless, and like that's what we've got to learn, and if we does then that'll bring us together, that'll make us sort of one, and that's weird or what? We'll only come together when we know we don't count, and that way we might make a difference, but until we does, it's like onwards to being the shit, a drip, a spot, a brief stain, and like I'm lying there on this beach thinking, 'Why doesn't anyone realise this?', lying there feeling the sand scraping at my back, making it's way between my 'T' shirt and shorts, and suddenly I'm swallowed by the size of it all, just staring at the stars, feeling useless, feeling empty, and because it's so empty, I'm joined to it, I recognise it, and like, with the waves crashing for a soundtrack, I feel myself drawn out of me, like being pulled thin, spreading out, across the beach, over the sea, onwards and upwards, and as I go, as I drift into this darkness, I realise that at last I'm falling asleep, and like, I don't know why, but all night long I dream of ants.

On Top

I woke up at about 4.30 with the sun warming my face, and I realised that I got to walk fast to get to work on time, and so I was off, straight up from the sand, and away.

Now there's something about early mornings that makes things look different, so this time I saw all the things I didn't notice the night before, you know, because I was looking now, not sort of just wrapped up in anger, and it was all sharp and stuff because of the new light, and looking at it sort of made life seem simpler again, I mean it's all there, beaches, sea, sky, trees, insects, and they just seem so much more important, so much more of a miracle sort of thing, like clean, and me, well, I soil all that, I dump on everything, destroy it all. And then bits of last night started coming back and all, and I hated the fucking stuff, like I remembered Ruth's creased face and it were sort of clear now how much I'd hurt her, and I remembered lying on the beach feeling all hippy about the stars, and like the anger and the uselessness, and as the memory started to build so did this tightness at the front of my head, and it was fucking strong, and it was a sort of lonely 'I don't like me', a sense, a thought, a belief, that I'm fucking crap, a wanker, ignorant, blind, not half as smart as I reckon, like I set myself up to be told to piss off, like it's all my fault, it has to be, because, I mean just look at the evidence, and it crashes on top of me, my parents, my school, my employers, my mates, all of them, all of it, like if it keeps happening to me, it MUST be my fault. And I kicks out at a stone, and I watch it as it skids out across the road and crashes into the side of a passing car, and as they stop and get out, I reckon this just about proves my point. And as they come towards me shouting, I run.

I ran for longer than I've ever run, and I didn't even think about stopping, you know, each step just led to the next and somehow this movement, like feeling the strength, sort of took me over, carried me away from the road, running alongside the beach, up and down, over the half grassy half sandy mounds, running and running, sort of drowning my thoughts with sweat, and I was coming back, not feeling so useless. And then suddenly I see the camp site, and I'd forgotten that that was where I was going, and that was a surprise, but not as much of a surprise as when I arrived at the depot, because first of all I was on time, and secondly, well, one hell of a lot has changed. One: Ruth has left, like last night she decided to go, and Dick the Dick drove her to the station, and right now she'll be thundering towards Paris – I can't lie, it were like finding out you got parole. Two: Maureen's not working with us no more because Dick the Dick has asked her to work with him in the delivery van, and so it's only Artois and me and the poofs, and we've got to work double hard to get things ready because there's no replacements yet, and even Albert is giving us a hand. Three: Artois is not a happy woman, like I see something is wrong with her, I mean she looks real pissed off, and when I asks if it's something I've done, this is her, loud like, 'Don't be so fucking stupid, you couldn't upset me, dickbrain', and I'm left standing in the middle of the depot, looking a berk, and Sidney comes up to me and says, this is him, quiet like, 'She found Antoine in bed with another girl last night', and this is Tony, 'Doing it doggy', and well, you got to laugh, because Artois really does look punctured. But I tell you, I'm not going to complain about none of it. It's what travelling is all about. I mean back home a problem can't just go away, but here, well nothing is permanent, everything is coming and going, like whatever lands on our beach has got to go back to the sea eventually, I mean it's a sort of rule of the road. And there's another rule and all, which is that if you've got a short time to do things you got to pack them in, like those dragonflies who only live for twenty-four hours, and so hell, what I reckon is that if I play it right I might even get to do it with Artois.

Things was quiet for a couple of days, and Albert's two younger brothers came to work with us, and they was a bit lazy but I don't mind, because I reckon working with Frogs who don't speak much Anglais is better than working with people who ignore you, and we hardly seen nothing of Maureen neither. She just appeared from time to time, but she wouldn't tell me what she was up to with Dick the Dick, so I didn't really push it, like fuck her then, playing the mystery bit, I mean that got right up my nose, and like I reckon she's still trying to get even about Ruth, which is pretty small, because I've told her I didn't know what I was doing, and how miserable I got, but she weren't interested. So I've smoked a lot of Hope, sat around, gone down the beach, thought about swimming, walked back, smoked some more, and it's been a bit boring really, which is not too bad I suppose because a load seems to have happened recently. The only real problem is that my Hope is running out, like I'm down to raiding my hiding places, you know, the bits I put away for when the main lump run out, and I'm sure I had another small lump but I can't find it. I mean I know I put three bits away, but I can only find two, and this is a real pisser, because I've turned the rucksack inside out, I've turned my plastic

136

bags inside out, I've searched everything I've got, and I still can't remember where I put the other fucker, and this sort of takes a bit of pleasure out of smoking the other two bits because I don't know if they're going to be my last or not, and if they is it means I got to go back and see Adolf again, which would be well good if it weren't for Catherine the Snot being on the same camp site. So I've started asking around here, being subtle like, and I'm not having no luck. I mean, Artois can't even get none. Things with her are well disappointing and all, I mean I've not seen her like this before, not even when she was ignoring me, and I've tried to get things going but it's like trying to get a wasp to settle down for a chat, she's all over the fucking shop, and if you get too close it don't half hurt, and so I've given up on her really, just sort of accepted it's not going to happen.

Then suddenly one morning she starts talking again, like she's back from the dead, and it's like nothing's changed, nothing's gone on, she just says she's well rid of Antoine and starts to party. I mean talk about a turn around, hell, suddenly she's flirting again, suddenly it looks like the chance of a bit of percy parking is back on, and like this time I'm going to play it right, I'm going to be cool about it, not all sort of eager and panting even if that's what I feel, I mean I'm not going to humiliate myself again, and so I don't make no moves or nothing, like I don't even go back to the caravan with her that night, well I go and gab with her and stuff but I don't stay or nothing, and hell she was dead surprised and that felt good too, you know, I walked out In Charge, and it was peculiar doing that because when I got back to the tent and lay down I suddenly felt glad, like glad I wasn't doing it! Weird, huh? Just because I'd avoided the shit I'd got into with the other two, because this time I'd shown self-control, just because of that I felt good, well good. Of course it didn't last.

137

Next morning at work she stood real close, every opportunity she had she were beside me, sort of suggesting, and it made the job bloody difficult and all, like I was well distracted, and I could feel the hope sort of building up in me, the hope I'd put away as best I could, and it's almost like it's not fair, you know, that she can have that much power, and she knows it and all, and that pisses me off a bit, because it makes me feel like a sort of toy, but I'm not going to complain neither because there's something dead invigorating about being a bit out of control, it's like playing the horses, like a flutter, and that's the right word because that's what's happening in your gut, you're fluttering, and I tell you we weren't even out the paddock yet. We're pacing, circling, and then she asks if I want to go to the beach, just the two of us, and shit, what's a man meant to say? We're walking down to the starting line, two horses raring to go, all self-control out the fucking window, like my brain is a piss small jockey with a whip that I don't give a shit about. I mean, hell, I'd been wanting her for weeks, hadn't I? Like she even appeared in dreams, and it were understandable, weren't it? I mean, Jesus, moving next to her like this, did it make me desperate for the off or what? This was what I'd been crying out for, this was going to make all the waiting worthwhile. This was going to be It. Hell, we'd've fucked right there in the sea if there hadn't been so many people out swimming. In the end though we just had to make do with talking dirty, psyching each other up, and then it was no good, we couldn't hang around no more, and we're out of the sea, and we're half running back to the caravan, and we're laughing and shouting, and we're coming up to the starting post, and I'm aching something chronic by the time we get there, and then the door is open, flung open, and we've flung ourselves on the bed, and our clothes are off in seconds, like wrenching, and hell we was all over each other, like a dream come true, and I could hardly believe it, rolling onto the floor, like this was real, dragging back up to the mattress, this was more than I've ever known, like there's so much happening, and she's exploding wanting it, and suddenly she's pulling me on top of her, and I'm being pushed inside her, her hand scrambling with my cock, shoving it in, and the warmth and wetness take my breath away, and then her nails dig into my back, like real hard, and suddenly I'm not thinking about sex, I'm thinking about pain, and she's moaning and groaning, and thrusting me inside her, and Jesus Christ, she's squeezing my balls like in a clamp, and I'm telling her not to, and she shoves her gob over mine, shutting me up, and she's driving me backwards and forwards, and am I confused or what? Because this is agony and ecstasy, because she's gorgeous, because she's killing me, I mean fuck she's hurting me so bad she's murdered the whole bloody point of the thing, but she don't know it because she's so gone and I can't stop her now, I mean that'd make me look a wimp, but Jesus I don't want to go on, I'm in pain like I don't know, feeling the blood coming out of the scratches, fighting the stabs as she tugs the hair from my head, ripping at the roots, my balls screaming for freedom from her thighs, and so I can't think of any pleasure, and I can't come, I can't come, I can't finish it, and that's all I want to do, and she's driving on, and her screams are lust and mine are terror, but she don't know, and this is torture and it won't stop, this is the longest sex I've ever had and I'm hating it, like I'm totally shocked, and she's pumping, pumping, like an animal, and I can't get it to the end, and oh God I wish I could hurry up, and now she's coming, and relaxing, and her eyes are opening and like there's fire in them, and she's spun me over, and I can't resist or nothing, and suddenly I'm falling to the floor all her weight following, and she's on top, and oh thank God she's released my balls, but it's no better because now she's bouncing so hard they're being crushed against the floor, and she's got my shoulders pinned too, all of her pushing, so it feels like my body is being dislocated, and then suddenly without warning, with her driving up and down, my spunk comes to the rescue, I burst inside her, and I'm flooded with relief, almost with pleasure, because this means I can stop, but she don't, and it's like someone shoving a fish hook down my cock, like my nerves are screaming at this repeat order, and so am I, and she's off on her victory lap, and I'm desperately fighting for breath, and then as she raises her arms to the crowd she sort of releases my shoulders and I have a split second to pull myself out, knob dribbling, to push her away, and she's off me, on the floor, at my feet, and I'm scrambling away, back towards the kitchen, but trying not to let her see, and this is her, 'What's wrong with you, you bastard?' But I'm too exhausted to answer, my hand cradles my red raw skin and I just sort of laugh, and I can hear the terror in it, and she gets up and walks over the top of me – me, flinching – to get some water from the fridge, and all I want to do now is get out of there, but I can't, because I can't move no more, I'm trapped by my muscles, like they've gone into spasm, and the only thing that helps is that she's looking at me like I'm an insult, that she's lost interest, and inside I can hear this sort of cheering, this sort of weeping relief, because I know I'm not going to have to do it again, because I know it's over. But I mean, Jesus, is life one sick bastard or what?

From Behind

It took me half an hour to get myself together enough to get out the caravan, and by then I reckon she'd realised that I was a bit shocked by it all, but something about her made me feel that that made the whole thing even better for her, and that was the most frightening thing of the lot, because I could see it in her now, like there was something definitely unhinged in there, something screaming at the world, something sick – I mean, hell, I thought I had problems.

My only real problem now is what to do if she comes on to me again – just the idea of it filled me with fucking terror. I mean, boy, was I praying for something to come along. I needed rescuing. And then just that happened, something came along to change it all again, something to turn everything on its head, and like was I pleased or what? Too right I was. To start with.

That night I'm sitting outside the caravan, it's about seven, and I'm having a beer, and I still can't get the morning out of my head, it's like it's on a loop, round and round it goes, making me cold each time, and I'm lost in this when suddenly I hear my name being shouted, and walking towards me are two people, and I know them, but it takes a moment to click into place, and then on a sort of wave of joy my brains clear – it's Ralph and Don. RALPH AND DON! But they're not here to party, I mean they're onto me dead quick, and they are looking sort of concerned, looking around, as if they don't want to be seen, and this is them, 'Ken, grab your stuff fast.' 'Don't ask why, just do it', and any other time I'd have said fuck off, but like now, now was now, and all I needed was a reason – any reason – to get the fuck out of here, so I stopped celebrating and was packed in two minutes. I came out of that tent quicker than you'd believe, and then – checking the coast were clear – my stomach sunk. They were gone. Where the fuck were they? And then I saw them over by the gates, sort of waving from a clapped-out Morris Minor van, and it felt so bloody good as I rushes over and dives in the back, and I'm telling you, they drove away from there like Hollywood stuntmen, and all I kept thinking was, 'Are these blokes angels or what?'

The further we drove the happier I was, like I was laughing my sodding head off by the time we hit the main road, one hundred metres was all it took, and then Don slapped me down, this is him – wham – 'Nothing for you to laugh about, mate', and he started to explain, bouncing about as Ralph threw the filthy green van that stank of fake leather around the road. 'You know what you gone and done, don't you?' He paused, then hit me, 'You've lost us our jobs.' And this is Ralph, in the mirror, 'You're a right fucking mate, you are.' And they were serious. They've been caught with the extras I'd slipped into their boxes, like I'd been a bit overgenerous, and Albert and Dick the Dick had got suspicious and called Maureen in. Shit, she was their spotter, their spy, their ice cream detective! And Don turned again, and this is him, 'She got Simon nicked.'

And this stopped me, like really stopped me, like I didn't believe it, but I had to, because you just needed to see Don's face, and it were a shock, because suddenly Si's name had been shoved back in front of me, after I'd pushed it away, here it were back, all fucked up, and it was my fault. I mean I'd been helping him every day, not occasional like these two, and he'd not asked or nothing, and now he was in the shit, and I'm so put out I'm not really listening to Don no more. This is my life. If the world wants a shit, it's going to do it on me, right on top, from very high up, hitting and sticking. And if it were on form, like the world would send the gendarmes after me and all wouldn't it? Yes, it would. And that of course is exactly what the world has gone and done. I mean fucking hell, or what? I'm on the run! Me, Ken White, a wanted man. And when I laughed this time it was more from shock. I'd never been wanted before, not by no one. You know, I'd done some shoplifting, and a spot of vandalism, I'd been in fights and shit, and there was the time I'd nicked that motorbike, and once, right, I'd kept guard while a mate did a house, but none of it had got serious, and this, this was a joke, like fuck – I hadn't done nothing wrong! It had just been a perk of the job. But Don and Ralph, they was well worried, and they was sure that I really did have a problem, and they was right, because, fuck, Simon really was inside, and he'd be in front of the local beak in the morning, and if they got hold of me I'd be stood there with him and all – I mean, Jesus, I tell you, I didn't know what the fuck I was supposed to do.

Don and Ralph reckoned I'd be alright back at their site, because hell, no one was going to look there, they'd think, 'Why should he go there?', no one would think these two would help me, not after I'd got them into the shit, I mean no one would think they'd still look on me as a mate. But that's the whole point because I'd proved what a mate I was by giving them extras without them asking, and so they did want to help, which meant that probably the safest place was their camp site, so that's where I went.

We pulls into the place, and all I was really worrying about was Si, because I mean he wasn't the sort of bloke who'd ever expect to end up in the nick – me, I'd always half expected it – he's as honest as you get. Hell, he probably asked to be arrested because he felt so guilty, and now I'm feeling guilty because I reckon I must've given him the ice creams to make him feel guilty in the first fucking place, like it was my way of getting my own back – even if it does sound stupid – and now I'm feeling well responsible about all this, and as the lads drive down to the tent, I'm all silent, bumping around, and reckoning, like hoping, that the worst they'll do – because, hell, it's not exactly major crime – is to deport him. But that still didn't stop me feeling shit, because right now he is – he must be – feeling well miserable, the poor sod.

The van came to a halt, and I get out, like slow, and head over to the lads' tent, and I feel I've got two tons on my back, and then I realise that someone is in Si's place, and that the someone is fucking well coming out, and shit, a bloody gendarme's hat is coming through the zip and I'm stood in the open like a zit on your forehead, and Ralph yells, and I takes this huge running dive and land in this ditch full of tall grass and shit, behind the lads' tent, and my heart is going like morse fucking code and I'm trying to lie so fucking still and praying to God that the grass is covering me and that he didn't hear me landing, and I can see his back now, and he's talking to the lads. They're both playing dumb Anglais, but he speaks English and he's definitely a bit narked, and looking around, pointing, waving his arms like Frogs do, as if he's in the six yard box calling for the ball, and suddenly I realise I haven't breathed since I landed and I'm getting desperate and I got to do it, and as I suck in the air it's dreadful, because it sounds like I'm screaming 'OVER HERE MISTER COPPER!' because boy is it loud, and the gendarme does turn around and he does look at the grass behind the tent, and like I'm almost wanting him to see me, to get it over with, and I'm having to fight this stupid fucking urge to stand up and walk over to him, but like I'm not that thick, so I doesn't. I lie

144

with my eyes half closed, like if I don't see him he won't see me, and then I don't want to open them because I'm sure he'll hear that and all, but I hear footsteps and I can't help myself and my eyes open, and I can see his bottom half, and he's only five feet away, and oh shit is his hand on his gun or what? It's fingering the holster, and I can just see it now, I can see him pulling out the fucker, bringing it toward me, pulling the trigger, like I can see the bullet on its way, and I'm a statue, trying to sink into the ground, like invisible, and still the air through my nose is shouting and still my heart is yelling and still he's not seeing me, and then he walks away, quite sudden, and this is him, as he goes back past the lads, 'If he comes here, you telephone.' And this is Ralph, 'Oui, monsieur, I'm a telephone.' And it were bloody difficult for me not to laugh, and like that'd be about right and all – nicked because of a joke. But it didn't happen, the copper was too interested in this German leather slag riding her bike into the camp site – his perfect woman. Bet she stank. But right then, I could have kissed her.

Of course because he went to check her out I was stuck in the grass-filled ditch for another half hour, and except for a spliff that Ralph lobbed my way I was bloody uncomfortable. For starters I now realised that I'd taken most of the top layer of skin off my left leg when I'd flung myself into hiding and that I was lying on thistles and all. For seconds I realised that the bottom of the ditch – where my bag was – was filled with water. I could have cried. None of it had mattered when the copper was there neither, but now, like now I had to put up with it, I couldn't even fucking complain, not a word, nothing, and what I reckon that goes to show is that pain is relative. Of course when I said this to the lads later on, Ralph just grinned, and this is him, 'All my relatives are a pain', and like that was when I know – I were back with blokes. Know what I mean?

Up Yours

It weren't easy to relax that night because we knew the gendarmes might come back, but what was I meant to do? So we all sat around on guard sort of thing, keeping a lookout, gabbing, and I sort of stayed behind the tent so I couldn't be seen from the road, and hell, it were a good thing we done all that too, because at about 12.30 that night Dick the Dick turns up and he must've parked the van down the hill so we wouldn't see him coming, because he sort of comes sneaking down the path, and he's dreadful at it, I mean it were like watching a cat stalking a pigeon in the middle of a park – like everyone can see the cat including the pigeon but the cat thinks he's being dead bloody clever. I mean he looked a right bloody prat, and like that were my hardest moment and all, because I never want to have to hide from a shit like Dick the Dick, specially when he looks so fucking stupid. But this time I had to. So back into the ditch I went, with a mat, so I was more comfy, and there I lay as the thick dipshit clown tip-toed his bloody way down the path, and like this was bollocks I didn't need.

Dick the Dick finally decided he was close enough when he realised that Don and Ralph weren't just sort of vaguely glancing in his direction but had been staring at him for bloody ages, and like he sort of straightened up, trying to be Dick the Dick again, and this is him, 'Ah, the unemployed', and you could see he was going to look down his nose at the lads more than ever because he felt he'd been so bloody clever in catching them on the fiddle, and this is Ralph, 'Oh golly gosh, and who might this be?' and this is Don, 'Why if it isn't that Dick, our former employer', and this is Ralph, 'But where did he come from?' and this is Don, 'It's as if he appeared by magical means', and like I really wanted to join them, I wanted to be giving the lip, because it was crying out to be done. And this is him, this is Dick the Dick, 'He's here, isn't he?' and this is Ralph, looking around, 'Where? Where?' and this is Don, 'It must be his magical powers again', and this is Ralph, 'But oh great magician, we are weak and puny mortals and we have only five senses', and this is Dick the Dick, 'You certainly don't have common sense', and the lads laughed and laughed, like rolling around at this, slapping the ground, out of control, with Dick the Dick confused, until Don suddenly stopped, and this is him, sitting up, 'It must be wonderful having 'A' levels.' And so it went on until Dick the Dick realised he was wasting his time – which I reckon he's been doing ever since he were conceived – and he turned, all huffy like, getting ready to leave, and you could see he wanted to save face, to be grand as he left, and this is him, 'Well, let me tell you, you will never sell ice creams in this part of France again', and this is the lads, 'No, because we've got jobs selling nuts', and like Dick the Dick's face falls for just a second before he realises it has fallen and tries to pull it back up again. And I got to say it, I was pretty surprised about their job and all, because no one told me that neither – obviously they wanted to make me feel more guilty, and like it had worked, because, hell, I'd even let them smoke the last of my Hope – sneaky little shits – so now finding out they'd got the job sort of released me from responsibility, I mean I didn't have to be grateful or nothing no more, and like now I knew what I wanted to do, no way could I resist it.

147

And I was off, I was running along the ditch as Dick the Dick stormed off up the slope, and I ran up to the road, and then along, down to where his van would be, and then I scramble up the hillside that ran along the road and hide behind the bushes up above where the van is, and I waits, but only for a couple of minutes, and then there he is, walking down the road, slowly, stopping at one point, turning to look back, and then he moves on again, quicker this time, and I wait and wait until he is inside, and still I wait and he turns on the engine, and I wait, burning to do it, and I hear the cough, and the judder, and the rumble, and I do nothing. And then he winds down his window, like he always does, with his left hand speeding until the glass thumps home, and then I let go, then I scream into the night, and this is me, dragging it out, louder than a fucking claxon, 'DIIIICCCK!', and he stops, he leaps out of the van, staring all around and I can see the useless fury in his headlights and this is him, 'I'll get you, you little bastard!' and he stomps back into his van and drives off, and I come down to the road, and wave at his tail-lights, and this is me, quiet like, 'No you won't. No you bloody won't.'

In Waiting

Just to make sure Dick the Dick didn't get me Ralph and Don reckoned I should move over the road again, back to the pock-marked fascist patron's site, and into Adolf's tent, because no one was going to look there, and like Adolf was quite happy about this and all, just as long as I kept out the way of Le Walking Smell and Catherine the Great, and like there was no way I wanted them to see me neither, so I told him he could rely on me, and Don and Ralph said they'd be back when they got any news on Si, and I settled down with Adolf and started smoking some stormers. It turned out it were a good bloody thing that we did risk the move and all, because Dick the Dick came back to the other site the next morning with the gendarmes, and they looked all over the bloody place, but by the end – and Ralph grinned when he told me this – it were obvious the gendarmes were as fucked off with this pompous English prick as we was. And that's the best, because, hell, it's like having them on my side.

I spent most of the day gabbing with Adolf, and he was dead good to me, specially since I was well nervous for Si, and you know, he saw that – I mean it's not nice knowing your mate's in the dock and it's your fault, especially when you're on the run and all – and it weren't easy neither because every time someone came close to the tent I had to dive under a camp bed, and

149

like Adolf gets a lot of visitors and all, and he don't want me out in the open to cramp his style, which is fair enough, and obviously I didn't want no one to see me neither, and so I had to spend loads of the day crawling in and out from under this bed like a mouse scared of its shadow – and I got to tell you it were turning into one of the longest fucking days ever. And the shittiest part about it were that I couldn't stop thinking the worst, like what could happen to Si. It were dreadful, especially because you've heard of those weird stories about foreign courts and foreign jails, and how they always want to make an example, specially of the English, and like I could just hear the judge now, doing his worst, rubbing Si's face in the law. I tell you, I almost wish I'd never left home. Well, I say that, but like me and Adolf got dead stoned, which sort of made it a bit better.

At seven there was another knock at the tent, and I'm diving under the bed when in comes Ralph, and oh shit, has he got a face on him or what? It's about twelve miles long, and he's shaking his head. And this is him, 'They told me they couldn't do it', and this is me, like horrified, 'What? What?', and this is him, 'Sit down, marrer', and now I'm gone, I mean I have never felt so terrible in my life, and this is Ralph, 'Two years, mate.' And like there's silence in the tent. Total silence. And this is me, 'Two years for a few fucking ice creams? Two years?! They can't do that.' And Ralph comes over and he puts a hand on my shoulder, 'They said they had to make an example', and my stomach is empty now, my head is shaking with the shock, and rising up – like uncapping a bottle of Coke – is the question, and you can't stop it, it's spilling out, disappearing into the air, 'Why? Why? What have I gone and done?', and it keeps coming up, ripping on the way, and I'm feeling sick, and desperate, and all I want to do is go down there, I want to say sorry. Sorry, like how do you say sorry? I want to swap places, let him go, because it was me, it was me,

150

and Ralph just shakes his head, and this is him, 'They reckoned they'd have gone easier on him if you'd shown up. Sorry.' And this is me, 'Well, I'll turn myself in then, like now', and I'm up, 'Jesus they can't do this to him.' But Ralph kills it, this is him, 'It's no good, Ken. It's too late now. Anyway mate, Si said he understands. He didn't want you in the same mess. He said to me, "Why should two lives be ruined?" He don't want you there, mate.' And I'm slumped so low now it feels worse than death, and this is Ralph, 'Look on the bright side, eh? Two years is only . . . 712 days', and this is Adolf, 'Next year is a leap year', and this is Ralph, '713 days', and this is me, 'Jesus, 713 days.' And that's it, the thought of it just hangs there, swelling up, like a balloon inflating, filling the room around us, and I can feel it pushing up against me, stretching around me, like taking my air, and there is only one pinprick of hope, like Si's strength, and this is me, 'What about good behaviour?' But Ralph shrugs his shoulders, and I don't know what to say. There is silence in the tent, for what seems like a lifetime, silence, and hopeless fucking thoughts.

And into the silence comes a slicing noise, a tearing, a ripping, and the zips peels the canvas apart, and then through the hole comes a head, a head I recognise, a face I know from somewhere, and the face is sort of half coy and half grinning and its jaw is moving, and I can hear the words, and this is Si, 'Des glaces, des glaces, beignet aux pommes', and I sort of go insane, everything sort of explodes, my brain dances, everything dances, and I'm telling you and I know it sounds dumb, I know it sounds girlie – I've never felt so much sort of 'Jesus I've fucking missed you' for no one, never. And Ralph and Adolf are pissing themselves, and I don't give a shit, because this is my mate, My Mate, and I'm so fucking happy to see him, and all that fear is dropped in an instance, like it's burst, but the feeling of it is still there, shaking me, and I grab at the man, I hug him to me, and I have to hold onto him, to prove he's real, and I'm mumbling, 'Mate, thank God, I'm so sorry', and shit like that, and he's laughing and saying it's alright, and like it's only after a couple of minutes that we realise what we must look like, and a sort of embarrassment sneaks up on us, and we separate, but like we know that we're back together, and that there's so much to talk about, and that nothing else matters. Well, one or two things – but we'll get round to them later.

Simon's Story

Si had not been having a good time. It started with the night of my fight with Catherine, when he felt this urgent need called lust. He'd taken one look at her shoulder-length black hair, her emerald green eyes, her five foot five pertness, and thought, 'I want this woman.' Now Si had wanted women before – not that he'd had any – but he wanted this one even more. This was his first flood of love – that's how he saw it – Love, and it threw him into one hell of a confusion. Here was his best mate, me, slagging off this woman that he thought was perfect all over, and he was trying to find some way to get her to accept him, but his best mate, me, kept blowing it. He saw that she was a bit stuck-up, he saw that she was a bit pompous, he saw that it looked like she liked herself a lot, but he liked her a lot more, and there was nothing he could do about it. He had to go for it. Well, you can understand that, can't you?

So he went for it, and he was doing quite well, until I turned up with Adolf, his guitar, and a joss stick. He was horrified at what he saw, like her exploding about fuck all, but was praying that I'd let it go, that I wouldn't make a fuss over a half stranger like Adolf. I mean he knew what I was like and all, that now I'd taken Adolf's side there was going to be no stopping me, but he was desperate to forgive her, even though she was behaving like a wanker, and he knew he was caught in the middle,

153

and just wanted this nightmare to go away, he wanted me to be someone else, and then I hit Dexter, and Si felt his life draining away. No way could he win her back now, because she thought Dexter was a really nice person, she'd told him, and he knew all this, saw it all, and he felt like he was stood on a hill staring down at things he could do nothing about, watching his life being fought over – there she was, heaven sent, and me, and Dexter, floored, and then he was sort of being picked up in the hurricane of it all, and we were being dragged out of there, blown away, gone, and it were like being kicked out of heaven. She had spoken to him, she had accepted him, she had even laughed at a joke of his and put her hand on his knee, and even though he understood what had made me do it, he felt like I'd stolen something from him. He thought I was a bad-tempered fool who couldn't begin to control any emotions, and this made him depressed because I was his oldest, best, friend, who obviously couldn't see what this woman meant to him. So he went to bed, like trying to escape into sleep, but it weren't any better there neither, because the snooty cow was there and all.

Next morning he was really nervous about going over to the camp site, but he had to, he was determined this woman wasn't going to slip through his fingers – hell, he was thinking marriage here – and when he got there he was shattered to find that she did not think bad of him, just she couldn't understand why it were Dexter and not him who had stepped in, and like he wasn't expecting that. He tried to explain about being mates, but she didn't see it, couldn't understand about us, and he found himself apologising, like he almost felt embarrassed he apologised so much, but she gave him this distant shit, this 'and now you are dismissed' feeling. But like she had left it open that he stood a chance, she had offered him a little hope, and so he went back the next night, and then started doing it regular, and even went over to her beach from time to time – I wondered where he'd gone – and they built up this friendship, and then he got Dick the Dick to move him to her beach, and hell, he just wanted to be with her all the time, and that's why he was finding it tough being with us lot, you know, finding us on a different sort of wavelength, but like from the sounds of it, I reckon she was just playing hard to get. I mean would it surprise you to find out Catherine was a pricktease?

A few weeks after we'd got there he finally got invited back to her tent, and she'd even made her tent-mate go out for the night, and this was like an invite from the Virgin-fucking-Mary, and that night he had got real close. Closer. He'd touched every bit of her, and she touched every bit of him, but it had still got no further, and he was ready to suffer the agony of long-teased balls, and then suddenly she said she would make love to him as long as he had a condom, and he had one – which surprised me – and they'd done it, out of the blue, there in the tent. And all of this was shocking, like he'd stopped expecting it, and he was nervous and ecstatic, and completely gone, because this was all his dreams come true – I said nothing – and then when it was over she wanted him out of there. And like this got to me, because I could see it, like he wasn't worthy of her, wasn't good enough, but I stopped myself again, I didn't say nothing. Si was real cut up by her dismissal, rejected and dejected, but he understood that she wanted her fellow students to think him and her was just good friends – but she wouldn't tell him why, would she – oh no. She just told him that they liked him and shit, but that they sort of felt sorry for him because of me. He found that real difficult, he had to fight that one inside. And so he came back to the tent, a mixture of joy and misery, and decided he was still not going to tell me what was going on, because he reckoned that was diplomatic, but like he says it was the hardest thing he'd

155

ever done, because he wanted to tell me real bad. I reckon that's bollocks though. I mean he hadn't told me nothing before, so why start now? I reckon he just didn't want to blow a shag – but I can live with that. He reckoned not having told me nothing for weeks had made it all worse though, because if he told me now he'd look a right shit for not having told me before, and so he was sort of stuck standing in a fucking hole he'd dug himself, and he couldn't see no way out. Of course the fucker about life is that while you're totally wrapped up and pissed off in one thing, trying to sort that out, someone else's life brings you down from behind.

Two nights after Si's first fuck we went to the disco, and he'd forgotten about it, like he'd arranged to see the stuck-up tart, and he was now in deep shit, because he was under heavy peer-group pressure and all. And so he went across to her and told her that he'd been asked out by some people and he was going and she probably wouldn't want to come because it were a disco and he knew she didn't like them but that he'd love her to come but he understood that she was planning to go out with friends and so he'd understand if she didn't want to join him, and she of course said thanks but no thanks. So he told her where we was going, but not that I'd be there – he left that out because she wouldn't trust my sort of night out – and then he came back to us, where the fun had already begun. I really does believe him when he says the last thing he expected was for her face to appear through the bodies on the dance floor, like he wasn't even hoping for it to happen. That of course was half the problem, his defences were down, and so when he saw her he was all over her, out of his drunken haze came love, and it took a while for him to realise what was going on, that he was in the middle, and like that were it, now he really was pissed and confused – you got to feel for him – and then she's dragging him out of there, and that WERE it, like within seconds the confusion left him, and he passed out in the back of the Golf GTI.

Next morning, he woke up in her tent, and she was 'indignant'. Not only had this been the only place they could get him to go back to last night, not only had he thrown up in one of the flowerbeds, not only had he made it quite clear to her friends that there was definitely something going on between him and her, he had also gone out with half-wits. I'd blown it for him again, just by existing, and this time he really couldn't understand why. He could understand that vomiting wasn't a good image, he could understand that being all over her was embarrassing, but he couldn't understand why getting pissed with me was the end of the world. And for a fraction of a second he saw the stupidity of all this, had a glimpse of the bitch, and then she started on him again, lecturing again, and he couldn't move, he was sucked back in, listening to the shit, and he can't say nothing back because the only answer is fuck off. He says it were like being hypnotised, there was this fury coming at him, and he was caught in it, like his brain had things to say, but his mouth wouldn't open, because all it was was fuel for her fire, and so that made him shut up even more, and merely mumble and mutter apologies out of good manners like, until finally she stopped – pissed off with his silence – stopped, because they had to go to work.

It were the feeling that he'd lost her that started it off again. It were her half-turned back. He now began to try to win her round, to be forgiven – what for? I don't know – and because I'd gone, moved to the depot, this should've made things easier, like he didn't have to worry about me no more, but of course she did. She'd bring me up all the time, like a whip to beat out any pleasure that might have snuck in, and like he was lost. He missed me, felt he had driven me out and all, and for what? She was still 'making love' to him occasionally,

157

she'd let her guard down now and again, so that he could see what he was chasing, and then all his old feelings would flood back, and she'd put up the fury again, and he'd be back in the front line, struggling for a ceasefire. And that was his problem – the ceasefires seemed worth waiting for. Bollocks – that's what I reckon. I mean, that's like walking naked in the snow so your sitting-room feels warmer, I mean nothing's worth that much hassle. And on top of all that you can't sit and listen to someone spouting crap about you every fucking day without starting to believe some of it. And that's what started to happen. He started to think he was doing dreadful things to her, he started to feel that maybe he was better off without me, that maybe I was more trouble than I was worth, but like the small sort of voice of our history wouldn't let him change that easy, it bit back, knifing him with guilt, and he had to suffer some more.

The day when I was doing the ice cream run was one of those days when he was stabbed from every side. First he had the shock of seeing me, the sudden return like, then the panic that I'd realise he was filling her cooler box, then the embarrassment of having to talk to me, and then the guilt of hoping I wouldn't come down to his beach after all, and like all morning that was all he was wanting, me not to turn up, but of course I did, and I backed up everything she had said about me, I flipped, and behaved like a dick – I reckon I had good bloody reason, but that weren't important right now – and of course, I gave her more ammunition for her mind-games. I played right into her hands and right out of his. And of course he had to make up for it. So what did he do? He bought her tickets for a rock concert, a concert he knew she wanted to go and see, full of old rock bands he'd never even heard of, and he was dead excited, he knew he had won this round, and he could just sit back and enjoy himself, this gift was not going to be rejected.

He was right too, she did not reject the tickets, she was 'quite pleased actually', but she was also amazed, like she was amazed he had been so selfish, he knew half of her friends 'wished to see the concert too', why didn't he get them tickets while he was there? 'Really', she didn't understand him sometimes, so she got on with ruining the evening.

About a month after I left the site, Si was reaching a kind of breaking point. It were the night of the concert, he'd managed to get tickets for her friends, and she had not spoken to him all day. She was pissed off with him because the night before he hadn't got it up. This had happened three times now. The problem was simple, but she didn't see it, he was terrified of failing. She'd already told him he was crap in bed, and now he knew it. His knob was dead, and rigor mortis refused to set in. All he wanted was a bit of sympathy. Wrong woman, Si. So the night of the gig he weren't exactly relaxed when he went up to her camp site, but he was still hoping that she'd be there and in a sort of gentler mood. She was there, but not with what you'd call open arms, you know, she was sat in the front seat of the car looking at her watch, and as the Golf pulled out of the camp site – Si and the others fighting to make room for each other in the back – she turned around and said, 'I hope we can still get a decent seat.' And that's when it began to rain, buckets of the stuff, and it didn't stop, down and down the fucking stuff came, and like when they arrived at the open-air stadium it were still pouring, and he knew that her whole evening had been ruined, and that not even the hot dogs that got wet, or the waste of space souvenir programme she insisted she wanted were going to cheer her up. It was all his fault of course, because if he had got tickets for the night before none of this would have happened, and as he followed her into the stadium he wondered if she was right, and he looked up into the

159

rain and wondered if God were punishing him for trying
to fuck a goy.

The concert finally began about two hours late, and
the first band did come on, but it were a waste of time,
a 'make sure we don't have to give them their money
back' kind of gesture, and after twenty minutes the show
was over, and all there was were rain, and that brief
moment when you wait to see if they're going to change
their minds. And in that moment this woman sitting
behind Si, a stranger, leant forward and started talking
to him about selling ice creams because she'd seen him
on the beach, and Catherine, the dear kind open-
hearted soul, stood up in a fury, and screamed 'Don't
pay me any damned attention then', and disappeared
into the rain with her friends trailing behind her. As he
caught up with the last of them, the last of her friends,
she put a sympathetic hand on Si's shoulder, and this
was her, 'She comes from a broken home, you know',
and Si did know, but it still didn't seem like much of an
excuse, and there was a sudden thickening of the rain,
like some bastard had opened the tap full, and everyone
started running, running, and among all the people Si
got delayed, like only for a minute, but when he got
back to the car, all the doors were shut, and they were
driving out the car park – like dripping fucking hatred
in a GTI can. He stood there, watching, desperately
trying to believe that at least one of her friends had tried
to stop her, but, I'm telling you, the shit-heads hadn't,
none of them, they was stuck together, they was stuck
up each other's arses. And at last he could see it for
himself.

Si was now stuck two hour's drive from home, wearing
a 'T' shirt, shorts, and espadrilles, in the hurling rain,
without a fucking centime to his name. No one was
going to stop to pick up this lost sodden animal. He had
to walk through the night – trudge trudge trudge trudge
– alone and miserable, on and on, until he was looking

on puddles as a break from the routine, until he had forgotten what he was fucking doing and was simply doing it, until he got back to Sainte Maxime about mid-afternoon, and even then it was still bloody well raining. He walked back up the hill to the camp site, a stream charging down the road past him, and his spirits sort of lifted, every step was making him better, like his shoes had collapsed, his 'T' shirt was two inches longer, his shorts were part of his body, but he didn't care, he had made it. Up the hill, that was where he had to go, and then he was there, above the camp site, looking into the field down there, ten feet below the level of the road, and it weren't a field no more – it were a lake. Everything was floating in a foot of water, everything of his, that is. Everyone else had got their stuff out. Hell, Ralph and Don had tried to move his stuff and all, but Si being Si, he'd padlocked his tent shut. Si stood looking down into this mess and he wished he'd trusted his fellow campers more and the 'people' on the other site less. Si looked down into the shit, and he wept. Fury, misery, loneliness, despair, like all of it mixed in with the fucking rain that wouldn't stop hitting him on his fucking head. It took three days to dry everything out, and even then his sleeping bag smelt like a cat had pissed in it.

It were at this point that he thought about coming to me, but he felt so shitty about the way he'd treated me he couldn't pluck up the courage. Hell, I'd been right about the bitch, I'd been right about her friends, I'd been right about mates, and I'd proved it all, day after day, by slipping him the extras that paid for his assault on the peak that was Catherine – and is that more poetry or what?

So he stayed where he was, felt like a fool, and just sort of got on with his days in a time-killing way. He moved beaches again, cut the bitch out of his life, and even spent a bit of time with Ralph and Don – he can't have been a happy man. Stuff was just passing him by. And then Maureen arrived on the scene, and he felt what happened next was like 'just punishment'.

And this is where Si stopped talking. This is when he stood up from the bed and started to sort of pace the tent, and the lads all stopped their gabbing and all, and there was this silence, and Si turned his back, and I could see he was trying to get himself under control, I could see that his twenty-four hour brush with the law were something he hadn't sorted out in his head yet and then he looked back at me and I could see him fighting with himself, like he was determined not to show me how bad it had been, determined not to make me feel guilty or nothing. And he starts explaining how he didn't think nicking a few extra ice creams was evil or nothing, but that he'd deserved what he got because he'd accepted the extras for all the wrong reasons – for Catherine – and because of the way he'd treated me, because he'd been such a dipshit, because he'd deserted me – I reckon that's a bit heavy myself, but you could see he meant it. So when he got arrested – he choked over the word – it were frightening, but right.

He turned away again now, sat on the other bed next to the lads, and like they was all watching him closely, and he starts telling me that the police thought his crime was a bit of a laugh really, that they took the piss quite a lot, that they told him they thought Dick the Dick was such un grand merde that they was going to take it out on him, that he was going to suffer for the hassle the wanker had given them, and Si took a deep breath, and looked up at me, straight at me, and told me what had been really worrying him though – get this – what had been really worrying him was that I'd get nicked and all. I didn't deserve nothing like that, I'd only been trying to help him out, and if he'd have told me to stop none of us would have got in trouble, but he'd carried on, guilt and all, because he was greedy for money for the blood-sucking one, and I hadn't made nothing out of it, he'd taken the lot and not even said thanks, and like even though they could only do me for sort of aiding and abetting, he knew I didn't even deserve that. And him saying this sort of stopped me, because being on the run had made me build up the crime and punishment in my head, and I mean now I looked at it, it were fuck all! All the hanging around had made it what it weren't.

And then Si stopped talking, like he couldn't go on, he were shaking, his face were buried in his hands, and I thought I could almost hear him strangling a sob, and I felt dreadful, I could see how difficult all this had been for him, all that time waiting in the cells, and I went over and sat next to him, sort of putting my arm around his shoulder, and he half pushed me away, and this is me, 'It's alright mate, you don't have to go on', and he shook his head, but didn't look up. It were Don that stood up, dead serious, and started to explain what had happened in court, how Dick the Dick had rubbished Si, had told the court what scum he was, how he was a man you couldn't trust, a man who deserved to be locked up for a long time, and then how Si's lawyer had got up and started pushing the mitigating circumstances, about Si's obsession with Catherine, about the lack of proof that Si had initiated the scam, about the fact that they couldn't prove any excess earnings, and then how suddenly it was all over, and how the beak spent what seemed like ages making up his mind, and then looked at Si, straight at him and began to lecture him about what is expected of a guest, about insulting your hosts, about an Englishman in France, and it weren't looking good, because the beak seemed to be winding up to something nasty, and Si had looked terrified, and then the beak suddenly changed, said that he reckoned the night in the cells was the main punishment – I reckon he were right and all – and that what Si needed now was to pay a 2000 franc fine.

But of course Si didn't have 2000 francs, he didn't have fuck all, and so he was taken back down to the cells, and he had to wait there while Don went and got some money, and that waiting was the worst because Don didn't have the money neither because him and Ralph had bought that green van last week, and so they had to go round loads of people borrowing money, and that had taken ages – why didn't they come to me? – but in the end they'd got it, and Don went back down the courts and paid off the fine, and Si had been handed over, and Don hadn't never seen someone look so shook up in all his life, and like he was fairly gone himself what with all the worry and shit, and he'd wanted to go for a drink with Si to calm things down a bit, but Si wouldn't have none of it, all he wanted was to get back here and see me. And Don shrugged his shoulders, and I looked round at the lads and they was all looking at me, and I knew all of this had been my fault, I knew it was because I'd wanted to feel important, that I'd gone over the top, tried too hard to prove myself, and I couldn't think of nothing else to say except sorry, and this is me, 'I'm really sorry lads. I really am.' And there was a bit of quiet and then Si sort of fights a smile and gabs about how it's history now, and they all nod, and this is Ralph, 'Ours as well.'

And it's like we're all waiting for something to happen now, something to break the atmosphere, and then it does happen, like the worst possible nightmare, suddenly there's this tearing noise, and the tent zip has been wrenched down, and the flaps are opening and through the gap comes a hat, a gendarme's hat, and my stomach just buckles and I'm diving under the bed so fucking fast that I don't hear it for a moment, I don't hear the explosion of laughter, and everyone, the whole tent, the lot of them are pissing themselves, like weeping, and I looks up proper from under the bed and I can see why, I looks up under the peak of the cap and it becomes obvious, because it's Dexter, and he's wearing the crappiest version of a gendarme's uniform I have ever seen, and this is him, 'That'll teach you to get us the sack, you dumb arsehole.'

I did laugh. But not for about ten minutes, and even then I didn't really want to. But it were a start, I suppose.

Out Of It Again

None of it had been Si's idea of course, it was Don, he was the bastard who done it, but hell, had they put me through shit or what? Now I'm not one who gets pissed off at a wind-up, because if it's good you got to accept it, and this one, well, it were bloody good – I mean hook line and sinker – and like maybe I'd deserved something for getting them the sack and all, but talk about pushing it to the limits. The bastards really had got me going. But of course they'd done more than that, hadn't they? Oh yes. They'd gone and pushed the thing right over the bloody limit. Right over. Because guess what? Dick the Dick HAD gone and reported me to the gendarmes – just because I called out his name. Typical, huh? The joke was over but the real shit was still going to hit me right in the middle of my fucking face. But hell, every cloud eh? I mean at least Si and me was talking. At least I'd have someone who'd come and visit me inside.

Si and me reckoned it was probably a good idea to get out of Frog, like there weren't a lot of point in hanging around. I mean the Frogs aren't exactly going to be searching for me, but there's a chance I might get nicked, and it's not going to be easy for Si to get another job round here neither – there is only so many peanut-sellers the world can take – and we still got the dosh we left England with – well I got a bit more actually – and so what I reckons is that we should sort of pick up where

166

we left off, you know – and I get a bit excited about this
– let's get out there and meet the Slow-Mos and Bobbys
of this world, get out there and travel, hit the road and
burn the fucking tarmac! But Si didn't get off on that
one, he reckoned I was a sitting duck if we done that,
he reckoned we should just catch a train and get the hell
out, and the others agreed and all, which was a bit of a
pisser, because I got into that hitching lark last time,
but I suppose they're right, and so I agrees, but not
with much sort of enthusiasm. The problem with a train
is that it's not as easy as a car, you got to choose a
destination, and that weren't exactly simple, not when
you're as stoned and pissed and speeding as we was, I
mean we'd been talking for fucking hours before we got
to this point, like it was five in the bloody morning and
neither of us had even noticed. It's not surprising we
struggled really, because I didn't know none of the
places Si mentioned, and all the places I mentioned
were just plain stupid – Bongo Bongo land and shit like
that – and so after half an hour we'd been round half the
fucking world and still got nowhere, and then we came
up with Spain. Spain. Shit, it's where all the fucking
Brits go, I mean my aunt – stupid cow – she always
wanted to go to Marbella. And that's how it happened. I
mentioned her and everything else just sort of followed,
this is me, 'My aunt always wanted to go to Marbella,
let's go there, then I could send her a postcard, and that
would really piss her off.' But Si don't laugh, suddenly
he's somewhere else, like he's got an idea, and then he
grins, and now he really does want to go to Marbella,
because his parents knows some people who's got a
time-share there, and he reckons the sons might be at
the place right now, and he's known them for years, and
like I've met them and all, and Si's mum had said 'Oh
pop in and see them, they're always talking about you',
and we've got the address, and he's real excited about
it, and like that's what sells it, because fuck it, what the

167

hell, it's a gift horse, know what I mean? And if they're not there, well, it'll be a piece of piss getting a job in a place like Marbella. I tell you, we were well pleased with the choice, especially when Adolf pulled out a wad of pesetas and offered us a pretty good rate of exchange.

The lads drove us to the station that night, and like all of us was wrecked, and it was weird knowing this was over, and having to say goodbye, because before it had just sort of happened, but this time I got to think about it, sort of wondering if I'd see them again, which would be good, right, but I didn't expect it, and so we swapped addresses and shit, and then did our au revoirs, and this is them, 'Fuck off', and this is me, 'Drown in your own vomit', and their crap green van doors closed, and away they went, the smell of Hope the last thing they'd left us. I passed it to Si, but he didn't want it, so I lugged deep, stamped on it, and we headed into la gare.

Si has this idea about getting us couchettes so we can lie in proper beds, and I'm all for this, so he goes and books them, and then we heads down to the platform to catch the midnight train. There it is, sitting there with signs stuck all over the windows, and on we get, and why not? It's nearly midnight. Our couchettes turn out to be piss small, but what's that matter, we're getting out of Frog, and so within five minutes we've unpacked our stuff, set up shop in the bedroom box, and unplugged a bottle of cheap red shit. Midnight, the train pulls out, chug chug chug, and we're having a bloody good laugh, and like it's just me and Si, together again, and that feels well good, even if things have sort of changed with us, like we're both trying a bit harder than normal. I mean we weren't like that when we first got back together, but now we're on our own, and all that – the things that happened – well, they are there, on the seat beside us, and hell we both know we got to talk about the anger and shit, but both of us is going to avoid it because we want it to be the same as it was. I mean

168

we both know it can't be yet, because too much has gone on and like too many experiences, and we haven't been there to talk about them, so they're only stories and no way's that the same, no way's that like sharing them, and we both know it, but like what the fuck can you do about it now? And that's what half the feeling is, like we lost something, but shit, we've gone and found it again, even if it is a bit different, and twenty years from now the being lost bit will be part of us, it'll be something only we understand, and that's the main thing, we're back on fucking course. This is me, 'Cheers, mate.' And I swig from the bottle, and then so does he.

About twenty minutes after the train pulled out there's a knock at the door. It's the guard, a fat bastard, with a scalp like a snow cloud, armpits like he's just played extra time, a moustache like Stalin and he wants our billets. Si is straight into his best GCSE French, and it's good because I can understand a load of it now, and so I settle back into my bunk and start taking the piss. Stalin is not amused though, he's agitated. It turns out that he's a fascist. He's got his nice dark blue uniform on, and he's God. Well, isn't that a surprise? He's got a problem and all, like he reckons we shouldn't be in the couchettes, because the train that was waiting by the platform at midnight is not the midnight train, no, the train waiting by the platform at midnight is the eleven o'clock train. The midnight train leaves at one o'clock. Well that makes sense. And guess what? This stupid dead fascist doesn't like the Anglais, particularly Anglais who are younger than him, and who are having a good time, and so no way's he going to do nothing to help us, oh no, the stupid fascist dead brain wants us out – not that any other bastard has booked our couchettes, not that we haven't paid good money, not that there's any fucking reason whatsoever, just that that's what he wants. And he's got his uniform on. I can feel myself getting cold at the bastard, but I know I got to control

169

it, because I'm sort of on the run, and he's an official sort of thing, but it's fucking hard not to floor the shithead, and so I get hold of my anger and I shout it in my head – Fascist dead brain arsehole, Fascist dead brain arsehole, Fascist dead brain arsehole, Fascist dead brain arsehole, and I grin, and my only pleasure is that he can't see my fucking fury. And Si? Well, what a surprise, Si sees Stalin's point of view. I mean, he's so fucking nice. I couldn't open my mouth without shouting, but he don't even argue. Jesus, why's he got to be so polite? It don't get you nowhere. Well, it does, it gets you out in the fucking corridor of an SNCF in the middle of the bloody night! Dickhead.

So here we are in the corridor, my arse is in agony, and my oldest mate is hogging all the oxygen, noisily, like he's flat out and snoring as bad as a road drill. He reckons it's his sinuses, but I reckon it's because his nose is so fucking big. The air isn't breathed in like with a normal nose, with his nose it's sucked in, it charges in, rattling like cappuccino, a nightmare noise that screams at you to wake up and stop enjoying yourself. So that's what I've done, I've woken up, and I feel shit, like I've had two hours sleep and I left my head at the fucking party, and with him and the train making such a racket I know I'm not going to get no proper sleep, and I'm getting bored now, and I've got that first-light horn and all, so I shakes Si up, and suggests we go into the toilets and have a wank as we cross the border, like at the same time, and Si looks at me in total shock, because like – I wake him up for this? But you got to give it to him, he goes and does it, and it's great because we're in two toilets opposite each other, and are we laughing or what? Wanking on a train, wanking into Spain – I reckon it could catch on. I slept better for it and all.

At about six in the morning we arrive at our first Dago changing place, where we gets to swap trains, and like it's total shit. On the Dago train we're squashed into this compartment that's got plastic seats that should hold six but hold eight instead – and all of them smell. And this train is slow, mind-numbing, stop, start, chug, chug, like an old man out for a walk, worse, it's like being the old man, it's like being frustrated, and the sun is coming in now, hitting us, and it's getting so fucking hot in this box we can't move and our legs are stuck to the seat, our whole bodies a claggy sticky oozing mass, I mean we can't get comfy or nothing. This is the slow train to hell, and both of us has given up talking. All there is to do is to watch dry land – just wishing it would go away quicker – and to try and not smell the people. What is it with their bodies? I mean hell, I'm sweaty as shit, but I don't smell or nothing. And there's no let up on none of this neither, because every station you get to, people come along the platform selling, and if you want to get anything you don't get out, you got to do it from the window – I want to get off this fucking train! – and so like there we are, eight of us, hanging out of a window made for two, feeling like a blunt sword is forcing you in half, and all we get for it is a dry sandwich with sweating cheese and a warm bottle of water, and it don't matter how much you drink of it, you won't get rid of the thirst. Mind you, you never need to piss or nothing, because the temperature is rising, like it's never going to stop, and you really can understand why people out here take a day to move, and then when they do it's to shout, because does this put you in a knackered foul mood or what? Thirteen hours we were in the train. Thirteen hours until at last we reached Malaga, thirteen hours of shit. It would have been quicker to swim, and fuck that's what it feels like we done. I've never got so wet in a dry place in all my life – never. And then, when we does at last squeeze out of this can of people, ooze from our tube of exhaustion, we at least expect to be lifted by a blast of fresh air, but no, no way, we're slapped down by a fucking glove of heat like you wouldn't believe.

171

Heat just settles on us, and it's a shock, I mean this is meant to be the cool part of the fucking day, and all I got to say is – please please please, just let me get to the sea.

The walk to the bus station was like going through the pain barrier, the bags felt like they were gripping on for life and were never going to let go, like they was heavy, and every step the straps dug in, and sort of made time go on for longer, so that when we did get to the station and dropped the fuckers there was this light feeling, like life rushing to catch up, and it were full of relief. But then we had to find the bus we wanted, and that was a chore and all, because like this place is not home, there's signs in a language we don't speak, and names that's not spelt proper, and people who is hanging around in a mess, not in queues or nothing, so you never know what bus is going where or when it's leaving, and so it's not all that surprising that it were ages before Si found the right one, and when he had, of course, we had to face those fucking bags again. It's like you'll never get to that seat, there's all that tarmac to fight your way over, the battle just to get to the door, the battle to get through it, the bodies down the aisle, the twisting and turning in a fucking small space full of heads, and finally that brief moment of victory when you finally gets to sit down and you're ready to feel comfy, and you realise you got no fucking leg-room. We were getting closer though, and that did make it easier.

Two hours later at nine we are stepping out of the bus, and we ARE by the sea, and there is a cool fucking breeze and I could sing I'm so bloody happy. In fact we does, all the way along the road, and no one seems to give a shit, they don't even look at us, and after asking a few of them we finally finds the right street name and all, and we head up it, searching for this time-share complex, and then finally we sees it, the last block halfway up the hill, and it's this huge white concrete mass of boxes and it don't look bad, not bad at all, and it's new and clean and fuck it's a load better than some crappy Frog camp site. Hell, I'm impressed because I didn't reckon the Dagoes could build nothing like this, but, you know, here's the proof, and the closer we get the smarter it gets, and hell we're really starting to hope these lads are there, and that they do talk about Si all the time, because this really could be shit hot, and we're both feeling a bit sort of nervous and bit sort of excited, and we sees these stairs and they've got the number on that we wants, and so we start up them, and like we both decide that we've got to play this dead cool, and so we put down the bags, check out what we look like, laugh, and then Si rings the doorbell and steps back and knocks one of our bags down the stairs. And that really sets us off. We're staring down the stairs, pissing ourselves, when the door's opened, and like this isn't the best way to introduce yourself, but as it turns out, it's the coolest, because the lads ARE there and this shows them that we don't care, that we don't need them. But the real joke turns out to be that we don't even need to do nothing to look cool, because they already think we are – get your ears round this – because I'm part of their folklore! I walk in through the door and they all know who I am! Shit, is the world weird or what? They rated Si because of Me! Because – wait for it – I was so 'street'! Si has got a well sharp reputation because of Ken, like he was painted with my fucking brush. Ha! Am I feeling a dude or what? I mean, fuck, someone remembered me for good reasons!

Into Ken

So let me tell you about my fan club, because as soon as the door opened it all came back – I remembered the whole fucking lot of them. First thing you should know is that these berks are all nice North London Jewish boys, and that their mothers have lived and breathed for them from the moment they were spilt on the earth. These are boys who will never say 'fuck' if their mother is in the room, and who reckon she'll find out if she is out of the room and all, hell even if she's out of the country. These are boys whose idea of an exciting party is having their name put into a hat, so the girls can pick their partners for the dancing. These boys will be bought their first moped, and a year later their first car, and it will be insured. These boy will marry into the faith. These boys are sweet, clean-cut, will never divorce, and are unlikely to catch anti-social diseases. Their wives will be called Jessica, or Diane, or Rachel, or Ruth, and there's a good chance they've met them already. They'll work hard for charities, will visit Israel at least once in their lives, will be upright citizens, and will always be able to get things on the cheap. These are boys mothers dream about, and fuck it, it's because they are really Nice. These are the boys Si grew up with, boys he introduced me to, and the ones he'll spend the rest of his life trying to get away from. Hell, these boys are already discussing their fathers' businesses. These are boys who are looking for excitement now because they won't have it later, but wouldn't know excitement if it walked up and sat down next to them, dressed in a catsuit with 'screw me rotten' tattooed all over it. These boys would think it was a furniture restorer. These are the kind of boys who see me as their chance to taste the thrills of life, who want to watch me blow myself up, so they can applaud, come to the funeral, and be terribly grateful that it weren't them. They want to talk, not do, they want tales, not real stuff. These are the kind of boys who make up my fan club. Great.

So who are these deeply disturbed people? Well, there's David, he's the eldest brother, about seventeen, who'll go to somewhere like Cambridge and make his family very proud. He's tall, slim, dark and hairy, and takes after his mother. The next brother is Samuel, he's sixteen, doing 'A' levels, and is short, fat, dark and hairy. He takes after his dad. Their best friends – forever – are Daniel, Paul, and Solomon. I mean hell, try a new name why don't you? These other three are in their late teens somewhere, and will probably make their family well proud and all. There is only one dumb one, and that's Paul, but he's already begun working for his grandfather's fur coat business – so that's alright.

These are my five boys then, the boys who was sat around in the all-white time-share apartment playing Monopoly when we arrived at 9.30 on that Friday night. On the table in front of them was one nearly empty bottle of wine. Need I say more?

Long and Short

It was David who answered the door, and he was particularly pleased it was us, because he was worried the neighbours were coming to complain about the noise. Like, what noise? Breathing too loud? So we're invited in, and they all stands up – I mean, fuck me – and introduces themselves. And then – Jesus – they shake our fucking hands, and it had only taken ten seconds but what I knew would happen had happened, like we'd just stepped onto Planet Polite. Si looked at me, and I knew he knew too, I mean wondering why the fuck he'd wanted to come here, but he couldn't help it now, and so little bits from the Polite Solar System kept sneaking out of him and all, but hell, at least he fought it, like he sat down without being asked.

So when they offered us a drink, I pulled out a litre of red shit we'd bought on the way, and the boys all look at each other and smile because you can see this got their blood going good already, and then when I pull out a lump of Adolf's Hope, well that's it, I mean they really is sinning now, and hell, they got to try it, but you can see they're worried that one of their aunts might turn up, suddenly, and like as soon as I'm rolling the thing David has gone and got us an ashtray each – I reckon he wants us to hold it underneath the spliff, like eating soup – and so I'm rolling and I'm thinking, and I'm thinking evil. I know what I got to do, and I know I

176

have to do it, I got to put no Hope in this spliff, I've got
to just put some in the top bit, my bit, just up my end,
and like as I'm doing this Si is telling them what's been
going on with us, and I can feel them watching me while
he gabs, this sort of cautious feeling, checking out what
I'm actually doing, and there's this thrill in the room
and it's building, and you can feel them, nervous, taut,
and then it's finished. I play with it a bit, rolling it in my
fingers, and then just holding it, like I've forgotten about
it, and you can see them watching it in my hand,
desperate for the off, and then finally I does light it and
they're watching it so fucking closely it's a joke. They
watch it going from my hand to my mouth, from my
mouth to my hand, waving in front of me as I talk,
drifting smoke up past my eyes as I listen, and it's like
they're a crowd at one of those crap tennis games you
get on TV, backwards and forwards, up and down, and
it's so fucking obvious my fans want to make sure they
knows exactly what they're meant to do, and so when I
feels the Hope come to an end I pass what is now a fag
to Si, but he don't take none – because he's like that
sometimes – and he passes it on, and now the fun really
begins. They suck at it like it will bite them, try again,
harder this time, trying desperately not to cough, and
then they nod their heads trying to look knowledgeable,
not breathing mind, and then the smoke just sort of
seeps out of them, and then they start to talk about it,
and like I'm desperate not to wet myself, because this is
them, 'Oh yes' 'My this is good' 'It's better than the last
stuff I had' 'Yes, this really is strong' 'Do you buy this in
Dalston? You can get it there, can't you?' 'Hey, don't
smoke all of it' 'He's a hog', and then they starts laughing
and shit, and they really ARE Stoned, like they've
thought themselves into it, and this is them, 'My head's
spinning' 'I can hardly stand up' 'This must have cost a
lot' 'Pass it on' 'Mind the sofa, mind the sofa', and fuck I
can't help it, I like these boys. No one's ever tried so

177

hard to impress me, not never. And then it hits me, and I feel a sort of wave of embarrassment inside me, like fuck, this is what I must have sounded like to the blokes at school when I first lugged their gear. Jesus. And like then I start laughing, because is life weird or what? And they all join in, and so the next time I roll one I don't piss them around, I pack it, solid, and this time there's none of the chat, because they're off their trolleys.

About midnight we heads out to the swimming pool, and I tells Si what I done with that first spliff, and he pisses himself, and pushes me backwards into the fucking water – mates know how to stop you getting cocky – wanker. But the pool's gorgeous, right, and the water's so fucking clean, and the underwater lights are so bright, you can even see your own piss, and like this is heaven, floating on your back smashed out your head, this is how it should be, I mean, this I could handle, like forever. The lads don't hang around outside too long though, they go back in after about fifteen minutes or so, and Si goes with them, and tries to persuade me and all, but I'm not moving till my skin starts creasing, because is this swimming at night weird or what? You feel hidden out here, any sound you make is sort of sucked up by the night, and there's all the crickets cricketing, and stars starring, and hell, I don't give a shit no one else is doing this with me because the rest of the universe is having a party and all. Mind you, it's probably not as smashed as I am.

When I does get back inside the lads have gone to bed, and Si is lying on one of the sofas, and he tells me to talk a bit quieter and to stop dripping on the carpet, and like I tell him to piss off. He don't say nothing, so I get my sleeping bag out and bung it on the other sofa, and just the look of it makes me happy because it's going to be the softest thing I've slept on in ages, but it turns out it's too fucking soft and I can hardly get a wink, and like Si's the same, so I gets up and raids the parents' drinks cabinet – which was packed – and like Si sits up and tells me to put the bottles back and to stop being a dick. He's never done that before. He reckons I shouldn't start nicking stuff from the parents. He reckons I've done enough damage waking up half the time-share complex. He reckons I should stop showing off in front of a bunch of kids, and if I'm so fucking desperate I should have a fucking spliff. So I take out a thousand peseta note, and wave it at him, and he wants to know what I'm doing, and this is me, 'I am paying for what I drink. Tomorrow with this money you and me will go down the shops and we'll replace what we used, alright Mummy?' And like I poured him a whisky, put it down in front of him and then swigged from the bottle, and that shut him up. After three drinks he'd come round, and I started making cocktails – great big steamers – and like it weren't till I threw up that I realised how strong they were. Si passing out should have been a clue, but there you go, it did the trick. I mean, fuck, did we sleep or what?

Next morning I was woken by a surprised David, this is him, 'What?' He's confused – he hadn't left the room in this much of a mess – but he don't say nothing, he just starts clearing up, and I could see he was annoyed, but he was being so bloody polite about it, I mean he didn't even ask me to help, he just kept looking at me now and again, with a tight sort of face, and it were well funny, because he didn't have to be like that, he could've just waited till we were up, because we'd have cleaned up the mess with him, but there was no way we could help right now, I mean I felt like shit, and Si still hadn't moved. I reckoned the only thing I could do to cheer him up – and me – was to roll us one lovely recovery spliff, and offer it to him first. He was a bit surprised, I got to say, but he did take it, I mean he did give it a shot, but then he started wincing and choking on this cough and passed it back, not talking, you know, strug-

179

gling with his lungs, and I said thanks, but like you could see he weren't cut out for the party life.

About an hour later the rest of the boys appear and I join them for breakfast, and we get gabbing about what they're doing for the day, and I can't believe it, because they're planning to spend the day stocking up on food and then playing some tennis! I suggested we hits the town and have a few beers instead, and maybe find some women, and they're a bit unsure to start with, but like after a bit of a row with big brother David, Samuel and Paul agrees and so the three of us leave the rest to their games – and Si to his coma – and head down to the town. And like have these boys got dosh or what? They're loaded, and quite happy to spend it and all, which is the main point. By six I have them so faceless Paul is flat asleep, ear to the table, and Samuel is giggling like shit because he's almost plucked up the courage to go and speak to a right little gland-spanker at the table by the bar, and I'm telling him he can do it, he can go over and talk to her, but he just doesn't know, and it takes about an hour of persuasion before he goes and does it, and then he gets up, swaying, crossing like a pinball, staggering into the seat beside her, and he looks ridiculous. But she's not fooled, oh no, she takes one look at his wallet, and makes him real welcome real quick, and hell, I got to grin, because this makes me a sort of matchmaker, you know, Ken, your very own computer dating service.

By eight, Paul has moved from the table and is propped against the wall in the corner, snoring like a mate I know – thank fuck the stereo is louder – and sometimes he stops the noise, I mean now and again, and he starts this shuddering, a sort of heaving, like his chest is fighting his body, and it looked bloody funny at the time I can tell you, you know, if you was there, and like me and the barman couldn't resist it no more neither and so we covered him with those pink and blue

180

umbrellas that stick up your nose when you drink crap cocktails, and I'm telling you the place pissed themselves. Samuel didn't notice nothing though, because he were still sat with the lip-flapper, trying like you wouldn't believe, and you could see it, you could see he was desperate, overexcited, slurring his words, and you could see she was bored and all, bored but sort of amused at the same time, and like I wasn't going to put no money on it, because it could still could have gone either way.

But I'm afraid that's it. I can't tell you much more after that. I met this bloke, whose name has completely disappeared from my head, and he and me started playing darts, and in the middle of one of the games I pointed to the double nineteen so he could see what he was going for, and he threw the dart, and my finger was still pointing, and the dart stuck my finger to the board, you know it went clean through where the nail meets the skin, in the double, and like it came as one fuck of a shock, because he hadn't thrown nothing right before that, and like then I hit him and he hit me, and I hit him again, and he hit me again, and we both sort of fell down, and couldn't get up, and when we did we both wanted a drink so bad that we stopped fighting, and that really is it. There's nothing after that.

I woke up at about 5.30, flat out on the beach, opposite the bar, sort of right beside the road, and Samuel was fast asleep on my legs, and Paul had his head under my armpit and I felt like a bitch covered in puppies – but Jesus did these puppies smell or what? I pushed them off, and they woke up, and you could see they'd never felt like this before in their lives, that it was all one fuck of a shock, and like these were newborn puppies, like they didn't know where the fuck they were, so I rolled us a wake-you-up spliff, and they lugged on that, and they both passed out again, and I laughed a bit, but that hurt, so I decided to go home – I

181

mean I didn't want to hang about here no more. I tried
to wake the boys again, but they weren't around, so I
left them on the beach, and spliff going nicely wandered
back up the hill to the time-share. The real pisser of
course is that the front door weren't open – I should've
nicked Samuel's keys – so I had to go down the pool and
crash on one of those sun-bed things, but it turned out
to be bloody comfy, and so I had very nice kip thank
you, which were exactly what I needed.

David must have spotted me from the flat, because at
about eight he comes running down and shakes me
awake, and starts going on, 'Where are they? Where are
they?' and so I tells him, and roll over, but he's not
having that, and this is him, 'You left them beside the
road? How could you? Samuel's only sixteen. I think it's
terribly irresponsible of you. For starters you must have
known that he shouldn't have had more than a couple of
drinks. Really, I mean really, I think you have behaved
appallingly.' And this is me 'Who are you then? Cane or
Abel?' and like I reckon that was pretty good considering
it was eight in the morning, and so I rolls over again,
and this time – with a huff – he does let me go to sleep,
well for about ten minutes, then he comes back down
again, ready to go and find the poor lost sheep sort of
thing, and this is him, 'The least you can do is go back
upstairs to sleep. I don't know what the neighbours
would say if they found you here . . . looking like that.'
And that last bit took him a bit by surprise, just sort of
came out, like training, and I reckon he heard his
parents saying it as he were saying it because he went a
red colour and turned and went away bloody quick, and
I had to laugh, but that still hurt so I stopped, and did
what he asked, because the sun was starting to get a bit
hot, and I knew Samuel's bed would be empty and all.

About nine I got woken up again, and like all of them
was there, sitting around in the sitting-room, waiting,
even Si, who looked at me with a 'you stupid bugger'

look on his face, and I grinned at him, and he just said he supposed I'd want a coffee, and went to get me one, and I reckons he were glad to be out of the room and all, because that's when David started, full of the eldest male in the family kind of shit.

It turns out that Paul and me got thrown out of the bar at about two, and that the leg-spreader then asked Samuel if he wanted to go down the beach for some 'hunting and fishing', and like this fucking amazed me, because that means he was still going after me, and the last thing I remember he looked well gone already, completely gone, and like you got to hand it to him, I mean fuck, you never know who's going to be able to hold their drink and shit does you? I got to look at the lad in a new sort of a light now, because fuck it, credit where credit's due, he did go over to the beach and all, and he done the business, and like even through his death-white face you can see he's feeling a bit good about it, which is right I reckon, but is not how David sees it. This is him, 'Not only did you encourage him to drink excessively, you persuaded him to pick up a woman of seriously doubtful morals when, and I must say this is what I think is worst of all, when he was carrying no contraceptive sheaths of any kind.' And you got to laugh. But David's not stopped yet, oh no, this is him, again, 'I don't see what is funny. Sleeping with a woman who is willing to sleep with you that quickly, must surely make you doubt the safety of the sex. On top of that . . .' – and he looked really put out now – 'sleeping with a woman who then makes off with your wallet, most certainly proves that the sex was patently unsafe.' And this came as a bit of a bolt this, but I was getting pissed off with the tone now, so this is me, 'Oh stop being such an up-your-arse prick.' And this is him, straight back, sort of shouting, 'He had his wallet stolen because you did not look after him! If you hadn't have taken him down there, none of this would have happened!' And this is me, 'He wanted to go. He wanted to drink. He wanted a fuck. He's a bloke. Lay off it. Grow down a bit.' And he didn't understand this and that slowed him, stopped him, just for a fraction, and I suddenly got this second wind, like a burst of energy, and this is me, 'You're just jealous, like he may look like shit now, but he had a fucking good time, and you didn't, you went shopping, and I reckon you should be grateful, because he will be, even if he did lose his wallet, because what he's got now is a fucking brilliant thing, a memory, he's got something to talk about, he's done something, and like you'd like to have a story like that, but you're not going to get it, because you're seventeen and senile. So give it a break, get off my fucking case – and get on your own.' And he just looked at me and walked away. Never mentioned it again. But it sort of spoilt the atmosphere a bit.

We went and played tennis with them that afternoon, and people sort of looked at me with shit in their mouths because I was in black shorts, a string vest, football socks, and purple pumps, but what the fuck eh? And I did keep hitting the ball out the court and all, and the people in the court next door did move along a couple of courts, but hell, it were a good laugh, and like it turns out that Si's pretty good at it, which, you know, was a bit of a surprise, because he never told me he could play, but I weren't going to complain or nothing because he was on my side. I say my side, but like I was starting to get this feeling from him, like a distance, and I sort of recognised it this time, it were the same as when we were at the camp site, sort of not laughing as much as he should be, and like he was talking to David and all, which was dead weird, because there's not a lot to talk about with him, and so I tell you what it felt like, it didn't feel like he was abandoning me or nothing, it felt like he thought he had to make up for me. He only did it a couple of times, but it hurt, I got to say, it did make

184

me wonder, you know. So after the game I went off for a walk, to have a think about it all, to bury myself in some Hope, and at first I thought maybe he was jealous, you know, because this lot rated me, but I knew he's not like that, and so I had to find another reason, and I reckoned it must be me. Me, what I'm like. I'm too loud, I mean, it's obvious. I don't make life easy for people. And I looked at them all, sort of avoiding me, and I wanted to get Si back on my side, like, my mate, and so I decided I should back off a bit, and so when I'd finished the spliff, and got back to them, I tried to be a bit quieter, you know, like for the rest of the day I just sort of swum, and went for a quick drink with him, and just sort of accepted that I'd knocked the stuffing out the lads and their party days were over – though they still drank a bit of wine at supper, and smoked my gear – and like at the end of the night Si and me is talking, quiet like, and he reckoned it were best not to 'outstay our welcome.' I wasn't going to argue, so like I told him I was getting sort of bored and all, you know, and he told me that one of the neighbours had complained a bit, and another had asked what that smell was when I was down by the pool smoking, and so we decided to hire a couple of bikes and drive down the coast, and I was suggesting we find a beach to crash on and Si was talking about maybe getting a room somewhere, and things were sort of up in the air really, which is a good place for things to be I suppose, and so the next morning we got the bikes and headed off, and like I didn't get the feeling they were sad to see me go. I tell you what though, Samuel came up to me before we left, and this is him, 'Sorry', and this is me, 'Why?' and this is him, 'Well, you know.' And this is me, 'No', which sort of shut him up, but I didn't mean it to.

185

Together Again

Now there is nothing much better than driving a bike on empty roads that have long straight bits to let you open up and tight curves to make you work your nuts off, and this is what the roads south of Marbella gave us, particularly after we'd passed through Algeciras, and like we had no helmets or nothing neither, just a naked head, and the sun all over us, and it were all well good – just Si and me again, bitching. I tell you what though, I never smelt nowhere like Algeciras before. There was this market we went into, and it were this big round building, and there's animals all over the place, live ones in cages, tied up ones, dead ones hanging from hooks – heads, skin, everything – and like when people buys chickens they choose one from the cages and the fucking thing has its neck cracked there and then, and like is this place full of weird shit or what? I mean you can smell the death, and the people are charging all over the shop, grabbing things, examining things, screaming at each other, talking to twelve people at once, and hell it's all going on, like life. We bought these things called churros and all, and are they like gorgeous or what? Strips of deep-fried batter they are, and I ate so many of the buggers I burned the top of my mouth off and made myself feel sick, but it were worth it, because the bloke in the stall pissed himself, you know he loved this sort of customer, and he let us cook some of our own churros, which was well fun.

And then we're driving out of the town, and the next smell hit us, and it were like putting your head down the toilet to smell someone else's dump, I mean it were bloody difficult not to gag then and there, but we keeps going, and the stench is getting stronger, and suddenly we're driving over this river, and it can't be a river, it must be neat shit, but it says river on the sign, and all the Dagoes are walking past without a turn of a single fucking nostril, and I can't believe it because this really is a smell from hell. But then, as soon as we're over the river the wind starts bringing us this new air, like the old smell stops, and a new smell arrives, a fresh one, a clean sort of mouth-watering musky type of thing, and it starts to get stronger, and I could live in this smell forever, and then we comes up this hill, and there's this factory, and stacked outside it are piles and piles of bark, and they must be burning it or something, because smoke is pouring out the chimney, and I have to stop to breathe it in, because I'm telling you, this one was a smell from heaven, like you could eat it.

We rode on for another half hour and then we comes over this hill, and there's this view and it's fucking Africa. We stop the bikes, because like this is a view to savour, and I light up, and I breathe it in, and it really is shit hot. On the left's a few houses running down this valley, and to the right there's more houses running up this hillside to a rock face half a mile or so back. Above this rock face are these huge birds, and I reckon they're eagles, but Si reckons they're vultures, but what's it matter because they know what they are, and they're circling around, sort of soaring, and like I'd love to join them – not as a career move – because, shit, it must be good, but I can't keep watching them, I got to turn back, I'm sort of called back, I got to look at Africa again, and is it a mean looking mother or what? I mean it's just there, this huge lump of ROCK. And hell, would it be good to have a house with a view like this? Shit, imagine living in one of these places, surrounded by all these trees, and all the crickets, and the birds and shit.

And then I see the pools, the swimming pools, and it hits me, I mean there's people sunbathing on top of these houses, and I feel sort of pissed off, because like these aren't for people to live in, these are holiday homes, they're places for the rich, this is 'fuck you, aren't we wonderful' territory, and it ruins the view.

I lobs away the spliff and gets back on the bike, with Si telling me that I shouldn't lob away spliffs like that because of fires and shit, and I tells him I knew the thing was out but I'll be careful, because would you feel a total bastard if you started a fire in a place as beautiful as this or what? And we head off, along these twisting roads with straight bits, and like after about ten minutes we see this round sort of building, and we have to stop, because there's a load of people piling into the place, and Si sees this poster on the wall and it's for a bullfight, and we realise that this is the bullring, and a fight must be about to start. Now Si, he's not keen, because he's seen them on TV but I reckons it would be a gas, and so I tells him to stop being a wimp, this is me, laughing a bit, 'Stop being a wimp', and so we parks the bikes and heads into the place, and it's round inside too, and it's a lot smaller than the ones Si's seen, I mean it's piss small, but what I reckon is that it's because it's a piss small village, like this is the Dago equivalent of Accrington Stanley, and then to shit on my theory out come piss small bulls. Jesus, it's a fucking joke, the poor buggers would only just come up to your gut, I mean they're kids, not fully grown or nothing, like the matador is huge compared to the bull, and the whole thing looks so fucking stupid I got to laugh, and then on comes this horse and rider, and the bull looks even smaller, and the bastard on the horse he starts to lunge at the bull with this spear, and all around me the crowd are cheering their fucking heads off. I mean, hell, they actually seemed to like it. But I didn't. I reckoned it were weird, I mean the poor little fuckers, it's like watching a licensed bully. They didn't even kill the bulls or nothing, they just stuck the spears in and then pretended to finish them off, like a joke, I mean is that fucking off or what? Do they reckon that don't hurt or nothing? I mean bollocks, it must hurt like buggery. I mean you can see the poor little thing all twitching and shit, at the shock, you know, the shock of his skin getting split right open, the shock of feeling the blood that's coming out of him like jam, frothing jam, and are you telling me he don't know? I mean it's sick, I tell you, it's sick. And the bloke in the crowd next to me must have seen the look on my face, because he laughed, and this is him, 'English?' and this is me, 'Too bloody right', and he laughed again, and told me it were a practice for the young matadors to learn their stuff, and I said, this is me, 'What about the bulls? This practice for them and all is it?', and I was a bit angry really – I don't know why – but he didn't notice, and this was him, 'No, no, now they fight no more, now they know the ring', and I thought that was typical, and so this is still him, 'Now they are put out in a field to live long and happy, until you want to eat steak.' And he laughed again. And I reckon the shit had a point, but I don't know if he meant to make it.

We watched about three of the poor little buggers go through this bollocks, and then we'd had enough. I mean hell, even if there had been a few deaths, it's not the most exciting thing watching a load of Gary Glitter lookalikes running around a sandpit, charging in and out and up and down these little wooden walls, you know, hiding, while some half insane creature runs around in circles like a dog eating its tail, then runs straight at an old tablecloth and misses. I mean who needs that shit? Not us. Anyway I was hot, and next door to the bullring was this hotel with a swimming pool and we reckoned

189

we could get a swim there – well I did, Si wasn't so sure, but I just walked in confident like, and no one seemed to mind, and then Si almost blew it by asking a waiter if it was alright . . . and I had to sort of cut him off, this is me, 'to have a couple of beers?', and it was, and Si gave me this hurt look, because he insists he weren't going to ask for permission to stay, he was going to ask for beers and all, but like I reckoned it were better to be safe than sorry. And it were worth it. The pool was well good, like huge, and so we had a couple of swims and a couple more beers and both of us lay back on the sunbeds and relaxed, like this was summer.

Si was just starting to think about where we should stay that night when I saw something I didn't want to see. Drifting up from behind the hill, over Si's shoulder, I could see this smoke, a column of the fucking stuff rising up like stairs of cloud, going upwards and upwards, climbing towards the sun, and it was grey, like deep grey, and I got this feeling, this immediate sinking feeling, in my gut, and I didn't want to tell Simon nothing about it.

Now sometimes you've done something and you feel so guilty about it – even if you don't realise that it's guilt you're suffering from or nothing – that when you see something else happening that sort of fits in with your guilt you immediately reckon it must be your fault, even if it's not. You did something wrong, and you know it could have consequences, and now you can see consequences consequencing, and like it could be coincidence, but you don't believe that – it must be your fault. You just grab at that, with a desperate panic inside, praying for it to be coincidence, but that just makes it worse, because you know you're only trying to make yourself feel better, you know you're just trying to deny the fucking truth, and the truth is, you started that fire because you threw away that spliff. I felt like shit. I knew it was still burning, because it had made a pretty arc, and sparks had jumped off when it landed, I had seen it, just before it died. But they always does that and then goes out, like it's the last spray of their short life, and what I told Si were a guess sort of based on experience, it weren't fact, and like there was a sort of 'oh fuck Si, get off your white horse' thought going on in my head and all, and of course now, now it was coming back to haunt me, a great big fucking sheet of cloud, and as we watched it spread I knew I couldn't tell Si about the spliff because like we'd just agreed for a second time that it was a good thing that I'd made sure it was out. Shit. There was nothing else for it – I had to go back. I had to go and see the damage for myself. I had to follow Si. I wish I hadn't.

It were the lower side of the valley that were on fire. It were blazing. Tops of trees were like engulfed. There were three deep red-yellow flames, one moment the red were winning, the next the yellow, and it were like they were fighting for control and out of the battle were coming puffs of smoke, rolling balls of the stuff, sort of changing shapes, building up into this column of smoke that were like hung above the valley, and like this fucking cloud was sort of sending its first fingers across the sun and it were like this huge shadow spreading, but this shadow were orange and it changed the colour of the earth. And all you could hear was the cracking of the trees as they burned, and the flames kept leaping from treetop to treetop, they would curve over, bending down until they touched the leaves, pull back, sway back again, touching, pulling back, swaying back once more, and then up goes the next tree, passing on my guilt, each burst of new flame, a new twist of guilt, and for some other trees the moment is more sort of sudden, a gust of flame suddenly leaps, wrapping around it, and it's like a total victory, and the flame swamps to the next to the next and, Jesus, it's running down the whole left-hand side of the valley, climbing the fucking sides, from

191

the road down, heading for the sea, and we are stood on the road, and the road is acting as a fire break, it's stopping the flames from carrying on up the mountain towards the rock face where the bastard vultures are waiting.

To the right, down in the valley, we can see two houses, and they are still untouched even though the flames have sort of come up close, like they're forty metres away, but it's like there's this invisible arm that is sort of holding the fire back, and the flames that leap across just sort of die, but that don't stop them trying, gobbing at the holiday homes, and then this tree falls and I realise there must be a stream or something down there, and the flames have only got grass and shit to jump across to and like there aren't branches reaching out for it, like nothing is stretching over the stream, and that's what's been holding them back.

But then I see something that changes all that, because this tree is falling, it's collapsing across the water, and it's landed in some bushes and if these go up the fire will charge through them and all, it'll run under some trees that lead up to the house, and like it's not a big step to the roof, and I turn to Simon, but he is already riding the bike down this dirt track and do I have to follow or what? And like I didn't know he could ride so well, and he gets there ahead of me, and when I pull up and leap off he's already got his towel out and he's beating the flaming bushes with it, and sparks are going everywhere, and so I grabs my towel, stamping on the sparks, thumping out at the flames, and every time they briefly sort of burn brighter before they get drowned by the beating, and we keep going for about ten minutes, him and me, working together, and we keep catching each other's eye, and it's our adrenalin, our excitement, our fear, working, and like then Si's shouting up to some people who've appeared round the corner of the house, and there's another tree falling further up the stream, and the people come running down with buckets and towels and they start beating at the new fire, and ours is pretty much under control, and when we've finished with it Simon charges over to help the others and as he goes I see this girl screaming at him, running towards him, and he sort of looks up, sees this next tree coming, and turns, suddenly diving away from the flames that have ballooned out as the tree hits the ground, but the girl's not judged it half so good, and I'm running now, and Simon is up and charging straight at the fire, and he's thrown the towel over his head and he's still going with a scream like you've never heard and then almost like immediately, he's coming back out from hell, running backwards, dragging this girl and I can see the flames burning up her hair and it's halfway up her back, and as I reach them he has dived onto her, his towel sort of hauled over her screaming head and his legs trying to swamp the flames that have caught her skirt, and I throw my towel down covering these final bits and then the rest of the people have come over, and Si is pulling away the towel, and the girl's face is covered in black shit, and her hair has stopped about half an inch from her scalp, and she has no eyebrows, and Simon is shouting at them about the tree and like I've already spotted that, and I've run to it because it's started the grass burning, and this is spreading, a patch, a black smoking carpet of hissing spitting grey-black spreading like oil across the lawn, eating as it goes, and I'm in at the tree and there's this woman beside me and she must be in her late forties and she's real beautiful and I recognise her from somewhere, hell, even through the flames I know that face, but like it don't seem the right time to say nothing, because these flames are sneaking out from all over, and the heat, the heat is worse than a Dago train, it's a wall, like standing right next to a huge fucking gas fire, burning to the bone, and you have to keep moving, you have to dodge, step in to beat, beat,

193

then jump back to stamp on sparks, to let your skin cool down, to breathe, and as the rhythm gets going there's an adrenalin burst, a pleasure to the danger, to the control, and you can feel it in all of us, like one body pulling together, one thing to do, to put out these fucking flames, and all of us dart in and out, some with buckets, some passing wet towels, some just beating, beating, beating, and half the lawn is burned away before it is out, and three more trees have come across the stream, but like then suddenly it is over. The trees along the stream has all gone, the fire has moved on down the valley, carried on the wind that carried it here in the first place. There is no more fire here, and all of us realise it together, and like all of us is gathered in a group, like at the end of a crap movie, watching the alien craft heading back home, racing out across the land to the sea, not sure if we shall ever see it again, not sure if we ever want to. And the fire is leaping, like lighting candles all the way down the valley, and the smoke cloud has completely filled the sky, and we are in this grey twilight, and like it's almost beautiful, all this destruction, it's so total, so uncaring, like it's not nothing to do with anger or hate, it's just to do with power, raw bloody power, and it's shocking, watching it go, now that our danger has gone, like we are nothing, only chance fucking objects in its chain reaction path. And we watch it change everything as it goes, and when it has taken all it can use, it just moves on, and on. And fuck, is it something or what?

Who?

I was the first person to speak, this is me, 'Fuck, eh?'
And like the old beauty just goes, 'Too fucking right.'
And this stopped me looking at the fire because, you
know, you don't expect to hear something like that from
a beautiful woman in her late forties. And then everyone
is talking, and laughing at each other, because we're all
filthy, and we didn't notice it happening, I mean, hell,
we weren't looking for that, and they're all thanking me
and Si, especially Si, and then they're inviting us back
up to the house, and as we are going I realise two things.
One: the girl without the eyebrows is leaning against
Simon as he 'helps' her back to the house and I can see
from his shoulders that he's not complaining. Two: the
beauty is like a film star. I know her, I mean I've seen
her on the box, and she is really famous, and I stops
walking, and suddenly I'm nervous, because I realise
who she is, I realise this is my dad's wet dream, and
shit, what the fuck do you say to someone like that? I'm
not going to tell you who it was – I'm not going to give
ammo to dad's mates – I'll just call her Marilyn. And
Marilyn stopped and turned and looked back at the fire,
and as she did so, she caught my eye, and she smiled,
like a huge welcome to her face, and shit, would that
have given dad a mid-dream groan or what? And she
comes over to me, like walking towards me, and she's
taller than me, and she's put her arm around my

shoulder, and I have to tense a bit, and this is her, 'You look like you could do with a cup of tea.' And this is me, and I don't know where it came from, 'I'd rather have a huge fucking spliff and a glass of whisky', and like my face froze as soon as I'd said it, and I knew then that my father had just woken, cold, ashen, his ejaculation caught short by that nightmare fucking son of his, and then she hit me, this is her, THIS IS MARILYN, with a laugh, with a fucking LAUGH, 'Right, one huge fucking spliff and a glass of whisky it is then.' And that's when I knew I was in love – like, what a woman!

I had the whisky in my hand and was out on the veranda watching her skin one up within two minutes, and like she don't look up, but this is her, 'So what you doing this far south?', and so I told her and like suddenly she IS looking up, like getting all excited and insisting that we should stay here with them, that there were plenty of rooms, and that it would be 'an honour and a pleasure', and I can't tell you but this filled me right up, and no way could I argue, I mean this was one of those things that don't happen often, and when it do you got to grab hold and ride it, and the only real problem I had was trying not to look too excited. Si – who was stood next to Marilyn's fully recovered but unnatural looking eighteen-year-old daughter, Nicola – looked like he might cry, and I reckon the fire must've affected him a bit, you know, delayed shock or something, because his face sort of stretched back, like everything opened, and he just looked into the sitting-room, and sort of toward Nicola, and said what a beautiful house it was, and hell, I had to agree, but I reckoned my reasons was different to his – and Nicola knew it and all.

So let me explain what happened to us, because is it weird or what? The house we just saved is owned by Marilyn and this famous writer bloke she's married to, and staying here is their three daughters and six of their mates – three flappers and three blokes. Just a bit up the hill is another house, and we've sort of saved that one too, and staying up there are mates of Marilyn's, this famous actor and his wife – who's a famous wife – their three kids, two daughters and a six-year-old boy, who'd got well stuck into the fire and all, which I reckon is good on the kids and good on the parents, and staying with these five up at the second house are a couple more mates, and like they're hardly famous at all. (One is an old politician husband and his young looking-after-him wife, and the other is a middle-aged dentist husband and his middle-aged school teacher wife.) All of this were well different of course. I'd only met a dentist, a school teacher and a wife before, like I'd not met famous people – well except for Nobby Stiles when I was five, and he's not exactly famous anymore, especially with his teeth in, and it's more something my dad remembers than me – and so like you'd expect that I'd be phased by all this, you know, overawed, but there's something about having a spliff rolled for you by a world-famous actress that breaks the ice, and then when all her mates lug on it, I mean, like what fucking ice? And I'm telling you, it were good gear – head, great big bushy fucking heads, and like you don't need many of them. Beautiful, crackling all the way down.

And that's how I spent the afternoon – stoned, with the big people. Like a couple of times I thought I was getting a bit boring, but hell they all laughed, and talked to me, and listened, and like everything was so fucking interesting, I mean to them and from them, and shit, it were well good just to shut up and listen and all, because boy could these people talk, and like the stories, and all the things they know, and like they were all socialists except the dentist, and like I reckon I am too, and I got to say it were the most fascinating afternoon of my life – well not quite, because the next time we gabbed it were just as good and all, and I weren't expecting that neither. Hell, I mean how often have you felt people's respect?

And they were discussing stuff you'd think I wouldn't understand and all, like perspective, and intention, and the prejudice of information, and this real good row about the function of charity when it's compulsory, and then one about football hooliganism, its historical precursors, and the creation and function of the teenager, and like there was loads of stuff about famous actors' private lives and all, and I mean shit, it were fucking brilliant! And when you got something to say, they look at you and you know you got to do it, like you can't cop out, and so you make sure you think before you open your mouth, well unless it's a gag, and they pick up on what you've said, they use it to move it on, and it's like watching a game of football, you know, a small pass can just build and build, like set things off, and that's the joy of watching it, and that's what hit me, that's what I suddenly realised, everything is about watching things build, everything is about seeing something change, grow sort of thing, like footer, or gabbing, or TV. And I had to say it, and when I had there was a silence, and they were smiling and nodding, because like that were truth, and the thing about a truth is that it's like a goal – you can't argue with it.

About seven they all head back to their house up the hill, and Marilyn suddenly starts getting all guilty because she hasn't shown me to my room yet, and here she is keeping me talking all afternoon when I probably want a wash and stuff after all that fire-fighting, and I tell you I had to laugh because I mean who gives a shit about stuff like that when you're with a woman like her? But she insisted, which was well kind, you know, and took me out to this sort of small house – the outhouse – round the back, and like this is where all the daughters' mates are staying, and there's this big sitting room with cushions and shit, and a stereo, and it's got these white walls and stone floor, and sliding glass windows that open onto Africa, and like it's huge, and they're all

198

there, drinking, Si and all, and Marilyn enters the room
with her arm round my shoulder, passes me to Nicola
and then she's gone, and like I can't help it, I got to turn
and watch her go. And this is Nicola, 'I hope you don't
mind, but you're sharing with Simon', and like I turned
back to her and just sort of smiled, you know, I stopped
myself from saying what I wanted to say, because I knew
it wouldn't help, but this is what I would have said,
'Who the fuck else would I want to share with you dumb
bitch?', because Jesus, what a dumb thing to say, I mean
I were travelling with the bloke for fuck's sake, but like
I could see she were just trying to be polite sort of thing,
and like her parents had been dead good and all, and
she and Si were clearly going gooey, and so this was me,
'Thanks', and then I stood there for a minute or so,
looking around the room, and there weren't nowhere to
sit or nothing and I was feeling well gone after all the
grass, and so this was me, interrupting, 'So where is it
then?' and someone told me, and I followed their
directions, but no one followed me, and when I got into
the room Si's bag was already beside one of the beds,
and so I dumped mine down next to the other one, lay
down, soaking up the comfort, and let the day keep
going through my head – the riding, the smells, watching the view, watching the bulls, swimming, fighting
the flames, the listening, the smoking, the excitement,
the anger, the fear, the guilt, the hope, the whole great
big bloody mess of a thing, and Marilyn, Marilyn,
Marilyn – like she must be at least twice my age and all,
but she was on top, bouncing me right into sleep.

About 8.30 there was a pathetic knock at the door,
and this head quietly stuck round the edge of it, peering
in, without a body, and it were Marilyn's youngest
daughter, Joanna, and she wanted to tell me they were
all going to supper, and did I want to come? But when I
got up off the bed and followed her straight away she
suddenly looked all shocked sort of thing, and this was

199

her, 'But, but, why aren't you going to wash?' and this was me, 'Oh it don't matter', and she sort of walked on a bit, and then this is her again, 'They always make me wash', and this is me, 'Well, when you're a bit older you won't have to', and I walked into the sitting room, and there they all were – clean and freshly dressed, not a smokey face among them. Like even Si had washed and borrowed some clothes, and they all turn and stare at me, and I mean what's a man meant to say? This is me, 'Anyone got any soap I can use? I can't find mine.'

By the time I'd washed they were all up at the house, and I hadn't been able to find no clean clothes neither – because my bag had got soaked when the gendarme was looking for me, and even though I'd dried everything I hadn't had a chance to wash it or nothing – and so I still looked a right mess when I got up to the main house, and like there were this mirror just by the door as I went in, and this was the first full-length mirror I'd looked in for two months, and it were a shock, a real shock, because it turns out I didn't look like I used to look. I was scrawny as shit, wiry, my hair was all over the place – past my neck, sort of shoulder level – my skin was a kind of shitty copper colour, my face was splattered in fucking freckles, and my clothes was so faded that all the stains on them just stood out more. I mean I looked like I'd been left outdoors for too long and could do with a good coat of paint. Hell, some places I'd've been a dude, but like as I turned away from the mirror and headed into the dining room I knew this weren't one of them.

They all looked at me as I came in. All of them clean, washed, in pastel shades. Summer-loving. Marilyn said hello, and so did some of the other big people, sort of nodding my way, but the conversation weren't stopping for me, I was only something sort of inconvenient, I was only something passing through, I was only something dressed wrong and heading for the seat right down at the far end of the table, in the corner, sort of stuck out of most people's sight, blocked by three of the daughters' mates, and they were looking away from me, their backs was turned, and they weren't going to come round. I could feel it, like as I sat down, I could feel the snigger run about my end of the table, half looking up to check that what they thought they had seen was what they had seen, and the conversation was busy at this end and all, and like they'd finished their first course, and so it were obvious that they were waiting for me, waiting for me to eat this silvery fish that looked like a sardine but might not have been, and as I picked up my knife and fork and hacked off the first bit, separating it the way me and Si did with Bobby, I sort of feel this snigger again, like hear it from unseen figures, and I look up, and they're all looking away, like really interested in each other, and not in me, and I know something is going on, but I don't know what it is, and like that just adds to it, that just makes me feel ignorant, and I don't like it. But no way am I giving in, I mean I reckon I got a right to talk and all. So I started on the blokes beside me, and they just watched me talk, and then went 'Yes', or 'I see', and that was it, like they don't pick the conversation up or nothing, like they turned away, back to their raised eyebrows and fucking smirks, and that's what they do, they smirk and like I weren't expecting this, because I mean straight after the fire they were quite friendly and I reckoned they might be different, you know having Marilyn as friend or relation sort of thing, but like obviously all that was really different was that they knew how to act nice.

I finished the fish as quick as I could, because I didn't want to keep them waiting no more, but I didn't really enjoy it, you know, I couldn't settle into the taste or nothing, I just had to get it down, I just had to catch up. Then suddenly there's this person who's appeared, like coming out of the kitchen, and Jesus, it's a servant, like a fucking slave, and she's older than anybody else in the room, and she's clearing up, she's serving, she's cooking, she's doing the whole fucking lot, circling this huge wooden table, and half the bastards don't even say thanks, don't even notice that their plate has gone, and I've never seen nothing like this, not even in a restaurant, like no one's stacking plates or nothing, and I really wants to get up and help her, because it's fucking typical, like there's always one poor sweating bastard, and shit, I'd like give her my seat sort of thing, just to show them what selfish bastards they all are, but like Si's not looking up neither, and so I don't know if helping her would be rude or something, and I tell you it's dead confusing because I was always told that rich people had special sort of manners and like if they have, and this is what they are, well fuck, they're bloody two-faced.

After about ten minutes of sitting there and no one saying a word to me, or even having a quick shufty my way, I'm starting to get bored and narked, you know, I feel like I don't exist, and so I tried to get Si's attention, but he was four seats up, and busy, and, hell, trying to get one person's attention at a crowded table's not exactly cool, because either someone else has got to shut up for you – and then they're going to have to listen to what you say, so what you say has to be good, but like it's not likely to be good enough because it never is if you've interrupted – or they're just going to ignore you. I should've thought about it before I tried to interrupt really, but I didn't. Guess what? Everyone ignored me. The only thing I got was from Si, like he turned sort of briefly, with half a smile, and sort of waves his hand – which was meant to be a message – and then he was turned away again, and was talking to someone else, and I couldn't see who it was, so I leant forward, you know to check it out, and I should have known, it should have been obvious, because he'd turned back to his new love, hadn't he? To his new dream girl, to his new queen, to his Nicola. And so I suppose I should have been glad he even half looked my way, but I wasn't. I felt a prat. I felt a total outsider. I felt I was the dog turd you can't shake off. And I felt the anger, I felt the need to turn the table upside down, to scream at all the fuckers that I was here, to freeze their conversation, to break up their words, smash their ideas, crack the fucking ice of their self-satisfaction. But I didn't. I looked down the table, I looked past the pumped-up egos of the children, down toward the big people, and I watched them in their world, helping serve the food, like passing it down, and talking, leaving us to us, and I remembered that afternoon, their respect, and I wanted to be back up that end of the table, and I knew I had to breathe deep to do it, I had to control the bollocks of being nothing, because I knew the dicks my end wanted me to fail, wanted me to have a tantrum, to demand attention, I could see it. They wanted me to be childish, that's what they expected, that's what they needed, so they'd have the chance to laugh at me, to get rid of me, because I wasn't them, because it were obvious that I'd used the wrong knife, because I'd been invited into their company without their permission. And that was it, that was what hit me. They didn't understand what they'd done to deserve me, they didn't understand why they had to have some wanker like me come along and destroy their holiday, like they reckoned you could control what happened to you, you could keep what you didn't like out of the way, and even though I was the thing they didn't like, all this was like a lesson, you know, and it sort of dawned on me, you can't side-step life, all you can do is try to face up to it or wait for it to go away, there's nothing else on offer, and like these kids had decided they'd wait for it to go away, they wouldn't face up to me. And because of that – and this was like one of those blinders – they wouldn't face up to themselves neither, I mean they'd made up their fucking minds and

203

the only thing they'd let me do was prove them right. So then, it was up to me, I had to face up to it, like there was just one road to victory. Me. I picked up my flat knife and forced the meat apart, into bitesize mouthfuls, and got on with watching Nicola and Si. It'd pass the time.

Even with a half-inch crop and no eyebrows, you could see that Nicola had snagged a bit of her mum's beauty, but she hadn't got it all – she'd got her dad's jaw – she hadn't got the oomph of her mum, but it were the right oomph for Si, and like he were gone, he couldn't get enough, and what really got me, you know, watching them, was that she couldn't get enough of him neither. I'm watching the two of them, right, and this is weird, because there he is, and it's like I don't know him, I know his history and shit, but I don't know him, like all there really is is a North London sort of Jewish boy, a Stamford Hill lad, an ambitious juggler, a magician, a contortionist, and there she is, a public school girl, a la-di-dah with training, and like she's got some style, you know, a bit of it rubbed off on her from her mum, but she's got an arrogance and all, like she can present all these fronts, I mean I can see her doing it as she turns among her friends. And then suddenly I see something else, I see her face clear as she turns to him, dropping all that shit, and it hits me, I see it like the sun, I know what they have in common, and it's simple – they're both fucking romantics. And I look up, and I catch Marilyn, and she's looking at me looking at them, and she just smiles and shrugs her shoulders, and like the smile keeps going so that I forget why, and I tell you – I could give her as many as she wanted.

The rest of the meal didn't seem half so much a problem, you know, I didn't give a shit about what the kids thought, I mean my end of the table didn't exist, and so when they'd finished eating and all got up and left – like millipede legs – I stayed where I was, sitting

204

there with the big people twelve empty chairs away, and it were like getting over claustrophobia, like suddenly I could breathe again, and I don't know if they sort of expected me to go and all, but I does know I didn't want to, I mean, fuck, this was where the interesting shit began, and what got me, right, was why the others should want to go and do a bunk in the first place. Couldn't they see what they were missing? I mean, not even Si? And I'm watching him go, sort of expecting him to look back or something, and then the dentist offers me a brandy, and like this is the first thing anyone's said to me since I sat down, so I reckon fuck it, and this is me, sort of surprised my voice still works, 'And I always said I didn't like dentists', which got a laugh, and so I moved down, got myself next to them, and settled in for a good fucking gabber, and like tried to keep my eyes off Marilyn.

Life is fucking weird though. There I am down the end of the table with the big people, desperately trying to get Marilyn's body out of my mind – which is not easy if you're looking at it – and suddenly I realise that for the last ten minutes sitting opposite me is somebody my sort of age who's not pissed off out of it to party with the kids neither, and I got to tell you, I don't know why the fuck I've not seen her before, because, Jesus, my penis just goes hard thinking about her, like this woman is shit hot, red-haired and see-through skinned, and she must be at least five ten, and her knockers are like winking at gravity – I mean they got to have some sort of deal going – and she's got these green eyes that just look at you, and she's sharp and all, telling good stories, you know, at the right time and stuff, but she's not shouting or nothing, she's sort of quiet as she does it, like she expects respect, and just being near her is sort of exciting. And then when I says something and she turns to me and I'm looking into that face, it's like we're looking down a toilet roll at each other, like we've been

205

blinkered, and when she finally turns away, I can feel myself shaking, like inside, shaking, and I turn round to look at who's talking now, and Marilyn is looking at me, grinning, and shit, I know she'll understand because Helen is nineteen and gorgeous. Of course, I don't stand a chance, but what the hell, eh? Where there's willy there's a way.

About two in the morning I got back down to my room, and Si weren't there. I didn't expect him to be, and he weren't. He was not in his bed. His bag had not moved. My mate was somewhere else – just like he had been since the fire – and I was on my own. I only had one mate now. So I lay in my bed and had a wank. And it were a dream of a wank, with Marilyn stepping into the light first, sort of catching her like it had done from the candles at the meal, and her clothes were being pulled off so that I could see her as she went down over me, her head bent, her eyes looking up, her hair trailing down my stomach, and from behind her comes another figure and I know it's Helen but I haven't caught her face yet, and then there she is, her hand slipping around my shaft, slowly wrapping as Marilyn's lips slide up and off, and the hand is stroking as Marilyn sits up, moves away, her pubes scraping at my shins as she slides, and Helen's face lowers down to meet her hand, her tongue flicking and her leg swinging up behind her as she straddles up and over as she swings round with her breasts her skin herself, and her hand runs down her chest lifting her tits and her fist guides me inside her, and I burst, a buttock-clencher of a spurt that means no way could I move, because shit, even a clean-up was more than I could handle, and like sleep were in bed waiting, kick-started by spunk, and now it was impatient, like Zzzzzzzzzzzzzzzzzzzzzzzzzzzzzzzzzzzzzzzzz, up through the mattress, a chain-saw through my nervous system, like immediate – cut off.

Next day I woke at about eleven and first thing I

thought about was Helen, she sort of did a dance out of my dreams and into that sort of waking up world just before dreams stop being possible, and she'd affected my groin and all, like she'd got together with my knob to build this stonker that was aching in seconds, bringing me back to the real world, and it were frustrating I can tell you. Then I rolled and saw the empty bed next to me and the fact of Si took over, and it felt like shrapnel in my throat, and I forced it down, pushed it down into my stomach, so it could rot, so I could shit out the idea, so Si could become just another part of my day, wherever he was. And I swung my legs out of bed, and sat on the edge, and thought 'I've got more important things to worry about.' Of course I didn't, but you know what I mean.

The house was empty apart from the old woman who served dinner the night before, and like she spoke loads of English because she comes from Gibraltar, and the two of us had a great gab, which was one hell of a surprise, because you never expect a creased person to be sussed, but there are some of them who, you know, have the gift, and this old dear, Isabella, she was one of them. Like first thing she says after she's introduced herself is 'Isabella necessary on a bicycle?' and I reckon that sort of summed her up, because she was full of really crap jokes, puns and shit, and she thought they were hysterical, like she screeched at that last one, and you could see she told it to every Engleesh she met, and so I screeched with her, and then she made me some eggs, which were like gorgeous, sort of swimming in olive oil. I ate them in the kitchen, and the two of us was still gabbing, and then I went to wash up the plate, and Isabella got all upset, like I was messing with her place, and she shouted at me to leave the plate and pan and shit, and to get out in the sun, this is her, 'Go, go, go eat the sun now', and she pushed me out the kitchen with a broom and a screech, and the door swung on its two-way hinges, and I was alone in the middle of the sitting-room, and all I could hear were the crickets outside, rubbing their legs together. And I stood there in this big room, with this huge black metal chimney hanging over the flat stone fireplace beside me, and I couldn't resist it, I had to drum on it, drum on the metal, and the rhythm sort of rang out filling the empty room, like me, the noise and the echo, and then I had to stop because my fingers were hurting and I headed to the door, going out to eat the sun when I hears another rhythm, this flip flap of flip-flops coming down the corridor, slapping the polished stone slab floor, and before you could say 'Who's this then?', Helen has appeared. And you won't be surprised to hear that I am not in the slightest bit upset.

It turns out the two of us is alone for the rest of the morning because like half of them have gone down the beach, and the other half have gone to the big round market in Algeciras, and so the two of us decides to go down to the pool, and on the way down Helen starts telling me all about it, because you see it's a famous pool, it's where some famous actor were found face down, dead, you know, and there's been a poem written about it and all, and like Helen says she read it and it's shit hot. So I gets her to read it to me, and it don't seem much, you know, it's not bad, and this is me, 'It's not bad', and this is her, 'It's brilliant', and she starts explaining it, sort of showing how words can have two meanings, like go either way, and that's what the poem is about, it's not really about a swimming pool at all, it's about how everything has two sides, like big and small, nice and nasty, rich and poor, above the water or below it, dead or alive, you know, it's just about which side you look at it from, and I got to tell you, this hit me, it made like loads of sense, and shit the poem was only sixteen lines long and all, and the two of us talked about these sixteen lines for at least a half hour, and like if

I'd've tried it at school you wouldn't have got two minutes out of me, and that says something and all, I mean it must be a bit depressing if you're a teacher. Weird thing though was that Helen was like a teacher, even though it didn't feel like that, I mean she made me want her to explain, and like I weren't distracted or nothing, just listening, and talking, and listening, and we both felt that there was something different about this pool, you know, the way places can have a feeling all their own, and like we both reckoned that this place had a feeling of death or something, like a battlefield, and then we reckoned maybe that was just us, because we knew someone had died here, and then we started to laugh because this was me, 'What do you reckon he died of? A stroke?' And so the conversation started to change, and we starts talking about swimming, and it turns out she can't swim, and she asks me if I could be her teacher, and this is a real compliment I reckon, and because I'm a pretty good swimmer I reckon I can teach her and all, and so we gets in the water and I starts to show her what to do.

Now there's something about teaching swimming that I didn't think about before we got in, and that's that someone who can't swim is going to sink a lot, like you have to hold them up, support them, make them feel safe, touch bodies – shit. It was alright to start with. Like to start with I was just thinking about the swimming lesson, I was really concentrating, I really wanted to teach her, but it were after about ten minutes, when she started to need me less, that I noticed what was going on here, and she sort of noticed too and stopped swimming. She rested in my hands, her weight pressing into me, and she sort of turned her head so she was looking up, and like the two of us held this position, like locked, and oh God, her eyes were just so fucking inviting! And this is her, in a deep sort of voice, a sort of husky version, 'What?', and this is me, feeling my

209

tongue go thick 'Nuffing', and I sort of choked on it, and this is her, 'It's something', and she was right, it were something, between us, and I knew what were going to happen next and all, and I didn't want it, like I didn't need to get this erection, not now, but it were too late, it were on it's way, any moment now she'd feel it pushing against her, and God I don't know why, but I suppose in this sort of panic, this flood of desire, this uncontrollable fucking urge, my eyes locked onto this face that was quite simply screaming 'KISS ME!' And it were like someone had stapled fishing wire through my throat onto the back of my neck, and they were pulling it down, reeling it in, and then my mouth met hers, and there was a wonderful sort of brief moment, a moment she held for a fraction of a second, until immediately after she pulls back, rolls off my arms and onto her feet, and slaps me, hard, across my left cheek, and this is her, 'Don't be so bloody stupid'. And I'm staring, like caught out, like it's the shock that hurt most, and this is me, 'I thought, I thought you wanted to and all', and this is her, 'I wanted a swimming lesson', and this is me, all buried panic and regret, spurting out words, 'I know, I know, I mean then, afterwards, not at first, when you were looking at me, then, I thought you wanted to just now', and this is her, 'Well, I didn't.' And it felt final, and I expected her to get out the pool and sort of piss off, but none of that happened, like she was still there, waiting for a lesson, and this is her, 'Well get on with it then', and like I'm confused, but I mean what's a man meant to do? By the end of the lesson she could almost swim a width, but my cheek still hurt – inside and out.

By the time the big people arrived back from the shops Helen and me was definitely mates again, and like I reckon I was the only one who was thinking about what had happened, like she'd just put it away as soon as it was over, and that made me sort of feel a bit childish because I hadn't put it away yet, but like it were also good, because it helped sort of thing, it meant I didn't have to make up for it, I just had to make sure I didn't make the same mistake again, which were fair enough I suppose.

We spent most of the afternoon together at the pool and sort of later on we were joined by some of the big people and that were good and all, and we had a good time, even though they wanted a siesta, and sort of gabbed about all kinds of shit. At about five me and Helen went up to her room, and lay on the bed and gabbed some more, and had a few spliffs, and like it were easy, like mates, even though I couldn't help looking at her tits from time to time – subtle like – and hell I'd even forgotten about the others, I mean I'd not thought about the way they'd treated me the night before or nothing, and then Helen mentions it, and she says she thought they were just a bit spoilt really, and like I had to agree, and what she reckons is that if you want them to take notice of you, you got to not give a shit, just sort of push your way in, and like I can see that and all, but the thing is I don't even know if I wants to be part of them, and Helen laughs and puts her hand on my leg and agrees, and I have to breathe deep.

I was still breathing deep at about eight when I went downstairs to change for supper, and like I could hardly believe it when I got to my room because there was Si, and it felt great, you know, just seeing him there, and so I'm straight into gabbing, like it bursts out, until I realises that Nicola's there and all, and immediately I sort of switch off inside, and everything becomes all polite, and within no fucking time at all they've left me to my clothes and gone up to the house. I mean, empty gut or what? I followed them about ten minutes later and like this time I'd made sure I weren't the last one up there and put myself in the middle of the table, and waited, and like sitting opposite me was one of Marilyn's

211

daughters' mates, Yvonne, and she sort of nodded to me and this is her, 'What school do you go to?', and so I told her where I'd gone, and she's not heard of it, but that's alright because I've not heard of hers neither, which surprises her but not me, and then everyone else turns up and the seats are filled, and there are a few odd looks my way, and it takes a bit for the seats either side of me to fill up, and like then on one side of me is the dentist and on the other is one of the blokes who ignored me all last night, and he looks like he's going to ignore me all tonight and all, but I don't give a shit, and turn to the dentist and ask him why all dentists have got bad breath, and he pisses himself, and we tuck into the starters. And like it's going alright, you know, the big people are near and so is Helen, and it's easy to forget the others, and like I'm just helping myself to some salad from this huge fucking bowl, when suddenly I feels these feet under the table and they're running down my calf, and back up again, and I looks up at the girl opposite, at Yvonne, and she's deep in conversation with the bloke next to her, but fuck I can tell it's her foot, and she's still not stopped yet, but hell, if she's not going to look at me, I'm sure as fuck not going to look at her, and so I get on with listening to one of the dentist's conversations. But I tell you, having your legs rubbed by unseen bare feet is bloody off-putting, and like I could hardly say a word for about five minutes, and then the feet slid away with a farewell tap, and I looked round and Yvonne was looking straight at me, and I couldn't think of nothing to say, so I smiled and she smiled, and then she turns back to her talk, and it were a bit embarrassing really, but I reckoned I'd just let it lie, and that's what I done, until we gets to the pudding, because then the foot comes out again, like dancing around my feet, and I look across and she's not looking, and this is a bit of a pisser because it's slightly confusing, slightly irritating, and slightly exciting too, and fuck it – I want an answer. But I don't get one. Even when I try to speak to her after the meal, like she's gone. And this is starting to get to me, it's eating at my head, and I need to talk to someone about this, and so I leaves the big people and goes after Si, but he's more interested in telling me something Nicola's said, and no way am I interested in that, and so in the end I reckon Helen's my only available ear, and I go round to her room, and I sort of knock – polite, eh? – and I hear Helen say something, this is her, 'Oh for God's sake, why?' and she sighs, irritated like, and opens the door, but then her face lights up, and I mean you can see she's pleased to see me, and so we starts talking and I can feel she's a bit holding back like, but it's not much, so I don't take much notice, and I starts rolling a spliff and sort of telling her about Yvonne, not boasting or nothing, but wanting to know what she thinks, and like she's making faces at me, and I don't know what she's on about, so I finish telling her, and then she says nothing, just, this is her, 'Really', and like this morning she was bitching about the others a bit, and hell, I'm expecting her to now, and so I tries to push her, and this is me, jokey like, 'So do you reckon she wants my body then?' And this is Helen, 'I doubt it.' And she opens the door, sort of shaking her head, and this is her, 'Do you want to go and look at the monkey?', and this is me, 'What?', and this is her, 'Follow me', so I does, and after we gone out she looks behind her a couple of times but don't say nothing about what was going on in the room, and starts telling me about the monkey that lives up at the other house, you know where the famous actor and the dentist is staying, and like we gets up there, and sure enough there is this monkey, and it's tied up by the back door, and Helen tells me to go over to it, and I get about five metres away and the thing is off its stool and with about four bounds has sort of landed on my shoulder and it's gorgeous, I mean, gabbing away, and I walks over to the stool and sits down, and it swings down onto my lap, and pulls open my shirt and starts checking out the hair on my chest, and shit you got to laugh, I mean like is this weird or what? You ever had a monkey going through your chest, picking things from the hair, things you can't even fucking see, and then sort of bunging it in its gob? I'm telling you, it feels well funny, and like Helen's pissing herself and all, and so am I and so is the monkey, and I tells Helen to come over and hold the thing, but she backs off, saying no way, because this monkey is a female sort of thing, and she hates women, like she's bitten half one woman's finger off just for feeding her, I mean, she's only interested in blokes, never harms them, and like Helen has heard this but not seen it in action, and so that's why she brought me up here, to see if it were true, and I can't fucking believe this, and this is me, 'You telling me I'm your fucking guinea pig?', and this is her, laughing, 'Yup', and hell, at least she's honest.

She hung around with me and the monkey for about half an hour, and then she said she was off, and like I got up to go and all, but it was bloody difficult to leave because every time I went the monkey started getting all miserable, I mean it were obvious, like you could see the poor thing were all sort of lonely and bored, but what you meant to do? You can't take it home with you, it's the gardener's pet. But it seems so unfair making it live like this, without choice, having to take what it's given and nothing else, it's so arrogant, it's so sort of treating it like it's not got a life except what we want, like we're so desperate to control everything, but I mean shit, don't this thing want to be in charge of her life and all? Of course she bloody does, but no way we going to let her, because we can shit on her so we will, we're going to prove that we can control things, and like I'm doing it now, by sitting and stroking her, like I make myself feel better than Helen, I mean I feel I can handle something she can't and that makes me feel special, and like as I sit there stroking away it suddenly hits me. Maybe the reason she attacks women is like a statement, maybe it's her way of proving a point, maybe it gives her a feeling of power, and I can understand that but it's really sad, because in the end the monkey can't really do nothing, it can't really fight, it can't really change nothing, it's got to lose, and like making that statement only makes the gardener chain her outside the back door, I mean every time she bites someone she bites herself.

About 11.30 I was ready to go. I'd been sat there on my own long enough, and so I decided I didn't care what the monkey did, I was on my way. I stood up and went, and the monkey followed me to the end of her chain, her chain to the wall, and then she grabbed at my leg, like quite tight, and I sort of undid her grip, and pulled myself away, and I started to walk again. And she began to wail, turning herself round, two hands tugging at the chain, trying to bend open the links, trying to wrench the pin from the wall, pulling, pulling, twisting to look up at me, to see how far I had gone, pulling, the chain tightening at the throat, pulling, knowing exactly what she wanted to happen, knowing that it never would, but every time, hoping – and I ran down the hill, running from the screams, running from the truth, because I knew there was nothing I could do.

Right and Left

I arrived back at the house, and I didn't want to be on my own, I couldn't handle listening to those screams, and so I found the big people still at the table, and I sat down beside them, and poured myself a glass of red shit, and I reckoned they must have seen something was up because they all went quiet like, and I was about to tell them about the monkey, when Marilyn gets up and comes over and sits down next to me, and this is her, 'I think we've got a problem here, Ken', and like I don't know what she's talking about, and this is her, 'It seems you've upset the others somewhat.' I still don't know what she's talking about, but this is me, 'Well, they've not exactly made me feel welcome', and she looks at me before she talks, and then this is her, 'I don't think that's exactly fair, Ken. You are staying in our house.' And I realise that she's not seeing it, and so I know I got to try to make it clear, and this is me, 'You've made me welcome, all you lot, but them lot, they're not interested', and she smiles, and this is her again, 'I thinks it's more than that. Maybe you've tried to do something you shouldn't have?' And so I told her I hadn't done nothing to them, I told her all I done was teach Helen how to swim, and I even told her what had gone on then and all – and like I don't know why I did that, because it weren't easy – but she laughed, patted my knee, and this is her, 'Well, it can't be that. That's her style' – which cheered me up, and pissed me off at the same time – and she carried on, 'If that's all you've done, then I don't understand it either, Ken. All I do know is that they were talking about you in very heated terms.'

And I don't get it, I really don't get it, I mean, what have I done? And Marilyn can see I'm not lying, she can see I'm as confused as she is, and so this is her, 'Maybe I should have a word with the girls.' And this stopped me, like as if what I'd heard had come from inside my head, like the meaning I got couldn't be what she meant when she said it, you know, it seemed like an offer of help, but why should she help me? I mean, she was Marilyn, and I hadn't even asked, and shit that idea was like magic, but at the same time I got that real crappy small feeling that I needed help to deal with people, and that the people would only be nice to me because they've been asked. So like before I knew the words, I'd sort of said, and this is me, 'No, no, no. It's alright', and she sort of sighed, and this is her, 'OK. Maybe you should go and talk to them about it then.' And it weren't an order, but it felt like one, and so I went down to the outhouse and into the sitting room, and like I did want to talk, I did want to take away the shitty thoughts, I did want to stay in this house, and there they all sat – well not Si and Nicola of course – all of them ignoring me, their up-their-arse heads turning away as I came in, like there was something hideous about me, something untouchable, and all of this was new, all of this was way beyond what had been going on before, this was not ignoring, this was not being pissed off by me being here, this was not people laughing at me, this was hate. This was their hate, and it filled the room, like walking into a fridge, and Jesus even Helen refused to look at me, and the three blokes stood up and moved so that their backs cut me off from the group on the chairs, blocking me, stopping me from getting to the tarts with their filthy fucking looks, and like these blokes are fresh out of public school, and they think they're so fucking smart, I can see it in their shoulders, and it makes my stomach knot with vomit, and my mouth goes dry and my jaw feels tight, and my fists get tense, and I'm desperately trying to think, like I've got to know, why's it become like this? Why has their lack of interest become loathing? And I'm staring at them trying to work it out, like aren't I even worth finding out about? Is this it? Am I worth hating because I didn't go to their type of school or nothing? Because I got no qualifications? Because I don't talk about the things they does? Because I'm too much like a stranger? Hell, maybe that is it. But shit, if I was some peasant from Afghanistan they'd spend a whole fucking week trying to get a sentence out of me! I mean if they could feel sorry for me, if they felt there was a story in it, and I look at them, and maybe that's it – maybe I'm not enough of a stranger. Maybe I'm a bit close. They've seen me, from their parents' knob cars, they've watched me in public places, and there's no story in me except the one that they can use to agree with their mates that they've met people like me, and we are thick, ugly, and bad-mannered oiks. And like that's all I can hold onto, that's the only thing I can think of, because I ain't done nothing wrong, I've not had the chance. And I know it now, like the only thing I can do is change their minds, show them another side, and so I hold my anger, I don't go and strangle the nearest fucking neck, I ask them if I can sit down. I humiliate myself. And they humiliate me back. This is one of the shit-head blokes, 'I suggest you just piss off', and he don't even turn and look at me. I feel the cold bite into me, I feel my fury turning me blind, and I rush to beat it, I rush to kill their chance of seeing me out of control, I kill it with words, and this is me, 'Why?' and I feel myself shaking, unable to move now, because I can't trust my body, and they say nothing, and I'm stood in silence, and it's up to me, so I try again, and this is what I says, 'I don't know what I've done wrong.' And this is Yvonne, 'Oh for Christ's sake, he's impossible. I'm going for a swim.' And she's up, marching out the room, and the others are following, and in seconds I'm on my own, and the silence is all that's fucking left, until from outside comes the sounds of the bastards' laughter and splashing, and I move over and slump down into the sofa. And as I sit there rocking, I can feel the misery building behind my eyes, and from far away I hear a screaming, from up in the hills, a scream that I know too fucking well now, and I can see her, I can see the monkey desperately strangling herself at the end of her chain.

I was still there ten minutes later when Marilyn came into the room. She stopped at the door, and a look of sympathy sort of dashed across her face, and then she came over and sat down next to me, and told me she'd just been speaking to Helen, and she knew what was going on. It turns out to be so bloody stupid I had to laugh, I mean it was all so pathetic. Marilyn's youngest daughter, the thirteen-year-old pretty-pretty deeply fucking irritating 'I've been in three films!' Joanna, was hiding under Helen's bed when I went in there earlier, and like Helen had tried to get me to shut up, but I hadn't taken the hint – why the fuck didn't she just tell me? Or kick the little shit out? – and sweet little Joanna had then gone back to the other oh so nice people, and told them that I was going round saying Yvonne wanted my body, and that she were playing footsie with me at supper, that she really fancied me, and that I'd been really rude about her – which I hadn't – and that I didn't like any of them – which were true, but like weren't what I'd said neither. And that was it, that was what had happened, like nothing. Yvonne couldn't handle it though, like it set her off, started a spoilt bitch with egg on her face sob, got her stomping around, proving it weren't true by hating me, and that was contagious and

219

they all started to catch the disease, and that was all. It's a fucking joke. Hell, even Marilyn laughed when she told me. And of course she believes what I said, and like she's checked it with Helen, and she's had a word with the others down at the pool, and like now it's going to be even worse because they're under orders and they won't like it, and neither will I, because it's going to look like I've sneaked, when I've done nothing at all, like nothing. I mean, fuck, I even tried to make peace, as if I might have done something wrong. I tried. Jesus, I tried!

And like you can guess it, all of this is starting to get me a little bit wound up. I mean, fuck them. Why are they so fucking special? They listen to crap music, they dance like they have piles, they wear crap clothes, they talk like they want to sound common but they behave like the royal fucking family, like total dickheads, they behave like they're special, and they're not, all they are is the rudest little shits it has ever been my misery to meet! And like I reckon Marilyn can see what I'm thinking and all. This is her, 'I was only trying to help.' And I had to look at her, and I know I shook my head, because, you know, it's just fucking amazing the way big people think they can make anything happen. And like hell, all this has confused me about her and all, because I get the feeling that even she's finding the atmosphere a bit difficult now, like it's entering her world, and I can see it now, I mean she's like everyone else, she wants to talk good, but she don't like it when it's real. And so for the first time there's this silence, like she don't want to find something to gab about or nothing, so I just let her go. And I waited. Sat on the sofa, waiting for them to come back. And I didn't move, because I was there.

And then in they come, and they all start to look for somewhere to sit, and I expected them to be awkward, but they're not, they're just wet, and like this makes it easier, because I don't even need to feel embarrassed,

220

and then Nicola appears, like she's been warned, and she comes over, and this is her, quiet like, with them watching, 'Look, Ken, why don't you move? They all want to sit together and you know what they're like. Come on, why don't you shift into the armchair? It'll still make the point.' And I'm looking at her and I'm looking over her shoulder and I can see all of them and they're grouping, and I can see Nicola, and I can see them, and the anger is turning towards her because like who does this fucking whore think she is, telling me what's good for me? Who does she fucking think she is with her gang of cold shit? Like what the fuck are they fucking staring at? And why, why should I do a single fucking thing to make these ME ME ME ME ME damp-arsed shit-stuffed dead brains anything but fucking irritated fucking put-out and fucking miserable?! And this is me, 'And what fucking point is that?' And I'm waiting for an answer and she has seen my eyes, and now she's nervous, and turning away, frightened, and I can feel the strength coming over to me, and I know I'm not going to fucking move, I'm going to wait, I'm going to push it, and the anger is there to do it, and the silence in the room is mine now, and they've fucking lost.

And then Si comes into the room, my oldest mate, suddenly he's here, to take my side, and he's got a fucking grin on his face, and he's saying watcha Ken, and I don't know why but I'm thinking of a tent that seems ages ago but was just a few days away, and I get that same rush, that same burst of love, and hope, like it's a shock, it sort of knocks my anger, thieves my attention, and like he's coming over to us, and he's talking to me, and it's like innocence walking in, and you can see he don't know nothing about what's going on in here, and a sort of relief floods in, filling me up, relief, like crossing to me, and I'm only thinking here comes my mate, and it pulls me up, I'm standing and like I'm going to talk to him and he's going to talk to me,

221

and he does, this is him, 'Watcha mate' and 'You left your glasses by the pool', and he gives them to me, and goes past to Nicola whose face goes so fucking gooey it's disgusting, and he's put his arm round her shoulder and he's saying see you later, and the two of them are going out the door, and Nicola only looks back once, and it's to see me staring after them while her arsehole family and friends dive into the seats all around me, smirking like fucking corpses who have gone to some crap fucking undertaker. And I'm left standing in the middle of all these filled seats, like it's a game of fucking musical chairs, and I don't know what the fuck to do now, looking around at them waiting to see what I'm going to do, and it's like someone's taken all my clothes and left me naked, and I'm only just realising, and when I does, I don't fucking care no more anyhow.

It's like Si's thirty second interruption changed everything, because now I'm standing there in the middle of the circle of chairs, and I realise what I've known all along, they're kids, the lot of them, Kids, and like they're so young, so stupid, and none of this was done by me. I was the bloke trying to get on with people, I was the bloke who hadn't done nothing bad at all, and like when I met these people it were like on equal ground, it were proper, we'd been introduced, I'd done something with them, we'd done something together, we'd shared it, we had respect from it, and the big people they'd seen that, they'd tried a bit, they'd looked for what I was, and they tried to understand. But this lot, this lot understood nothing, they have no ideas, all they have is this belief that they know a lot, that they have a lot, and that they're going somewhere where they'll get a lot more. They are kids, vicious, nasty, ignorant little nappy-crappers, with the fucking planet made in their sodding image, and hell, I felt better than them, wiser, and as I looked at them victorious at having got their seats, I almost felt sorry for them, and that felt good. So I walked away, I walk out the room, and as I go one of the funny little public school messiahs presses play on the stereo, and I hear the music, I hear these words, 'Arsehole, bastard, fucking prick and cunt', and they are laughing, all of them, and it were Yvonne whose pig snort started it, and it stopped me, and I turn, I look at them, and this is me, 'Why does this make you happy?', and then I was gone. Well, I told you they played crap music.

I went and sat by the swimming pool, and then after a few minutes lay down on one of the sun-loungers and looked up at the moon, and I wanted a cloud to go past it, but it didn't, and instead I heard a buzzing in my ear, and then I saw a mosquito land on my arm and begin to suck my blood. I didn't kill it or nothing, because Dago mosquitoes don't carry malaria, I just waited. I didn't even go back to my bed, I mean there didn't seem any point, like there was no one there. And so I looked up at the stars some more, and I remembered looking at them so many times in the last couple of months, and as far as I could see they hadn't changed a bit, but like I knew they had, I knew something was going on up there, but I just couldn't see it, and I lay there, with my brain gabbing, and I thought of Si, I thought of history, I thought of the little boy stood beside his mum, the little boy giggling with his dad, the boy in the shower without his foreskin, the boy chewing his own piece of bacon, the boy on the bike, the boy in the darkness of his bedroom talking from the bed above me on the floor, the boy and me, the hours and hours and hours of us that meant fuck all if you want them to, and I've never felt so fucking miserable in my life. I had no one, because no one understood me, understood what I was going through, what I felt like, what I thought like, no one who really gave a shit, and here I was stuck, nowhere, with nothing, but me, on my own, me, feeding an insect.

And at the bottom of this pit were one thought, like one good thing worth going down to get, and I picked it up, turned it over, and I felt the grin coming, because I was still here, it hadn't killed me, I could handle it, like I'd proved to me what I really needed to know, like 'I don't need no one, and no one needs me', and shit does that make you feel better or what? And that's when I came to my decision, and it were simple – I'm out of here. Shit, it might even wake Si up, it might make him see what's been going on, bring him back – shit, it might even make him want to come with me! And for the first time I realised I were doubting it, really doubting it, like suddenly it was well possible that my mate might dump me, because he'd done it before, and hell why shouldn't he do it again? And fuck it, I found myself going down again, like slipping back, and I could see that idea down there at the bottom of the pit again, but until I got there it weren't no good to me, because like I was fighting the slide, and that's what irony is, isn't it? I needed to know I didn't need no one, but I didn't want to believe it. Shit – history, can't live with it, can't live without it. And I must've been thinking all this as I fell asleep and all, because like I was surprised when I woke up the next morning, like I didn't even realise I'd been asleep, and like I woke up thinking the same kind of shit, not even a pause, just straight in with 'He can't let me go off on my own', and like straight back with 'I wouldn't fucking put it past him though'. And so I got up and slowly went back to my room, and packed, and put on a clean 'T' shirt.

I thought about missing breakfast but in the end it seemed a bit dumb, so I went up, and there were a few people there, including Marilyn, but I didn't say much, and neither did no one else. When I'd finished I went over to Si and told him I wanted a word, and like he was a bit put out because like Nicola still hadn't finished her toast, but I pushed him a bit, and he gave in, and sort of followed me down to the pool, and he was really happy, going on about Nicola and what a wonderful place this was and how he could stay here forever, and I told him I was leaving. It took a moment for his face to make up its mind, and then he looked at me like he's never looked at me before, and it were like I had told him I had fucked his mum, because the shock were total, you could see the disbelief, it were screaming out for me to tell him it were a lie. How could I want to go? What did I mean? Why did I have to? Why? Why? Why? And never once 'What way we going?' Never once 'The bastards'. Never once 'Oh shit I'm sorry mate, I've been so wrapped up in Nicola I've not seen what's been going on.' Nothing. He just panicked. And then I saw it again. I saw desertion. I saw he was gone.

And the anger was on me like I reckon only love can produce and I hated like beyond caring, like beyond nothing, and Nicola is coming down the steps, and she's coming up to me, and she has seen nothing, because Simon's head is hiding mine, and this is her, this is the holiday romance of Simon's miserable fucking life, 'Ken. Thanks for moving off the sofa last night. I think it was for the best. Things aren't that easy for you around here, are they really? Maybe, perhaps, it would be easier if you kept out of their way for a while.' And then she saw my face, and her's fell, and this is me, 'Don't worry, I'm going', and this is her, desperate now, 'Oh I didn't mean that, I didn't mean it that way, honestly, you're welcome', and Simon joins her, and I watch her change, I see her suddenly realise that if Simon's on her side I might be persuaded to stay, I see her dreadful little brain, click click click, and what am I supposed to do now? I look at her – and I know my hand could take her by her sweat-shirt, and I wouldn't be hurting, I'd be frightening, pushing her back – and this is me, 'I was going, not for you, not so your little fucking holiday can by happy happy happy' – shaking her, 'Happy' 'Happy'

225

'Happy' and I knew she'd begin to sob – and this is me – as Simon could have reached my back – 'I'm going because you have nothing here to offer me, you have no life, no party, no fucking soul' – and I feel inside, I feel myself turn swinging, I feel my half fist slap Simon backwards, I hear him stumbling back into the pool, and I know that she is slumping – and this is me, 'And if you think for one minute that any little shit coded message from you would penetrate a skull as thick as mine then that is the biggest fucking compliment you have paid me since I came here and you started to fuck with the bastard who deserves to drown in that pool. Do you understand? I wouldn't wipe your snot if you was a spastic.' And as she turns dripping tears into Simon's fucking shoulders, both house loads come spurting down the stairs, slowing as I stepped back, dripping over the last two steps, drawn by voices, halted by the lack of physical violence, and this time I went beyond words, took my actions out my head and put them in front of her, and I spat into the pool, big and brown from coffee, hoiked from the back of my throat, and it were good, and it were floating, and this were me to Simon, his latest mate in the crap memory of his arms, 'You should get some fucking glasses', and I pushed past the audience and went up to my room, where my packed bag was waiting, patiently.

I went through the main part of the house on my way out of this dump, and I found all the big people were sitting in their sitting room talking, about me, and sadness, and no hope, and the culture of violence, and shit, and when I came in, they all went quiet, and Marilyn stood up, and she walked over to me. And this is her, 'Whatever provocation you may think you had young man, your behaviour was entirely inexcusable, and I am deeply disappointed.' And I looked up at her, and this is me, 'Do you know what I'd like now? A huge fucking spliff and a glass of whisky.' And she shook her head, and this is her, 'You cannot joke your way out of life, young man.' And this was me, because like I reckoned I should still try with this lot, 'Look, I could have done a lot of damage to all those people downstairs. They've treated me like shit. Every time I've done something, said something, they have been completely uninterested. They have shat on me all day long, all night long, they have made up their minds about me, when I didn't about them, and like because you lot up here was pretty decent, I reckoned it were worth the effort. But let me tell you, you've fucking failed with that lot. Just like all of you do. Like this is as much crap as I've seen shoved down anyone's throats, all of it. Look at it all. Fuck me – do you really think they're that special, that you're that special?' And I saw them staring at me, listening, and I realised, and this is me, 'You do, don't you?' And Marilyn's husband coughed, and this were him, 'Not really.' But I could see he didn't mean it, and when I turned to leave, I could feel them relax, like just one more fucking sigh at having got away from anything like real fucking life.

Gone

The motorbike started at the first kick, and I didn't look back as I climbed up the hill to the main road, except to glance across at Africa, because like it were one hell of a view, this rock across the sea, and I didn't expect to be coming this way again, not for a long time. And then I opened up the throttle and rode, twisting and turning, the movement sort of killing off all the thoughts, until I was back in Marbella, and still on I went, out the other side, till I reached my hitching spot, and then I stopped the bike with a skid of dust just for the hell of it, got off, put the keys under the seat with the spanners, and stuck out my thumb.

I wasn't expecting much, like I didn't care who came along, and I reckon I was still sort of numb from what had gone on and all, you know, with all those words coming back, running through my head, changing slightly as I thought of what I should have said, but like in the end I didn't really care now. I mean, what was the point?

And then I saw it, coming down the road, my first chance of a lift, and it were like a thrill, an excitement, and I was waiting to watch them go past, on their way, and I didn't care, but it were unbelievable, because the buggers did stop, the doors of the Volkswagen Combi did swing open, and as I looked in at a van load of Aussies and Kiwis, out wafted the smell of Hope. And I mean, like, is life weird or what?